THE JOURNE

Conrad Jones

Red Dragon Publishing LTD

ISBN: 978-1-7393036-5-5

RED DRAGON BOOKS

Chapter 1

The wooden gate was hanging from one rusty hinge, its salmon pink paint blistered by the Nigerian sun, cracked and peeling. Oke pushed the gate with her knee, her hands occupied by the bundles of clothes and bedding she was carrying. The gate resisted for a few seconds before the hinge squealed in protest and gave way. She pushed harder and the wood splintered; the gate fell to the ground in two pieces with a clatter.

'Make some more noise, why don't you?' her sister Isime said, quietly. 'We're supposed to be keeping our arrival a secret.'

'A secret from who?' Oke said, gesturing to the deserted street. 'Everyone left here a long time ago. We're the first to return.'

'We still need to be quiet.'

'Tell the gate, not me,' Oke said, shaking her head. 'I touched it, it fell off. That's not my fault and there's no one here anyway, so stop worrying.'

'That's an omen,' Isime said, biting her lip. Her black skin glistened with a sheen of sweat.

'It's not an omen. It's a gate, Isime,' Oke said, tutting. 'It's broken, not haunted.'

'I told you we shouldn't have come back here.' Isime picked up a jerrycan full of water from the handcart that they had commandeered to carry their belongings. 'This place is cursed and they say you should never go back to where bad things happened,' she added.

'They say this and they say that. They say we shouldn't go back where, home?' Oke asked, open mouthed. 'Do they say you should never go home?'

'They say that you should never go back to a place where bad things happened.' Isime insisted.

'Bad things happen everywhere. Have you been sleeping for the last ten years? Don't you listen to the news?'

'Never. It's depressing.'

'Whatever happened here, it's our home. This is where we belong,' Oke said. 'The past is the past and we're going to make our future here.'

'You mark my words, sister,' Isime said. 'We were here a long time ago and bad things happened here. They say you shouldn't go back.'

'This is where our family lived and we were forced to leave this place, a place we loved. We had a wonderful childhood here,' Oke argued. 'This is our home where we grew up. Stop talking superstitious nonsense.'

'I'm just telling you what they say.'

'I have heard enough about what they say. Who exactly are they?' Oke snapped. 'Who actually says that?' Oke asked, sighing. She made her way to the back door through knee-high grass, which was straw-coloured and dried out. It hadn't rained for months. 'I'll tell you who says things like that,' Oke added, dumping the bundles onto the dusty porch. 'Old women with nothing better to do than chitchat their superstitions and religious nonsense to anyone stupid enough to listen.'

'Are you calling me stupid?' Isime looked shocked.

'If the cap fits, wear it,' Oke said, nodding. 'I for one, have had enough of living my life by rules, folklore and myths made up by men trying to control us poor people, women in particular.'

'It's not a rule. It's advice,' Isime argued.

'If it's advice, I'll ignore it if you don't mind,' Oke scoffed. 'We're home and this is going to be a happy home. I'm not having any of your negative nonsense in this house, understand?'

'I'm not being negative.'

'Superstition and imaginary deities are not welcome here,' Oke said. 'Understand?'

'Imaginary deities, like God?' Isime whispered. 'Have you lost your mind?'

'No. I've freed it. If there really is a God, he's been pissed off with us most of our lives. I've decided not to rely on God anymore. He's a massive let down.'

'You should be careful who hears you talking like that,' Isime said, hushing Oke with a finger to her lips.

'Don't you shush me, young lady,' Oke said, wagging her finger in reply. A smile touched her lips.

'Don't wag your finger at me,' Isime replied. She smothered a giggle. 'You're such an old bossy-boots,' she added. 'You sound more like mother every day.'

'She would be pleased that our family has returned home,' Oke said. 'What's left of us, anyway.'

She tried the handle but the door was locked. Oke picked up a plant pot, which her mother used to grow herbs like berbere and cumin. The odours of her mother's cooking drifted to her from her distant memory. They were such happy times. Her heart sank as she remembered the family eating together at the table. She could see her baby brother Beb smiling as he spooned food into his mouth as if he hadn't eaten for a month and her younger sister Kissie giggling when he stole food from her plate. Mother said his legs were hollow. He was always hungry. They were ghosts now, all of them. Nothing more than ghosts.

'Here it is,' she said, wiping a tear from the corner of her eye as she picked up the key, making sure Isime didn't see her tears. She wiped the dust from the key on her sleeve and slid it into the lock.

'Are you okay?' Isime asked.

'Fine. I have dust in my eye.'

'Dust?'

'Yes, dust.'

'You're crying.'

'Shush woman,' Oke whispered.

She felt the metal grating against grains of sand as she turned the key ninety degrees. It stuck and wouldn't budge. Oke wiggled the shaft and tried again. The lock clicked and she turned to look at Isime before pushing the door open. Isime nodded and smiled, encouraging her to go in. Sunlight penetrated the darkness and dust swirls twisted and danced in the beams of light. A sickly-sweet odour drifted from inside. It was the stench of decay. The air was rotten.

'Oh, no,' Oke said, covering her nose. 'Something has died in here.'

'I told you we shouldn't have come back here,' Isime said, her voice a whisper.

'Why are you whispering?' Oke asked. 'The dead can't hear you.'

'Yes, they can,' Isime argued. 'It's cursed. I'm telling you.'

'Then the entire town must be cursed, Isime,' Oke said, ignoring her. 'What happened to our family, happened to hundreds. Where else would you suggest we go?' She stepped inside and allowed her eyes to adjust. All the shutters were closed. She put her bundles onto a dining table, which she didn't recognise. It was handmade from different types of wood. The legs were all different shapes, topped with scaffold planks. It wobbled and creaked beneath the load.

She remembered her mother beaming with pride when her father bought a teak table from a local carpenter; it could be extended to seat more people and it had six matching chairs. Mother polished it every day and it took pride of place in the kitchen. She wondered where it had gone to. Probably sold or taken by Boko officers. The rest of the kitchen appeared to be intact as she remembered it although all the pots and pans were missing. Dirty cups and plates were stacked in the sink, covered in mould. The house had been lived in but the occupants were gone now. Probably a high-ranking Boko and his family. They had annexed that part of the town when they invaded and handed out the best houses to their officers. Everyone was supposed to be equal but some more equal than others.

'Oh, it stinks in here,' Isime said, entering the kitchen, screwing up her nose. 'Mother will be frowning down on this mess.'

'Shush and do something useful,' Oke said. She opened the shutters and the light poured in. Insects scurried for the shadows. A thick layer of dust covered all the flat surfaces. 'Bring in all the cleaning stuff from the cart. I'll open the shutters and let fresh air in, you can start cleaning.'

'Do this, do that, do the other,' Isime grumbled. 'You're so bossy,' she added as she put down her load and went back through the door. 'I'll stick a broom up my arse and brush the floor while I'm walking around, if you like?'

'It's a big ass, so it would be a big help.'

'I heard that!'

Oke smiled at her grumbling and walked into the living room. She opened the shutters and the light flooded in. There were two threadbare armchairs, one either side of the room, and a thin mattress on the floor. The walls were bare and the bookshelves which had belonged to her father were gone, their contents burned in the town square by Boko, no doubt. Their hatred of books and education were entrenched in their ethos, which was irrational and unexplainable. She pictured the room as it had been, cosy and comfortable with big fluffy cushions, colourful weaves on the walls and their television set, which had taken centre stage. Their father watched every kind of sport he could when he wasn't working and they watched films with the shutters closed, so the neighbours couldn't see them. Even then, the extremists looked for any reason to report anyone not deemed devout enough. Watching the wrong film could bring trouble to their family.

She pictured her mother and father holding hands on the settee, sharing dried fruit as they watched a film, their love for each other as strong as when they were young. In her mind's eye, she heard Beb and Kissie were amused by something, the sound of their infectious laughter drifted from one of the bedrooms. Happy times when everything was good and she believed nothing could take those people away. How wrong she'd been. How fragile life was. Her loss writhed inside her guts like a snake coiling itself into ever decreasing circles and sadness flowed through her veins. Memories of their loved ones, lost on the journey through life, never forgotten, always there. Ghosts.

'I don't know where to start,' Isime said, disturbing her thoughts. She plonked a bag of cleaning equipment onto the table. 'Have you found where the stink is coming from?' She realised Oke was daydreaming. 'Are you okay?'

'Yes, I'm just remembering,' Oke said, half smiling. She opened the door which led to the hallway. The stench was stronger and she nearly gagged. The air was stale and there was something else. A sense of foreboding touched her.

Stay out.

'I don't think it's an animal.' Oke ignored her instinct but self-preservation told her not to go any further.

'I think we've seen enough death recently to know what a dead human, smells like,' Isime said. 'I told you…'

'The place is cursed?' Oke interrupted, walking down the hallway, slowly. 'Change your tune, please. We have nowhere else to go, Isime.'

She stopped outside the first door and listened intently. Her breath was shallow and she felt sweat running down her back. She put her hand out and opened the bathroom door, looking inside. Light crept in through cracks in the shutters but the corners of the room were hidden in shadows.

'What can you see?' Isime whispered.

'Please stop whispering,' Oke said. 'You're making me nervous.'

She stepped inside to open the shutters. 'Oh shit!' she shouted. Oke put her hands to her face and spat onto the floor.

'What is it?' Isime asked, startled. She followed her quickly.

'I got a mouthful of cobwebs!' Oke complained.

'I thought something bad had happened,' Isime said, disappointed.

'It did. I swallowed spiders' web,' Oke said, opening the shutters. She looked at her sister. 'Oh no! There's a big spider on your shoulder,' she said pointing. 'It's huge!'

Isime began slapping at her clothes as she ran in a tight circle. 'Where is it?' she shouted. 'Get it off me!' She was frantically slapping at her clothing as she gyrated, a terrified look on her face. 'Get it off me!'

'There it is!' Oke pointed at nothing.

'Where?' Isime panicked. 'Where is it?' She let out a piercing squeal. 'Get it off me!'

Oke couldn't stop laughing; tears filled her eyes and she thought she was going to choke.

Isime stood still.

'There is no spider, is there?'

'No.'

'That is not funny!' Isime shouted. She folded her arms in disgust. 'I hate spiders and you know it!'

'I do know it,' Oke said. She burst out laughing again. 'You should have seen the look on your face,' she said, doubling over. 'That's the funniest thing I've seen for months,' she gasped.

'It wasn't funny!'

'Oh, it was funny,' Oke disagreed. She danced around in a circle. 'Get it off me, get it off, me, get it off me!' she mimicked her sister.

Isime couldn't stop a smile appearing, despite being annoyed. 'You're so stupid,' she said, laughing.

'It was funny,' Oke said, still laughing.

'So not funny,' Isime said.

'So was funny.'

'Not.'

'Was.'

Oke opened a roller bind, which covered the window. Insects scattered along the windowsill and woodlice and earwigs ran for cover beneath the bath. A centipede the size of a snake glided behind the toilet and disappeared down a hole in the floorboards. She noticed a single toothbrush on the sink, its bristles yellowed by time and a worn bar of soap in the bath, cracked and greyed.

'I think one person lived here,' Oke commented. 'This bathroom needs to be fumigated before I take my clothes off in here. I'm not sharing my bath with the entire cast of Bug's Life.'

'I remember watching that with mother and father,' Isime said, retreating into the hallway.

'That was a long time ago.'

'It was made in nineteen-ninety-eight, I think?'

'Your memory never ceases to amaze me,' Oke said. 'I can't remember why I entered a room or if I've just been to the toilet for a wee or if I still need to go and I never remember where my glasses are.'

Isime laughed and walked towards their old bedroom. She put her ear to the door. There was nothing but the sound of their breathing. Her smile was gone.

'I don't like this,' Isime said, whispering again.

'Whatever is in here, is dead,' Oke said. 'They can't hurt us.'

Isime paused before opening the door. It was dark inside and the stench of rot was strong. She held her breath and stepped inside, crossing the room before opening the shutters. Light filled the room and chased away the gloom. Dust floated in the air. There were small bones scattered across the floor.

'They look like chicken bones,' Isime said. She saw lines scored into the wall in sevens. Dozens and dozens of them in rows and columns, covering nearly all the wall. The room was devoid of furniture or furnishings. It smelled of stale sweat and urine. 'This bedroom stinks,' Isime said. Oke looked inside and turned up her nose. 'I think they kept an animal in there, maybe a dog,' Isime added.

'It smells like a human to me,' Oke said, shaking her head. She saw the marks on the wall. 'Dogs can't count. It looks like someone was counting the days.'

'Do you think someone was held captive here?' Isime asked.

'Why not?' Oke asked. 'We were.'

'I suppose so.'

'We weren't shackled but we were held captive for years. They made us marry their men but we were never free. We were prisoners nonetheless.' Isime nodded in agreement.

'Something terrible happened here in our old home,' Isime said. 'I can feel it.'

'I can smell it,' Oke said. 'We'll never know what the Boko got up to in this part of town. We were never allowed near it when they brought us back.' Oke closed the door. 'It needs bleaching and scrubbing. A lick of paint will bring it back to how we remember it, almost.'

Isime shivered but didn't reply. Her expression said she thought it would take more than a coat of paint. A lot more. They walked to the end of the hallway. Beb's room was on the left, their parents' room on the right.

'Which one first?' Oke asked, shrugging.

'Should we get help?' Isime asked. 'I'm scared.'

'I'm scared too,' Oke said. 'But there is no one who can help us. No one else cares, Isime. There is something dead behind one of these doors, we know that much.'

'Beb's room first,' Isime said, opening it. The unwholesome stench of decayed flesh hit them, making them step back from the door. Isime wretched and lost the contents of her stomach. The smell of vomit mixed with rotting flesh sent Oke over the edge and she had to fight to stop being sick.

'That's disgusting,' Oke said, gagging. 'Are you okay?'

'I told you we shouldn't have come back here,' Isime mumbled, wiping vomit from her face. 'I can't cope with this.'

Oke squeezed her hand. She took a deep breath and tiptoed inside. Something crunched beneath her feet. Despite the gloom, she could see dark shapes on the floor. She avoided them and opened the shutters. The light rushed in to reveal a dreadful sight.

'What on Earth?' Oke whispered as she backed out of the room, crushing hundreds of dead flies with each step. It was difficult to make out what she was looking at. Metal rings had been fixed to the walls. One either side of the door and one below the window. Skeletal arms were hanging from cast iron shackles. Long dark hair clung to the skulls and the skin had turned to leather, sightless eye sockets stared into the nothingness. Another set of shackles hung empty from the wall opposite. 'Bless their poor souls,' Oke muttered.

'They are all women?' Isime asked. The bodies were naked, their breasts withered but unmistakeably female.

'This is what Boko did to our young women, who didn't agree to their demands. They caged them like animals and starved them to death if they didn't conform.'

'This could have been us,' Isime said.

'We were already broken,' Oke said, nodding. 'We had no fight left in us.'

Isime stared into the room in disbelief. Oke pulled the door closed to hide their gruesome discovery. She squeezed Isime's arm and opened their parent's room. The odour of decomposition was so thick, she could taste it. A body was lying on a double mattress, shrivelled and reduced to leathery skin and bone. Grey hair and a thick grey beard still clung to the skull. Oke stepped inside, her hand covering her mouth. A wooden handle protruded from the chest. It had punctured the man and the mattress below him. She looked around and saw a broom, snapped in two. On the floor between the bed and the wall was the decomposed body of a female, the throat slashed, a curved blade on the ground next to her. An AK-47 was balanced against the wall in the corner of the room and two bullet belts loaded with magazines were draped on a chair next to his clothing. Gossamer webs hung between them.

'She fought back,' Oke said, shaking her head.

'And got killed for her trouble,' Isime said.

'It was probably preferable to being chained to a wall by a rapist pig,' Oke said.

'Shall I find the soldiers?' Isime said.

'Yes,' Oke said. She paused, looking around the room. 'But we hide the weapons first.'

'Where shall I put them?'

'Do you remember father's toolchest?'

'Yes. In the outhouse.'

'It was fixed to the floor,' Oke said. 'To stop thieves from lifting it. If it's still there, use it and cover them up with linen and towels.'

'I'll check.' Isime left the room and scurried down the hallway. Oke picked up the weapons and ammunition but left the blade where it was. She closed the door behind her.

'It's still there,' Isime said, returning. She took the weapons from Oke.

'Hide them and then find some UN soldiers. They will remove the bodies and document this. The world needs to know what happened here.' Oke shrugged. 'They will do nothing about it but at least we let them know.'

CHAPTER 2

She saw her mark walking out of the Skinners Arms and she crossed the road to follow him. He was fifty yards ahead when he turned to check the traffic before crossing on a zebra. She assessed his face, cheekbones, nose, jaw, all matched the images she had seen online. Today she was known only as Alice, which wasn't her real name. Tomorrow her name would be different again; all that mattered today was Harry Trainor. Harry Trainor was partly responsible for the death of Suzette Unganu, according to her auntie, Jet. Jet Unganu had employed Alice to capture Trainor so that she could exact revenge for the death of her niece. Jet was distraught at Suzette's death. Suzette had been in her care following the death of her mother to drugs. It was a drug overdose that killed her, drugs which her sister, Jet distributed, which was ironic, although the irony was lost on Jet. She was the biggest distributor in Soho and the West End yet she ignored the suffering she caused. Suzette had worshipped her auntie and tried to become part of her operation but Jet resisted and kept her at a low level where she was relatively safe. Suzette wanted the big money and had gone rogue and tried to go into the wholesale business for herself. She tried to double-cross her customer, Beb Sammi, but it all went horribly wrong and unbeknown to her, the drugs were switched.

Harry Trainor bought a kilo of cocaine from her, which turned out to be junk, switched at the buy. When he realised that he was the proud owner of a kilo of baking powder, he threatened to kill her unless she could come up with fifty-grand. Suzette needed to find out where the real cocaine was and was so frightened that Jet would find out, she attacked Kalu Sammi, Beb's father with a knife and was killed in the struggle. Jet wanted Trainor, Sammi and his family dead, which was easier said than done.

Alice took out a burner-phone and called the only number stored in it.

'Where are you?'

'We're parked up, waiting,' the voice said. 'The coast is clear, no feds or traffic wardens.'

'He's heading towards his car at the rear of the station,' she said. 'Can you see him yet?'

'I can see him.'

'His car is where it always is,' Alice said. 'He'll cross the road when he's opposite it.'

'Okay.'

The call was ended. Alice closed the gap between them and shadowed his movements. Sure enough, Trainor crossed between parked cars, stepping out between oncoming vehicles. A van slowed on the opposite side; the driver waved that he could cross. Harry waved back and looked away. The van accelerated and hit him full on, knocking him into the air. He landed bloody and bruised in the gutter and the van sped away. She jogged across the road and knelt close to his head, talking on her mobile to an ambulance controller, who didn't exist. Concerned onlookers approached.

'Is he okay?'

'Shall I call an ambulance?'

'I'm a doctor,' Alice lied. 'An ambulance is on the way.'

'Did anyone get the registration number?'

'I took a photograph,' she lied again.

'Do you need any help?'

'I'm on it,' she said. 'But thank you.'

'Lucky you were here,' someone said.

The concerned onlookers moved on and a few minutes later, an ambulance arrived. The paramedics were black with their hair in bangs, one male, one female, both wearing green jumpsuits. They lifted the injured man onto a trolley and strapped him in before lifting him into the back of the ambulance. She climbed in and sat next to him as they closed the doors. Harry was coming around, dizzy and confused.

'What happened?' he mumbled.

'You threatened the wrong woman,' Alice said. Harry looked more confused.

'What are you talking about?' he asked, trying to free his arms.

'You threatened Suzette Unganu and now she's dead.' Harry frowned as the situation dawned on him. 'Her auntie, Jet Unganu is devastated. You are so fucked,' Alice said, smiling.

Chapter 3

Oke unpacked the cleaning equipment and began to bleach the kitchen. She wondered who the dead girls were, their names, their age, their stories. They may have been people she knew from Monguno and they could also have been brought to the town from across the border. Women were trafficked there to be sold to Boko as slaves. They called them wives but no matter how they dressed it up, they were slaves. Not that it mattered to the dead females. Their suffering was long finished and she hoped they were in a better place but she wondered if their families were mourning them or waiting for them to come home one day. If the authorities could identify them, maybe their families could be told they were dead and the ache of not knowing would end. Somewhere, someone must be hoping they were still alive and would return one day. It made her sad and her own sense of loss bubbled to the surface. She found herself crying again. The home she grew up in had become a prison for those poor women. Her parents would be tormented by what their home had been used for. How could they rest in peace knowing what had happened here?

She tried to clear the thoughts of their suffering from her mind but the smell of decay refused to leave, lingering to remind them of the evil which had dwelled there. Whoever the bastard who lived there was, he got his comeuppance, good and proper. A broom handle through the chest must have hurt and it would have been a slow death. Good. Bastard. Rapist bastard. They were all rapist bastards. They strutted around as if they were untouchable, free from sin and holier than thou yet they didn't have a compassionate bone between them. They were pirates robbing communities and kidnapping teenage girls, while hiding behind Islam. She despised them. They had taken everything she held dear from her and then held her in a state of permanent enslavement. She was a cook, a whore, punchbag and breeding machine and nothing more.

The sound of male voices drifted to her and fear gripped her. Such was the effect men had on her now. She heard her sister's voice chattering away. Isime was talking to them and Oke relaxed a little. They came into view and entered through the back gate.

Oke met them at the back door. There was an officer and two sergeants. They were black but not Nigerian. Isime was waffling to them. She didn't know when to be quiet. Although the soldiers were there to keep the local civilians safe, she didn't trust them. Men were men and as long as they had a penis, they couldn't be trusted.

'This is my sister, Oke,' Isime said, fussing. 'She's the eldest and has been in hospital. She was infected with the virus and nearly died. It was such a terrible time. I thought she was never going to recover. It was the worst, wasn't it, Oke?' she rambled. 'I lost my son and my husband,' she added. 'It was such a terrible time. I don't know how we made it through alive but here we are.'

'Isime,' Oke said.

'What?'

'Take a breath,' Oke said. The officer smiled. 'I'm sorry. She could talk the hind leg off a donkey.'

'No need to apologise. It sounds like you have been through the wars. I'm captain Mane,' the officer said. 'Your sister has told us you've just returned to the town?'

'Yes,' Oke said, nodding. 'I'm sorry we can't offer you a drink but we have just arrived. I wouldn't trust the water from the taps. It's running but rusty coloured.'

'No problem,' Mane said. 'Can you show us where you found the bodies?'

'Down the corridor in the bedrooms,' Oke said, pointing. 'Please feel free to look around but we don't want to see them again.'

'Of course, you don't. Thank you,' the officer said. 'You can carry on with what you're doing. We'll try to stay out of your way and keep the noise down to a minimum but we'll need to use power tools to remove the shackles, no doubt.' Oke raised her eyebrows in surprise at his respectful tone. Isime smiled. 'This way men,' he said to his sergeants. They disappeared down the hallway.

'Did they say if we could stay here?' Oke said, whispering.

'They were surprised we were here at all,' Isime said. 'They said they weren't aware of anyone living in this area.'

'No one does,' Oke said, shrugging. 'We're the first people to return.'

'He was shocked, to be honest.'

'But did they say it was okay?'

'They said they weren't here to police where people live.'

'But they know people are going to come home?' Oke asked. Isime shrugged. 'People will return to the town. Where else do they expect people to go?'

'I don't know,' Isime said. 'They were telling me how stretched their men are. I didn't think they were going to come with me at first but when I said there was a dead Boko, they changed their attitude.'

The sergeants returned and walked through the kitchen and out of the back door without speaking. A courteous nod of the head was all they gave away. The captain appeared, looking tired and weary.

'What a terrible business,' he said. 'No one should have to witness such a thing.' He paused. 'I can't understand why they haven't been found before now.'

'The house was locked up from the inside,' Oke said.

'Okay. Tell me how you got into the house,' he asked.

'Through the kitchen door. We tried the front door but it was locked. The barrel must have been changed because the spare key didn't fit,' Oke explained. 'Mother hid spares beneath her herb pots at the front and back. The front door key doesn't fit anymore but the back door key did. But the front door has been padlocked too, from the inside.'

'This house belonged to your family?' he asked, walking to the front door. He held up a small bunch of keys. 'These were in the dead man's pocket.' A bolt was fastened with a heavy padlock. He tried a couple of the keys and unlocked it from the inside and opened the door. 'There you go. That will go a long way to freshening it up in here.' Sunlight and fresh air rushed in shifting some of the stench. 'You were going to tell me about your family?'

'Yes,' Oke said. 'Our father, Kalu Sammi, was a doctor. He was a junior doctor at Monguno general hospital and when he qualified, he had a surgery in the square and mother was a head seamstress in town.'

'What happened to your parents?'

'When Boko invaded, we tried to reach Europe. Father had a brother in London. He is a doctor too. Mother and father drowned crossing the Mediterranean,' Isime answered. 'Along with our younger sister, Kissie.'

'We were fished out of the sea and taken back to Libya,' Oke explained. 'We were sold to traffickers and then bought by Boko as wives.' The officer nodded and frowned. 'We were teenagers. Just young girls with no idea what was happening to us.'

'That's a very sad tale. I'm guessing those girls in there suffered a similar fate,' he said. 'I think one of them stabbed her captor and was killed herself in the struggle.'

'We thought the same,' Oke agreed.

'The others probably starved to death because no one knew they were in here and it was locked from the inside.' He shrugged. 'Boko were taken by surprise by the presence of UN soldiers and their numbers were decimated by General Basse's nerve agent disaster. When we arrived, they were in disarray and it was every man for himself. No one checked who was missing and no one cared anyway. They ran in all directions. His death went unnoticed and unfortunately, so did theirs.'

'What will happen now?' Oke asked.

'My men will remove the bodies and we'll clean and sanitise those rooms for you,' he said, half smiling. 'The clean-up teams have been busy since General Basse released his nerve agent. We'll have this place liveable in no time. After that, we'll keep an eye on you for as long as we can,' he added. 'How long that will be, I can't say.'

'You are very kind, thank you,' Oke said. 'We're very grateful. Are you stationed at the old barracks on the F258?'

'Yes. We have the run of the place at the moment but Nigerian troops are being billeted their too. It's a big place and most of it is empty and unused,' he said.

'We used to sneak up to the fences when we were children,' Oke said, smiling. 'Hiding in the grass was so exciting back then. Everything is so simple when you're a child. Are your troops planning to leave the area?'

'I don't know for certain,' Mane said, turning away. The lack of eye contact told Oke he wasn't sharing the truth. 'Just one thing I find strange.'

'What's that?' Oke asked.

'There are no weapons in the house?'

'We saw a knife in the bedroom,' Isime said, a little too quickly.

'A Boko officer would have at least one firearm,' he said, studying their faces. 'And the doors were locked, so nobody came in and stole them.'

'We hid his rifle in the toolbox in the outhouse,' Oke said, nodding. 'I thought it might be useful to protect us in the future.'

'I didn't hear that,' the officer said, half smiling. 'I appreciate your honesty but keep that between us, okay?' The sisters nodded. 'Do not tell anyone else, understand?' They nodded that they did. 'We're essentially a peace-keeping force. It costs a lot of money for us to be deployed. Sooner or later, they will pull us out and the Nigerian forces will be left to their own devices.'

'They will run away at the first sign of trouble,' Oke said, shaking her head. 'They crumbled when Boko first invaded this region. What will be different if they come back?'

'I can't answer that, sorry,' Captain Mane said. The sound of engines approaching interrupted them. 'My men are here. Please carry on with your cleaning and we'll be as fast as we can.' He paused. 'Don't you have any relatives who live closer to the cities?' The sisters shook their heads. 'It's so remote out here, I'm not sure the town can be protected long term. The government concentrate their resources in the more populated areas.'

'This is it, I'm afraid. All our family are dead and we have nowhere else to go,' Oke said. 'Just us and my children.'

'Where are they?' he asked.

'With a friend until we get cleaned up here,' Oke said.

'Boys or girls?'

'Two girls and a boy,' Oke said. The officer nodded and looked at his boots for a second, deep in thought.

'You need to keep a close eye on your girls,' Mane said. 'You know yourselves that they have value to certain people.'

'Boko.'

'Yes, Boko and traffickers,' he warned. 'They may never have the numbers they had before General Basse screwed up but they're on the prowl in small packs. Be alert all the time.'

Oke nodded and felt her heart sink into the pit of her stomach. Soldiers entered the back door and smiled hello. More entered with body bags and stretchers and others followed wearing full protective suits and backpack sprayers. The sergeants stepped in with bottles of drinking water and two crates of supplies. Oke saw fresh fruit and vegetables and tinned meat and beans.

'You're very kind,' Oke said. 'Thank you so much.'

'Our pleasure,' Mane said. 'I'll leave you to it.' He walked down the hallway and began organising the clean-up.

'He sounds worried,' Oke said. She looked at Isime.

'They said Boko are regrouping across the border in Chad and that there had been several raids in the area,' Isime whispered.

'Oh no,' Oke said, shaking her head. 'Where?'

'The captain said a supply dump had been attacked and weapons and ammunition taken,' Isime said. 'We're not safe here, Oke. Boko are coming back.'

Chapter 4

Alice sipped her coffee and waited for a sight of her mark. Latte with an extra shot and one sweetener. It was standard fare for a busy assassin. Her best customer had been on a revenge mission, which was good for the bank balance. Jet Unganu was her best customer and main source of income, which was ideal. The fewer clients, the better. There was less chance of being set up, ripped off or murdered herself. She felt no remorse or sympathy for her targets. They were mostly involved in the criminal underworld one way or another and as such, well aware of the risks and occupational hazards they were exposed to. Today's hit was slightly different in that he wasn't involved in crime. He was a doctor in a children's hospital and upstanding member of the community, which was a shame as most of her hits were total scumbags. It didn't sit right with her but that was the job. Get the name, do your research and eliminate the target. No questions, no guilt, no loose ends. Bank the money and move onto the next project.

Dr Kalu Sammi was the target today, the man who was attacked by Jet's niece. She threatened him with a knife but when Sammi struggled with his attacker, Suzette Unganu fell on the blade, which resulted in her death. His son, Beb had been murdered in a double-cross, carried out by Suzette but she was tricked herself. Beb didn't trust Suzette and had switched the drugs, anticipating foul play during the deal. His instincts had been spot-on. Suzette had been desperate to find the real drugs but she had killed the only man who knew where they were. She wrongly assumed Dr Sammi would have an idea where his son might have hidden them and confronted him. She pulled a knife and the rest was history. They struggled and she fell on the blade and bled out before the ambulance arrived, promoting Dr Sammi to top of the wanted list. It appeared Sammi was an innocent party, guilty only of being related to Beb. Could he be blamed for the death of Suzette Unganu? Not by any rational person but Jet was completely irrational at the best of times. Her brain was haggled by cocaine and alcohol. It was all academic in the long term. Once the dead are buried, questions may be asked but not for long. A tragic story lost in the mists of time with a million other tragic stories. Lives were cut short every day at the bequest of other human beings, no one really gives a shit about it and the few who do, are pissing against the wind. Nothing changes. People live and people die but the world keeps turning. Alice didn't care about Dr Sammi and how innocent he was. She cared about her bank balance and professional reputation. There was also the thrill of the hunt. She enjoyed every second of studying, tracking and hunting another humans. It was better than sex, not that she had much of that. Relationships didn't belong in her world. Emotionally, she needed no one and physically, a selection of vibrators brought her to a quick, yet satisfying climax. Having a partner was impossible in her trade. They ask too many questions and eventually become a liability. If they were to find out the truth of her occupation, they would become the next victim.

There he was, head down, collars up, beanie hat pulled low over his ears. He walked between two ambulances and headed towards the tube station. He was slightly later than usual by about forty minutes. He would cut through London Bridge Street, stopping at Starbucks on his way to the tube. London Bridge station was busy most of the day but it would be quietening down now; rush hour was over. The daylight had long since faded and bumper to bumper traffic crawled by through the drizzle. Headlights and streetlights sparkled in the darkness and exhaust fumes hung heavily on the breeze. Getting to Sammi had been infinitely more difficult than most targets. He didn't drive to work and he didn't go anywhere alone. The only time he wasn't with someone was on his journey home. She had him shadowed for three days and the information appeared to be solid but her source couldn't track him all the time. His place of employment was a children's hospital and out of bounds. No children. That was her only rule. Not even as collateral damage. A children's hospital was off limits but now he was out of there, he was fair game.

She followed him and almost walked past him while he went into Costa. Not Starbucks. She watched through the window as he bought his coffee but he didn't buy coffee. He bought tea. It was not his normal routine but hardly worrying. Sammi was talking on his phone when he came out of the coffee shop and crossed the road, heading towards the tube. Alice closed the distance, weaving through pedestrians like a downhill skier, zigzagging silently, closing the gap. The sloshing of car tires splashing surface water into the air drowned out any noise her footsteps made. Twenty meters became fifteen, then ten. He stopped at a zebra and waited for the green man to appear before crossing. There were people around him, people between him and her, witnesses everywhere she looked. Dr Sammi crossed the road and entered the station through the wrong entrance. Her information led her to believe he did the same things day in and day out. He wasn't following the pattern. Anxiety touched her senses. Any deviation from the norm wasn't good. He bought a ticket for the Northern line and turned around, catching her eye. Alice looked away and continued through the turnstiles. Had she seen something in his eyes? Her instinct told her to abort. Sammi drank coffee every day and travelled north from London Bridge tube station using a prepaid pass. Today, he bought tea and was heading south with a ticket he had paid cash for. This was not his routine. She watched as he descended on the escalator. The wrong escalator. At the bottom, he headed to the southbound platform, not the northbound. Wrong. Was he going to another hospital before going home or visiting a friend, south of the city or going on a date, maybe? There were a million connotations and she didn't have time to consider them all. Proceed or abort, simple choice.

Alice followed at safe distance and stepped onto the platform. Sammi made his way through waiting commuters to the far end of the platform. There were fewer people there and he found a space he was comfortable with and checked his watch. The train was three minutes away. She heard the roar of a northbound train arriving on the other platform, behind them. A blast of warm air announced its arrival. She heard the announcement but not the words. Her attention was on Dr Sammi. He stepped forward, closer to the edge of the platform. Several other commuters shuffled forward, stalking the arriving train, trying to pick the optimum position to get on and get a seat before anyone else. Competition between the herd of commuters was fierce. The train was approaching, a deafening clackety-clack noise accompanied the blast of warm air. It sounded like it would shake itself to pieces. Sammi took a half step forward. A man to his left moved close to his shoulder, another just inches behind him. She could see the light in the tunnel. A woman pushed in front her. Alice kicked the back of her knee, swift and unseen by anyone else. The woman's leg gave way and she stumbled to their left and cried out. Her face was a mixture of surprise and panic. It was all she could do to keep upright. Some onlookers helped her to regain her balance. She had no idea what had happened. The train was almost upon the station. Alice stepped forward and nudged the man behind Sammi with her shoulder. It was a hard shove and unexpected. The man lurched forward and crashed into the back of Dr Sammi. He tried to turn and grab something but the only thing there was the man who had stumbled into him. Sammi grabbed the man's arm, desperate to gain purchase but he was already falling. He pulled the man off balance. The two men fell from the platform and the train hit them before they hit the rails, catapulting them into the air. The impact was catastrophic and they were dead before they fell beneath the thundering wheels where they were crushed and cut to pieces.

Alice was already halfway up the escalator when the screaming began. Dozens of onlookers exited the platform in a hurry, heading for the exits. A death on the line would stop the trains for hours and the police would be interviewing witnesses all night. Most people didn't have the time or the inclination to waste their precious hours on fruitless investigations. Whoever was under the train was dead. Full stop.

Several police officers were running down the opposite escalator in response to the panicked noises from the southbound platform. She breathed a sigh of relief as she stepped out of the station into the night. The drizzle felt refreshing on her skin. Job done.

Chapter 5

Kissie ended the call and kicked the armchair, swearing at the empty room. She went to the fridge and took out a bottle of water. She placed the bottle against her forehead, enjoying the coolness. Beb called her, his timing uncanny. She unscrewed the top and gulped the cold liquid down before answering.

'Hello brother,' she answered smiling. Her life felt completely different with him in it. Beb had died but it wasn't Beb and the real Beb was alive, recovering from a bullet wound in Morocco. Shortly after, Kissie and her father had seen her sisters, who had been missing presumed dead since their transport boat was sunk. Isime and Oke were on the evening news from Monguno hospital. The sense of loss which had haunted her for over ten years had been replaced by such a feeling of love and excitement, she felt like she was going to explode. But it also brought a sense of longing. Longing to find them and be with them again. 'How are you today?'

'We're good. I'm almost back to full strength,' Beb said. 'Amira is shopping for clothes and food for the journey. Heba is growing every day. I swear she has doubled her weight since we came to Morocco.'

'I can't wait to see her,' Kissie said, smiling.

'Have you found Oke and Isime?' Beb asked.

'No, not yet,' Kissie said, closing her eyes. She sighed. 'Every time I think I have a lead it turns out to be a dead end. I have just spoken to a foreign correspondent in Nigeria and she said the last broadcast she did about the nerve agent was from Monguno General Hospital. I asked her about the patients in the background and she said she wasn't allowed to interview any of the patients or their families.'

'They're silencing the victims,' Beb said.

'It looks that way,' Kissie agreed. 'The Nigerian government is smothering the incident or they will have to admit that Boko was in control of the entire north-eastern border of the country, unchallenged for years.'

'And that would make them look weak.'

'Exactly. When I asked her for the names of the doctors who were dealing with the patients, she hung up on me.'

'What about calling the hospital directly?' Beb asked.

'The landlines are not connected,' Kissie said. 'Everyone there uses mobiles and no one has any numbers I can use.'

'What has father said?' Beb asked.

'We're trying to get flights as soon as we can,' Kissie said. 'He has a few cases that he needs to hand over before we can travel. He's been at the hospital all day, trying to get a colleague to cover him. It's so frustrating.'

'So, we know they were in Monguno?' Beb asked.

'Yes,' Kissie agreed. 'But we don't know how they made their way back there or if they are still there.'

'It's clear to me why they are there,' Beb said. 'I thought about going there every day when I was growing up.'

'What do you mean?' Kissie asked.

'They have gone home,' Beb said. 'That's why they're there.' Kissie felt tears trickle from her eyes.

'They think we're dead, don't they?' Kissie sniffled.

'We all thought the same thing,' Beb said. 'They will know we're alive soon enough. We're going to get a flight to Chad. N'Djamena airport is the closest we can get to by airplane. If we hire a jeep, we can cross the border at Fotokol and be there in around eight hours.'

'When are you going to fly?'

'Tomorrow.'

'Crossing the border isn't easy, Beb,' Kissie said. 'It's dangerous.'

'I have been crossing borders in Africa most of my life,' Beb said. 'Most of the time, you don't know you've crossed one.'

'I suppose you have,' Kissie said, sobbing now. 'It makes me so sad to think of you drifting in the wilderness all those years.'

'It was the only life I knew,' Beb said. 'Borders are just imaginary lines on a map. They all have the same requirements to cross.'

'What's that?'

'Money gets you into any country in Africa,' he added. 'We have enough money to get there and cross the border.'

'This is so scary for me to think about. Where will you go to look for them?' Kissie asked.

'Home, sister,' Beb said. 'Home is the most obvious place to start.'

Chapter 6

Detective Sergeant Alfred struggled into a forensic suit, cursing that the fucking things were getting tighter. It was probably due to a cost cutting exercise, using less material to save a few pounds here and there. They were disposable after all. There was no need to make them comfortable if they were being thrown away. Single use PPE didn't need to fit, obviously.

'That looks a bit tight, boss,' Detective Constable Coop said, grinning. 'Put a few pounds on lately?'

'Fuck off, Coop,' Alfred muttered, breathing. 'They've changed the supplier.'

'Funny, mine fits the same,' Coop said, frowning. 'Have the sizes changed?' he asked one of the CSI officers, who was working nearby.

'Nope,' she said. 'If it's tight, you're eating too much and not moving around enough.' Alfred glared at her. 'It's okay to be heavier than you would like to be. Lots of people are,' she added. 'It's part of the human condition. Some people are fat, some aren't. It's important to own the fact and that you're comfortable in your own skin.'

'Thank you very much for that incredible insight,' Alfred said, shaking his head. His face was flushed purple. 'You could be a fucking guru if you lose this job,' he said, nodding. 'Here's an insight for both of you. Some people have secure employment and some don't and some people are too fucking stupid to realise the difference!' Coop stopped grinning and put his overshoes and gloves on. The CSI looked away and carried on logging evidence. The lead detective popped his head into the van.

'DS Alfred?' he said. Alfred nodded, pulling on his gloves. 'I'm DI Stanton. I was told you wanted to be brought up to speed on this one?'

'Yes. Thanks for the call,' Alfred said. 'Harry Trainor is connected to a drug-related death on our patch.'

'So, I believe,' Stanton said, nodding. 'Suzette Unganu?'

'Yes. You're aware of it?'

'Jet Unganu is in the frame for this,' Stanton said. Alfred nodded in agreement. He was ready and stepped out of the van. 'Follow me. Is this your DC?' he asked, nodding to Coop.

'DC Coop,' Coop said, introducing himself. 'How long has he been here?'

'It could be as long as a week,' Stanton replied. 'Until we have the preliminary reports back, I can't say for certain.' They walked into a derelict warehouse and the smell of death floated to them. 'It has all the marks of a punishment killing. This isn't a hit on a rival, it's personal. The poor fucker was dissected by someone with knowledge of how to inflict maximum pain for the maximum length of time.' They reached a forensic tent, which was unusual for a body found indoors. 'We put the tent up because images were posted online and the pictures were taken from up there on that gantry,' Stanton said, pointing. 'Instagram, Pinterest, Youtube, Facebook, TikTok, and a few on the dark web all had images and video clips a few hours before we received the tipoff that the body was here. I have no desire to star in season two.'

'Jet has let everybody know what happened to Harry Trainor,' Alfred said, rubbing tiger balm beneath his nose. 'Have they been taken down?'

'The originals, yes,' Stanton said. 'But they've been shared so many times, they're beyond reach now.' He opened the tent flap and ducked inside. Alfred and Coop followed him. The smell of corruption intensified.

'Jesus Christ,' Alfred muttered.

'It's difficult to work out what I'm looking at,' Coop said, shaking his head. 'Feet here, hands over there, head missing eyes…'

'Okay Coop!' Alfred snapped. 'We don't need a fucking commentary, thank you.'

'Sorry, boss,' Coop said, shrugging. 'Just saying what I see.'

'I'm not Roy Walker and this isn't fucking Catchphrase.'

'The skin looks blistered,' Coop commented, ignoring the DI's moody response.

'We don't know for sure, but we think he was tortured with something caustic, a strong acid or alkali before they started cutting bits off him.'

'Fucking hell,' Coop whispered and turned pale. 'He must have suffered.'

'Do you think so?' Alfred said, shaking his head.

'It's an expertly dismantled human being,' Stanton said, smirking at Alfred's impatience. 'We've seen similar to this twice before. The acid burns are common to all three victims. One was a drug dealer in Southend in 2016 and the other was a CHIS found in Brighton in 2019. Both were in conflict with, guess who?'

'Jet Unganu,' Coop said, enthusiastically. Alfred looked at him and frowned, shaking his head. 'Obviously,' Coop muttered.

'She's using an enforcer,' Alfred said, studying the remnants of Trainor. 'The amputations are clean, no jagged edges. Bleeding was kept to a minimum by cauterising the wounds with the blowtorch, keeping him alive as long as possible.'

'I'm not buying the enforcer theory,' Stanton said, disagreeing. Alfred shrugged and waited for the inspector to clarify his thoughts. 'Jet Unganu may be a larger-than-life figure in Soho but in the wider scheme of things, she's relatively insignificant. She stays within her postcode and avoids stepping outside it, right?'

'Yes,' Alfred said. 'But she's no angel by any stretch of the imagination. She's a ruthless operator.'

'I'm not disputing that but look at her outfit,' he said. 'You know them better than we do but I don't see anyone on her payroll capable of this type of hit. They're thugs and steroid munching bouncers. This took planning, precision and skill. The wet work has been practiced and honed to a fine art. This is beyond the capability of her outfit. It's another level. Their knowledge of anatomy, nerve centres and how to dismantle the bigger joints is advanced. This is the work of a true professional.'

'Are you talking about a hitman?' Coop asked.

'Yes. I am,' Stanton said. 'It's the only way she could carry out this type of punishment hit and stay completely clean of any investigation. She's paying a real pro to do this. Someone who could carry this out with the confidence that they wouldn't be interrupted and the internet knowhow to take pictures and upload to multiple sites for maximum impact, quickly and irreversibly. This has all the hallmarks of practice to perfection.'

'Are you going to pull her in?' Alfred asked.

'Not yet,' Stanton said. 'We have nothing to link her to this that would get us a warrant. Trainor was seen arguing with Suzette in a pub but we know he didn't kill her. Dr Sammi was the only one there when she died. A judge would laugh us out of court.'

'So, what are you going to do?' Alfred asked.

'We're going to apply some pressure to the weaker links in her organisation and I need your help with that,' Stanton said. 'I want to shake every tree in her yard and see what falls out.'

Alfred felt his phone vibrating. He looked at the screen and saw it was his superintendent.

'I need to take this,' he said.

'No problem,' Stanton said. Alfred went out of the tent. 'What is happening with the Suzette Unganu case from your end?' he asked Coop. Coop looked towards the door, uncomfortable. 'I'm not asking you to talk out of school. It's just a question from one copper to another. How is it going?'

'It's stalled,' Coop said, shrugging. 'Dr Sammi was defending himself and his hands weren't on the knife at any point.' He lowered his voice. 'The delay has been because he pissed the boss off so we looked into the possibility that he knew what his son was up to but it was a ghost-hunt. The boss was being arsey about it but there was no substance to the enquiry. There was nothing to indicate he was anything but unlucky.'

'It sounds that way,' Stanton agreed.

'That was the superintendent,' Alfred said, stepping back into the tent. He looked shaken and a little bemused. 'Dr Sammi fell under a tube train last night.'

'Is he dead?' Coop asked.

'What do you think, Einstein?' Alfred asked, sighing.

'That's a massive coincidence,' Stanton said.

'My thoughts exactly,' Alfred said. 'Jet Unganu is exacting her own brand of justice on the men she blames for Suzette's death.'

Chapter 7

Oke and Isime were both delighted and relieved with the state of their house. The soldiers had been a blessing; their intervention had turned a dreadful situation into a bearable one. The bodies were removed discreetly, the shackles dismantled and the bedrooms were cleaned, steamed and disinfected in under two hours. There was barely a trace of the horrors that they had uncovered when they returned to their family home. The shock of finding the bodies was fading although the images would stay with them forever.

Unfortunately, the soldiers couldn't save the bed. The frame was rotten and the mattress was infested and it fell apart when the soldiers moved it. Not that the sisters wanted to keep it but furniture was in short supply. When the soldiers had gone, they had worked late into the night to finish cleaning the living room and kitchen. The bathroom was as clean as it had ever been and the water was running clear. They were exhausted when they curled up together on the thin mattress that had been left in the living room. Sleep found the sisters quickly and enveloped them until the sun came up the next morning. They felt rested and made sweet tea, eating some fruit for breakfast. After washing themselves, they set about finishing the job, so that Oke could fetch her children.

Oke opened the pantry door. It was cool in there, no windows or air vents. Most of the houses had them to store food out of the blistering heat. The pantry shelves, which had once been filled with jars of pickles, preserves, dried and tinned foods, were empty now. A faded mat made from reeds and twine covered most of the floor. Oke moved it and Isime rolled it up. A brass ring fixed to a hatch was the only clue that there was a storage cellar dug beneath the pantry. Her childhood memories drifted back. Her mother used to threaten to put them down in the cellar if they misbehaved; although she never did, the threat was severe. Being put in the cellar and locked in the dark was the nuclear option and never used. Oke pulled at the ring and the hatch opened with ease. She looked inside with curious excitement but was disappointed to see the shelves down there were empty too. It was hardly surprising. The pantries were common to most of the houses in town and wouldn't have remained a secret for long.

'There will be nothing left down there,' Isime said. 'It would have been raided by Boko.'

'You're right. It's empty,' Oke said, sadly.

'What did you expect?' Isime asked. 'The bastards took everything this town had to offer. Like a plague of locusts. Greedy selfish pigs, all of them.'

'I can remember how it looked and the smells in here, can you?' Oke asked, studying the space beneath the hatch.

'Not so much,' Isime said. 'But you're older. Much older.'

'Shut up,' Oke said, chuckling. 'If I'm older, I should be wiser too.'

'Should be,' Isime added. 'Maybe the wisdom will come eventually.'

'Cheeky woman,' Oke joked. 'The ladders are still here,' she said, reaching beneath the hatch. Wooden steps slid into view. They were fitted on rails. 'Mother used to threaten to lock us down here. Do you remember?'

'No,' Isime said, 'But I was a good child. You were naughty.'

'I was not naughty,' Oke said, frowning. 'Mischievous, maybe.'

Oke climbed down into the small cellar. She looked into the shadows. One shelf was filled with material, rolls and rolls of plain and patterned cloth. On the shelf below was a familiar object. She smiled with delight.

'Mother's sewing is still here,' Oke said. 'And rolls and rolls of cloth.' There was quiet for a few seconds. 'She taught me how to use this,' Oke said, excited. 'I can make things to sell. This is such a fantastic find.' Isime watched on, smiling. A knock on the back door startled them. 'Who is that?' Oke called.

'I don't know,' Isime said, ducking. She glanced through the window and saw a truck and men in uniform. 'Soldiers!'

'What do you think they want?' Oke asked, panting as she climbed back up the steps. 'I can't get my breath these days,' she added. Another loud knock frightened them. 'What can they want from us?'

'Don't answer the door,' Isime whispered. 'I'm frightened.'

'They know we're here,' Oke said. 'The lights are lit.'

'Don't answer it,' Isime said, squeezing her hand. 'I can't go back to where we were before, Oke. They'll make us marry another pig.' She was shaking like a leaf in the wind. 'Please don't open the door.'

'Clam down, sister,' Oke said. 'No one is taking you anywhere.' Oke peeked through the corner of the window and saw Captain Mane. She sighed with relief.

'It's the nice captain,' she said, straightening her dress. She opened the door and smiled. 'Hello captain,' she said, beaming. 'Come in and have some tea.'

'No, thank you. We're in a rush,' the captain said, nodding hello. 'But we have something that I think you will want.' He winked and tapped his nose. 'The Nigerian troops are refurbishing parts of the barracks and they have over ordered some beds and mattresses,' he said, lowering his voice. 'The old ones have never been used. I noticed you were short of a few beds,' he added. 'Would you like them?'

'Oh, what a kind thought!' Oke said. 'My children will be so excited to try a bed with a mattress.'

'We've brought two big ones and three singles,' the captain said. 'That is enough, isn't it?'

'More than enough,' Isime said, her hand to her mouth in shock. 'You're so kind, Captain Mane. We can't thank you enough.'

They stood back while the captain's men unloaded their truck. The two sergeants who had been there before smiled as they carried bedframes in.

'Shall we put them into the bedrooms, for you?' one of them asked.

'Yes please,' Oke said. She clapped her hands together. 'I haven't been so happy for years!' she laughed. 'Imagine what the children will say when they get here. They will be delighted!'

'They would have been put into a storage shed and left there to rot,' Mane said. 'No one will notice they are missing. No one knows what is going on at that barracks. There are more chiefs than Indians and none of them want to work. I am worried what will happen when they pull us out.'

'I hope it's not for a long time,' Isime said. 'We feel safer knowing you are around and we appreciate the help you have given to us.' She smiled. 'Do you and your men want some tea?' Isime asked.

'No, thank you,' Mane said. 'We're in a rush but I wanted to drop those beds off before they were moved into storage or thrown away. Equipment keeps arriving and no one knows who is ordering it. Three truckloads of uniforms and boots arrived this morning and no one knows what to do with them. It looks like they're expecting hundreds of troops to be stationed in Monguno but nobody can tell us when they are coming.'

'That's a good thing though, isn't it?' Oke asked.

'From your point of view, yes. It makes you more secure and it's less likely that Boko would return while there are troops in the barracks.'

'That is a relief,' Isime said, pouring cold tea into cups. 'Here, have some tea while your men are bringing the beds in. I insist,' she added. Mane took the tea and sipped it. Their eyes met for a second too long and Isime looked away and picked up a cloth, wiping at a non-existent stain on the table. 'We're very grateful. I can't remember the last time we slept on a bed, can you?' she asked Oke.

'In hospital,' Oke said. 'But I was ill, so it doesn't count as enjoyable.'

The sergeants walked back through the kitchen, smiling and nodding as they went.

'All finished?' Oke asked as they left. One of them turned and saluted. He winked and Oke blushed. 'You and your men have been more than kind,' Oke mumbled.

'We try to help where we can,' Mane said, placing his cup in the sink. 'As I said, we're in a rush, so I'll bid you good day, ladies.' He stepped out of the door. 'Sleep tight tonight,' he called.

The sisters hugged each other and laughed. It had been a long time since they had any luck but bad luck.

'I can't wait to get the children and show them our new home,' Oke said. Sadness appeared in Isime's eyes. 'I'm sorry,' she said. 'I know how much you miss him. It's insensitive of me.'

'No, it isn't,' Isime said. 'You nearly died. I'm so glad you didn't.'

A tap on the front door startled them. The second knock was more of a bang. They frowned at each other and Isime went to the door and opened it. A small woman in full burka was standing on the path. Her eyes were dark and wrinkled and something else. Angry.

'What are you doing here?' she asked, without introduction.

'Sorry, who are you?' Oke said, shaking her head.

'This house is not yours,' the woman said, shaking her head. 'What are you doing here?'

'This house belongs to the Sammi family,' Oke said. 'Doctor Kalu Sammi's family. There was recognition in the woman's eyes.

'You knew him?' The woman nodded. 'We are his daughters, Oke and Isime, not that it's any of your business.'

'You are disgusting women,' the woman said.

'I beg your pardon!' Oke laughed. 'Who the fuck are you and why are you knocking on our door?'

'You're behaving like sluts of the night,' the old woman said. 'I've been watching you. Men coming and going all the time. Foreign soldiers.'

'I think you need to go and annoy someone who gives a shit what you think,' Oke said. 'Because we don't.'

'You have a filthy mouth but most sluts do,' the woman said, pointing her bony finger. 'You think those soldiers are your friends?' she asked, cackling like a witch. 'They will want something in return for the food and furniture they brought for you,' she said, cackling again. 'Where do you think that furniture came from?'

'Why don't you mind your own business?' Isime said. 'We're just trying to get by and build a home. Leave us alone.'

'It wasn't theirs to give away but they will want payment for it,' the woman said. Her eyes were piercing, full of spite and hatred. 'They will want your filthy flesh and if you say no, they will threaten to tell that you have stolen property in your house. They want your vagina, nothing more. Sluts.'

'Just fuck off!' Oke shouted, her temper snapped. She shoved the old woman hard in the chest and she staggered backwards. 'Go and spout your hatred somewhere else.'

'You'll be sorry you did that. I've warned you, sluts.' The woman composed herself and walked closer to them. 'I'm going to inform about your behaviour. You'll be whipped to an inch of your lives. Just wait and see if you're not.' She pointed her finger again. 'I'll go to the barracks myself and tell them, right now!' she glared at Oke. 'You'll be in jail before nightfall. I'll make sure you are.'

'Are you going to inform on us, really?' Isime asked.

'Yes, I am!'

'I recognise you,' Oke said, remembering her eyes. 'You were like the morality police in the town, always interfering in other people's lives.' The woman folded her arms and nodded. 'You were poison then and you're poison now.'

'We'll see if you're so smart with your mouth when the soldiers are dragging you to the square by your hair. Sluts!'

'Why would you do that?' Oke frowned.

'Because you're unholy sluts and you need to be flogged,' the woman hissed. 'I hope they stone you to death!'

Oke felt something move behind her. She caught a glimpse of Isime and saw a flash of something dull. There was a sickening crack as a stone rolling pin connected with the old woman's skull. Her eyes rolled backwards and blood poured into them. A whimper erupted from her lips as her knees buckled and she folded in half on the path. Isime stood over her and hit her again, crushing the back of her skull. A gurgling sound came from her. Isime brought the weapon down twice more. The sound was slushy. The gurgling ceased.

'Isime!' Oke hissed, quietly. 'What have you done?'

'She's an informer. I've shut her mouth for good,' Isime said, grabbing the woman by the waist. 'Let's get her inside before more spying eyes see us. If she told the Nigerian soldiers we have furniture from the barracks, we would be back in slavery for the rest of our lives. I'm not letting that happen, sister.' They dragged the frail body into the house. She was the type of scum who collaborated with Boko and got people killed. It was only a matter of time before someone shut her up.'

Oke closed the front door and bolted it. She turned and stared at the woman on the floor. Isime felt for her pulse and shook her head. 'I can't feel anything.' She took the rolling pin to the sink and washed the blood from it.

'You have smashed her head in,' Oke said, sighing. 'I mean, I wanted to smash her head in but I didn't. You've actually bashed her brains out. What the fuck, Isime?'

'We have to think about us and your children from now on,' Isime said, drying her hands. 'She was going to inform on us. We have food and furniture from the barracks and we have a machinegun in the shed. Do you remember that?'

'What?'

'The machinegun that you told me to hide?' Isime said. 'If they search the house, they will find it and then we're finished.'

'Yes, you're right,' Oke said, staring at the lifeless eyes.

'We have a weapon in our house. It would be a death sentence and what would happen to your daughters then?' Oke leaned against the door as if she was about to faint. 'They would be subjected to the life we had.' Isime opened the pantry door and opened the hatch. 'They will not live the life we had to. Not while I'm breathing.' She stood over the body. 'Help me move the old witch,' she said. Oke stared at the body. 'Oke!' Isime clapped her hands. 'Snap out of it and help me move her.'

'What are we going to do with her body?'

'We'll put her in the cellar until we can work out what to do with her,' Isime said. 'The most important thing to do now is remain calm. No one knows what has happened, so we hide her for now and work out the plan later.'

'I can't believe you smashed her head in with a rolling pin,' Oke muttered. 'My sister bashed the woman's brains out. The world is mad.'

'Stop complaining. Grab her legs,' Isime said. They carried the woman across the room and into the pantry. Oke was struggling to breathe. 'Put her down there.' They placed her next to the hatch and Isime kicked her over the edge into the cellar. The body tumbled into the cellar with a thump, like a bag of cement hitting the floor. She stood up and closed the hatch, covering it with the reed mat. 'There we go. We're safe now, sister.'

'We have a dead body in the cellar,' Oke said, shaking her head. 'That is not my definition of safe.'

Chapter 8

London

Kissie was drying her hair when her mobile rang. She saw the name on the screen. Auntie Celia. She swore beneath her breath and turned off the Dyson. Celia was a snob and had looked down on them when they had arrived from Africa. She was patronising and had talked to Kissie as if she was retarded. Kissie remembered her asking what she wanted to be when she grew up, a hairdresser or beauty therapist, or perhaps an admin assistant. When Kissie had said she wanted to be a scientist, Celia had laughed, shaking her head in a patronising manner. 'It's charming that you have dreams,' she had said.

Years later, when Kissie was graduating for her MA, Kalu took the family for a celebratory meal but Celia made an excuse not to be there. Their relationship was strained and only maintained for the sake of her father. If she never heard from her again, it wouldn't bother Kissie. In all the years she had known her, Celia had never called her, which gave her an uncomfortable feeling. Something bad had happened. She answered the call.

'Hello Celia,' Kissie said, trying to sound pleased to hear from her. 'Nice to hear from you.'

'Is your father there?' Celia asked, without pleasantries. She sounded like she was crying. 'He's not answering his phone.'

'He's working a nightshift,' Kissie answered. 'He normally finishes about nine-ish in the morning unless he gets stuck, which is always.' Kissie heard her sniffle. 'Are you okay?'

'Chuk is dead,' she said, her voice breaking.

'Uncle Chuk?' Kissie said, shocked. She loved her father's brother. 'What happened?'

'He didn't come home last night,' Celia said. 'I was worried sick. He's often late but he's never not called. I knew something bad had happened and then the police arrived and told me he was dead.'

'This is terrible,' Kissie said, crying. Her stomach cramped with anxiety. 'What happened, Celia?'

'They don't know exactly. There was an accident at the tube station,' Celia spluttered. 'London Bridge station.' She was sobbing uncontrollably. Kissie listened to Celia's heart breaking and waited for her to gather herself. 'Chuk and another man fell under a train. They were both killed.'

'How could that happen?' Kissie asked.

'I have no idea. There will be an investigation. I need to tell your father his brother is gone. I don't want him to hear it from the news or social media. He will be devastated.'

'I have an emergency number at the hospital, where I can reach him,' Kissie said. 'Do you want me to tell him?' Kissie asked, hoping she would say no.

'If you could, that would be a huge relief,' Celia said, sniffling loudly. 'I can barely think straight. He can call me when he's finished work.'

'Okay Celia,' Kissie said, feeling gutted. She felt guilty for not liking her. It seemed so silly now. 'I'll call him now.' She paused and waited for a reply but Celia was whimpering. 'Are you alone?'

'No,' Celia lied. . 'I have family here,' she muttered. Kissie sensed she was telling lies. 'Tell your father to call me, yes?'

'I will,' Kissie said. 'Take care of yourself.' Celia hung up, leaving a deafening silence on the line.

Chapter 9

Beb had chosen not to fly directly to Nigeria as Amira was a Tuareg and would encounter hurdles to enter the country. They didn't have time to jump through hoops for visas. The closest airport was in Chad. N'Djamena is the capital city of Chad, situated on the northern border of Cameroon and just a few hours drive to the eastern border of Nigeria. It has over a million inhabitants, many refugees from rural areas where rebel groups kidnap male children to train as boy soldiers and young females for sexual exploitation and domestic slavery. Civil war had made the city a dangerous place to be. Beb was well aware of how fragile the society there was. Like most of the African continent, law and order wasn't a given and money was king. Flying with his wife and child would be simple enough and safe but the journey from Chad through Cameroon to Monguno would be treacherous. Amira was nervous about flying and Heba was oblivious until the plane began its descent and then she complained about her ears hurting. Beb gave her a lollipop and she settled down. They landed and cleared baggage claim and customs without incident. He had contacted several companies online, who offered vehicles for hire and for sale but only one had replied and their website was dubious. They had promised to send a representative to meet them at the airport. As they left the baggage hall, a dozen drivers held up cards with names on them but none of them were his. He scanned the waiting crowd again but couldn't see anyone waiting for them.

'They said there would be someone here with my name on a board,' Beb said, dragging two cases across the exit hall. Amira followed, holding Heba's hand and a small case. It was buzzing with activity and people talking loudly in different languages. Heba was wide-eyed and frightened by the noise.

'Shall I wait here with the cases while you look for them?' Amira asked, hugging Heba to her chest to reassure her.

'No. Absolutely not,' Beb said, shaking his head. 'We stay together every minute of the day until we know we're safe. We do not separate, darling. Not even for a minute. It's too dangerous.'

'You're frightening me,' Amira said.

'I don't mean to,' Beb said, kissing her forehead. 'But we need to stay together.' He noticed a man leaning against a barrier holding a piece of cardboard with 'Bob Sani' scrawled on it. 'Let's ask him if he's waiting for us,' Beb said. They crossed the expanse of tiles, navigating the tide of humans exiting the airport. 'Are you waiting for me, Beb Sammi?'

'Beb not Bob?' the man asked, frowning.

'Yes. Beb.'

'Are you on the Marrakesh flight looking to hire a vehicle?'

'Yes,' Beb said. The man was massively overweight and sweating profusely. He eyed Amira a little too long. His white suit was a few sizes too small and greyed at the cuffs and knees. It hadn't been washed for a long time. The smell of body odour was unmissable.

'Then I'm your man. My secretary needs to wear her glasses when she's writing. Call me Squire,' he said, grinning. His teeth were yellowed by cigarettes. 'Let's go to my office where we can talk. It's too noisy in here. Follow me, please.'

They weaved through the crowd to an exit marked, taxi and parking. The heat of the afternoon sun hit them like a brick wall. Horns blared and packs of taxi drivers swooped on everyone leaving the building. The smell of cigarette smoke hung heavy on the air. Some of the cabbies grabbed for Beb's luggage, offering to carry them for a small fee. Over-enthusiastic offers turned aggressive when he refused and pulled his cases away. Squire shooed some of the men away angrily as if they were seagulls following a trawler, stealing the catch, vermin to be driven away. Curious eyes studied them as they followed Squire past the taxi rank towards the carpark. Beb noticed the attention they were getting. A man wearing a scruffy white shirt jogged next to Beb. His name badge said he was Omar and he was a taxi driver.

'Hello friend,' he said. 'I see you're not from Chad.'

'Hello,' Beb said. 'We don't need a taxi, thank you.'

'Cool. Where are you from?'

'That's a long story,' Beb said.

'Do you know this fat thief?' Omar said, smiling. Half his teeth were missing. He pointed to Squire. 'Do not trust this man. He is not a good man.'

'Get away from him,' Squire shouted. He squared up to the little taxi driver, threatening to squash him. 'Go about your business and leave me to do mine.'

'Don't trust this man,' Omar said, turning away. 'He's a greedy man, you can see that by looking at him,' he added. 'Do you see how fat he is?' Omar shouted. 'That's because he's greedy!'

'Go away,' Squire growled. 'Before I beat you to a pulp.'

'Fat thief,' Omar called after them. 'Don't trust that man!'

Amira looked at Beb, her eyes full of concern. Beb felt uncertainty engulf him. The enormity of the precarious situation they were in threatened to overwhelm him. He had never met the little taxi driver before yet he trusted him more than the man they were supposed to be doing business with. Omar's warning resounded in his mind. They were carrying everything they owned in their arms and everyone around them knew it. They were vulnerable and they were exposed. Squire sensed their anxiety.

'Take no notice of that man,' he said, smiling. His voice was full of confidence but his eyes belied it. He looked nervous and shifty, like a man about to do something wrong. Beb had been around dishonest people most of his life. They had a furtive look in their eyes when they spoke. 'The airport is a magnet for crooks, thieves and beggars. You cannot trust anyone or anything they say, unless they're a legitimate business, like mine. We have a website as you know and that is how you know we're a company you can trust.' He beckoned them towards a reasonably new Mercedes. Beb felt a little better as they approached. 'We're established with a very good reputation.'

'Is this the vehicle?' Beb asked.

'What?' Squire asked, wiping sweat from his brow. He looked at the Mercedes and laughed. 'Oh, this one?'

'Why is that funny?' Beb asked.

'Because it's nearly new.' Squire shrugged. 'You can see it's a nearly new Mercedes?'

'Is it the vehicle we're hiring or not?'

'This is a hundred-thousand-dollar Mercedes,' Squire said, shrugging. He smiled widely and rolled his eyes. 'Come on, seriously. No one is going to hire this vehicle to a stranger at the airport, so close to the borders of three countries, plagued by pirates, rebels and extremists. Surely, you don't expect a vehicle like this?'

'I'm not sure what to expect,' Beb said, disappointed. 'Are you telling me you only hire vehicles to people you know?'

'Of course, not. We have to be sure our clients can actually drive a vehicle and are able to pay,' Squire said. 'The risk must be minimal or we would go out of business. You must understand that?'

'I can understand that. We need a vehicle,' Beb said. 'So, what are the choices?'

'Let's get to my office, where we can go through the details,' Squire put his hand in the air and waved. A rusty old Fiat pulled out from a parking space. 'Obviously, the vehicles available depend on where you're going and for how long.' The driver of the approaching vehicle smiled at them through a cracked windscreen. A single tooth was clinging on to his gums. 'Get in and my driver will take us into the city. Our office and carpool are half an hour away.'

Amira squeezed Beb's hand. Her eyes were pleading and frightened. She shook her head.

'We're not getting into any vehicles except the one we hire,' Beb said, shaking his head. 'No offence but we don't know you or your driver. Let's do the paperwork here and you can have the vehicle delivered to us here.'

'You're perfectly safe with Squire,' he said. Disappointment made his face sag and look dogged. He looked offended. 'There are a lot of questions to go through, obviously. We can't do it here.'

'We're not getting into a vehicle with you. We need some shade and we need water and something to eat. My daughter is tired and hungry,' Amira said. 'We'll be in the airport. You can ask your questions there and deliver the vehicle when we're done.'

'I don't have all the paperwork with me,' Squire pleaded. 'We must go to the office. You can be on your way in a few hours.' He steepled his fingers, pleading. 'Come to the office with me and you will see that everything is above board. We're a very trustworthy company.' He opened the door and leaned into the Fiat. 'Ask my driver. He has worked for me for many years.' The driver nodded and smiled a toothless smile. He looked clueless as to what was going on. 'Everyone knows Squire is a trustworthy businessman, don't they?'

The driver nodded enthusiastically and put his thumbs up.

'We're not going anywhere,' Beb said, unconvinced. 'Like my wife said, we'll be in the cafeteria. You can ask your questions there.' They turned and walked back towards the terminal, where they were hounded again by the swarm of taxi drivers. Beb caught sight of Omar. He was smiling and nodding his head.

'You're wise to listen to advice, mister,' Omar said. 'The fat man is a shark. Ask anyone here. He's well known for ripping people off. He's a dangerous man.'

Beb carried on walking but bowed his head slightly, as a thank you gesture.

'Where are you going?' Omar asked as they walked away.

'Ignore him,' Amira said. 'We don't know if he's telling the truth or not. You can't trust him either.'

'I don't trust anyone,' Beb said. They stepped into the terminal, welcoming the cooler conditions. The air-conditioning was installed on a budget and wasn't fit for purpose but it was better than being outside in the glaring sun. The fans whirled noisily, some of them rocking off balance. 'Let's go to that café over there,' he said, gesturing. They made their way to it and found a table with four chairs fixed around it. Beb put the cases against a partition, which separated them from the next row of tables and gave Amira a twenty-dollar note. 'I'll mind Heba and the cases. You go and see what you feel like eating, love.'

'What do you want?' Amira asked, handing Heba over.

'A couple of sandwiches and some juice,' Beb said. 'I'll let you decide,' he added smiling. Amira went to the counter and was served immediately. Beb watched her, while he chatted to Heba. She was beginning to relax a little but her eyes darted here and there, captivated by the array of brightly-dressed humans. Amira made her way with a tray full of food and drinks. She put them on the table as Squire reappeared. He looked agitated. There was no room on the table for his paperwork.

'Sit there,' Beb said, pointing to the next table. It would put a little distance between them and Squire's armpits while they ate. 'What do you need to know?'

'I have some of your personal details from your online enquiry,' Squire said, wiping sweat from his forehead with his sleeve.

'I need to see some ID; passport or driving license will suffice,' he said, without looking up. Beb handed him his passport and Squire scribbled the details in an illegible scrawl. 'This document is new?'

'Yes,' Beb said, nodding.

'How long have you been at this address?'

'A few weeks.'

'Weeks?' Squire asked, irritated. 'Where did you live before?'

'In the desert,' Beb said.

'In the desert?'

'Yes.'

'Which desert?' Squire asked, holding the pen above the paper.

'Does it matter?' Beb asked.

'Not really. This is most irregular. How long do you need the vehicle?'

'I'm not sure yet,' Beb said. 'A week maybe but maybe longer.'

'How much longer?' Squire said, shrugging. 'I need a return date, even if it's flexible.'

'Okay, say a week,' Beb said, biting into a sandwich.

'Where will you be staying?'

'We don't know yet,' Beb answered, chewing.

'You don't have any accommodation booked?' Squire frowned.

'Not yet.'

'I might be able to help you with that,' Squire said. 'We have apartments in the city. Let me make a call.'

'Wait, wait, wait. We're not going into the city. We're heading to Monguno,' Beb said, holding up his hand.

'Monguno?'

'Yes.'

'Monguno, Nigeria?'

'Yes.'

'Are you a fucking crazy man?' Squire said, raising his voice. 'Do you have any idea how far away it is?'

'It's a ten-hour drive,' Beb said.

'It's not just a ten-hour drive,' Squire argued, his jowls wobbling. 'You have to cross two borders, the first into Cameroon, which is a corrupt shithole full of rebels and extremists, and then into Nigeria, which is an even more corrupt shithole and has more pirates per square mile than Somalia, if that's even possible.' He rolled his eyes. 'And you want me to give you one of my vehicles when the chances of you surviving to return it are zero?'

'People drive that route every day,' Beb said. 'If we cross into Nigeria at Fotokol, people meet up and form convoys for safety and travel in numbers down the A3 to Dikwa.'

'The A3 is a single-track road through a hundred square miles of jungle and swamps, which is the home of hundreds of rebels hiding from the government. People are robbed and killed there every day,' Squire said, gathering his paperwork into a bundle.

'The convoys are rarely attacked,' Beb said. 'I have researched it.'

'Even if you make it through the jungle, the journey north from Dikwa to Monguno is along the F258. The government has put army patrols on it because of the pirates.' He stood up and tapped his temple with a fat finger. 'You're a crazy man, wasting my time. I can't hire you a vehicle. It will never come back.'

'Okay, we can't hire something,' Beb said, calmly eating his food. 'So, we'll need to look at the possibility of buying a vehicle?'

'You want to buy one?' Squire asked.

'If we can't rent, then we will have to buy,' Beb said.

'Vehicles are very expensive nowadays,' Squire said, sitting back down. His demeanour changed. 'How much do you have to spend?'

'That isn't the question I want to hear,' Beb said, chewing. 'Manual or automatic, petrol or diesel, two or four doors, any preference on four-wheel-drive?' Beb shrugged. 'They're the questions I want to hear from you, then when you know what I am looking for, you can tell me what you have available and how much they are.'

'I don't have a hundred vehicles for sale,' Squire argued. He was losing his temper. 'What do you think this is, car supermarket?' He sprayed spittle as he spoke. 'This is Chad. Cars come here to die. Most of the vehicles here wouldn't be allowed on the roads in other countries.'

'You're doing a good job of talking yourself out of a customer who is in the market for a vehicle,' Beb said. 'I need something that is going to get me to Monguno in under twelve hours without breaking down,' he said, remaining calm. 'Do you have such a vehicle or not?'

'Not,' another voice said from nearby. Beb turned around to see Omar sipping a coke on a table behind him. 'Don't give him any money unless you see the vehicle and have the keys or you will never see him or your money again.'

'I'm warning you!' Squire turned on him. 'Don't interfere in my business.'

'Show him a picture of what you have for sale,' Omar challenged him. Squire flushed red with anger. 'Come on, show him your vehicles.'

'Yes, show me them,' Beb said.

'You must have some photographs on your website or on your mobile, surely?' Omar said, shrugging.

'He has a valid point. Do you have any pictures of your stock?' Beb asked, frowning. 'If you do, I would like to see them.'

'Look, don't listen to this idiot,' Squire said, desperately trying to keep control. 'It doesn't work like that.'

'How does it work?' Beb asked.

'You give me an idea of how much you want to spend and I'll make some calls and see what is available in your price range,' Squire said, smiling uncomfortably. 'I'll get you the best deal.'

'Okay,' Beb said. 'Let me get this straight. You don't have anything we can hire and you don't actually have any vehicles for sale?'

'I don't have time for this,' Squire said, standing up. Sweat ran down his cheeks and dripped from his chin. 'You have my number when you need to talk to me. I'm too busy to waste my time here.'

'Why would I call you?' Beb shrugged. 'You don't have anything for sale or to rent, do you?' Beb asked. Squire stormed off. 'I guess not,' Beb said, watching him. He looked at Amira and she smiled.

'You negotiated very well,' she said. 'We don't have a vehicle but we still have our money. Well done.'

'He's a conman,' Omar said, slurping his coke. 'You've realised that for yourself.'

'We're not stupid,' Beb said, smiling. 'But we appreciate the tipoff.'

'No problem,' Omar said. 'I don't like seeing people being ripped off.'

'We're grateful,' Amira said. 'But we need to get to Monguno and our first option has just walked away.'

'Monguno is a ten-to-twelve-hour drive through dangerous territory.' Omar finished his coke. 'The last I heard the United Nations are keeping the extremists quiet alongside government forces. If you get there, what are you going to do?'

'We don't know yet,' Beb said. 'We're looking for family but there's no way of contacting them without going there. There're no guarantees we will find them.'

'They live in Monguno?'

'We think so.'

'Do you have an address?'

'Yes,' Beb said, nodding. 'I grew up there.'

'Aah, you're going home,' Omar said, slapping the table. A huge grin lit up his face. 'That explains why you're willing to risk the journey.' Beb nodded. 'My guess is, you're not going to want to drive a vehicle back here, so you need to buy one or hire a driver, who already has a vehicle,' Omar said. He lit a cigarette and inhaled deeply. 'I'll take you there for the right price.'

'In your taxi?' Beb asked.

'Yes. I have a Toyota Land Cruiser,' Omar said, nodding. 'It's big and comfortable, four-wheel-drive if the roads get wet and muddy and it has a three-litre engine in case we need to get out of trouble in a hurry.'

'How old is it?' Beb asked, grinning.

'Old but I look after it, myself,' Omar said. 'Toyotas are common here in Chad. When I need parts, there are plenty of broken machines to take parts from. It's very reliable and it will get me there and back, no problem.'

'How much to take us to Monguno?' Beb asked.

'It's four-hundred and sixty-two kilometres, so including fuel, two-thousand American dollars,' Omar said, holding up his phone, which was on Google maps. 'It's a nine-hundred and twenty-four kilometres round trip. I have to drive back, remember.' Beb shook his head. 'It's a fair price.'

'Not a chance,' Beb said, frowning. He shook his head again. 'Five hundred, including fuel.'

'Five hundred?' Omar said, closing his eyes. He put his hand to his head as if he was going to faint. 'Squire was right. You're a crazy man.'

'If we walk outside with our cases, I reckon we can find a taxi driver who will take us to Monguno.' Omar frowned. 'Five hundred American dollars.'

'You are insulting me,' Omar said, shaking his head. He put his hands on his heart. 'I thought we were friends. That hurts my feelings. Two thousand is a good price for a friend. It would be double for a stranger.'

'Paying a thousand dollars a day for a driver hurts me too,' Beb said. 'Two-thousand dollars is way over the mark. You need to do much better than that.'

'Fifteen hundred,' Omar said, holding out his hand.

'Seven-hundred and fifty is my last offer,' Beb said, holding out his hand. 'Including fuel.'

'One thousand,' Omar countered.

'Seven-fifty,' Beb insisted.

'Plus fuel?'

'Including fuel,' Beb said sternly.

'It's extra for the cases,' Omar pushed, grinning.

'Do you want this fare, or not?'

'Okay, deal.' Omar and Beb shook hands.

Amira smiled thinly at Beb but he could see the concern in her eyes. She was frightened. The truth was, Beb was frightened too but he couldn't let her see that.

Chapter 10

Detective Alfred and his DC climbed the stairs of a new venue, which had just been opened by Jet Unganu. Snooker, pool and darts, was the simple name, which was exactly what it said on the tin. A state-of-the-art pool hall.

'It says members only, guv,' Coop said, gesturing to a brass plaque on the wall. 'The website says it can only be used via a membership.'

'How much is the membership?' DS Alfred asked.

'Five hundred a year but you still have to pay to play. That's just for access or it can be hired out for stag and hen parties, birthdays and the like.'

'I remember when it was twenty-pence a game,' Alfred said, shaking his head. 'This is a front to wash money. She's not bothered about members,' he added.

The business was built inside a converted warehouse that had been derelict for decades.

'The word on the street is Jet has built an apartment here too, combined with some office space, which sounds like another counting house,' DS Alfred said, lowering his voice. 'The entire business is just another front to launder drug money.' Everyone knew what she did but evidence is required and witnesses had a habit of disappearing. She was known to buy and sell her properties often but always had over a dozen properties at any one time and she rotated where she slept to keep the police and her rivals on their toes.

The entrance was bright and smelled of adhesive and paint. The stairs were tiled with marbled porcelain more akin to a luxury hotel in the Caribbean than a Soho pool hall. A stainless-steel handrail ran up the staircase and four Velux windows fitted in the roof allowed natural light into the stairwell, which was decorated with huge black and white images of Soho at night.

'Those pictures are amazing,' Coop said.

'It's very impressive, indeed,' Alfred said, looking up at them. 'How do you blow up a photograph to that size, I wonder?'

'It's beyond me. How much do you think this cost?' Coop asked.

'More than we earn in a lifetime. We're batting for the wrong team,' Alfred answered, puffing. Sweat formed on his forehead. 'Why spend all this money and not put in a lift?'

'You could do with joining a gym, guv,' Coop said, taking the stairs two at a time. 'Your lung capacity will improve if you do a bit of aerobic exercise.'

'Thank you for the advice,' Alfred said, breathing in. 'But I would rather shove wasps up my arse than go to a gym. I'm in good shape for a man of my age.'

'Of course, you are,' Coop said, wishing he hadn't spoken. He opened the door at the top of the stairs. 'Fucking hell. Look at the size of this place, guv.'

There were four new snooker tables to their left and eight pool tables in two lines of four. Six dartboards were fixed to the far wall with electronic score boards attached. Each oche was raised into a stage. The bar was to their right. It was a chrome and glass masterpiece stocked with hundreds of boutique gins, rums and single malts. The walls were decorated with images of sporting legends. Boxers, sprinters, golfers, athletes and martial artists. Bruce Lee holding nunchakus dominated one wall and Mohammed Ali standing over the unconscious Sonny Liston dominated another. Four men were playing pool and the barman watched on, polishing glasses. He was wearing a waistcoat, shirt and dickie bow. All the men were black, their hair plaited into bangs. The detectives walked towards the bar. One of the men playing pool snorted like a pig.

'Can anyone smell pork?' he asked as he took a shot. The black ball rattled into the corner pocket. The men laughed raucously.

'Babylon, innit,' Another man added. 'Look out boys, we're likely to be searched, innit.'

'No fucker is gonna be searching anyone. Jet has the pigs around here on a leash. These jokers are just trying their luck,' the oldest man said, sipping from a coffee cup. He was greying but looked big and strong and he held himself as if he was in charge. 'Good morning, officers,' he said, politely. 'I'm afraid we don't open until two o'clock.'

'Oh, we're not here to play pool,' DS Alfred said, smiling. 'And these two pigs aren't on anyone's leash,' he added winking. 'The last funny guy who called me a pig is doing a five-stretch now because someone planted half a kilo of smack in his car. We know you drive a blue Audi, RS, don't you?' The older man looked taken aback and remained silent. 'We're here to speak to Jet Unganu,' Alfred said, his hands deep inside his jacket pocket. 'Is she around?'

'Afraid not,' the man said. 'Is there anything I can help you with?'

'Not unless you had anything to do with the murder of Harry Trainor?' Alfred, asked, smiling.

'Harry who?' the man asked, frowning. He shook his head.

'Trainor,' Alfred repeated.

'The name doesn't ring a bell.'

'Of course, it does. He threatened Suzette Unganu because she gave him a bag of baking soda and when he demanded money, she panicked, attacked Dr Kalu Sammi and ended up falling on her own knife,' Alfred chuckled, dryly.

'I heard he got his as well,' one of the men sneered.

'I beg your pardon?' DS Alfred asked. The man grinned but remained silent. 'Obviously, Jet is very angry about the death of her niece and she should be. We understand that. But you already know all about it.'

'We don't know nothing about nothing.'

'I can't believe that for one minute,' Alfred said, frowning. 'You all work for Jet, don't you?'

'We're just playing pool, innit,' one of the men snarled. 'You're a nosey motherfucker.'

'Nosey?' Alfred said, turning to Coop. 'Am I nosey?'

'All the time, guv,' Coop said, nodding.

'I suppose I am. I'll let you into a little secret. We know you work for Jet because you all have the same hairstyle, you see,' Alfred said, pointing to their heads. He tapped his nose with his forefinger.

'It gives us a massive clue, you see. Everyone that works for Jet has that hairstyle.'

'It's a fashion, innit.'

'Whatever. It's a fucking stupid idea because everyone knows what you do for a living and who you work for.' The men glared angrily at him. 'You would have to be as thick as pig shit to think it's a good idea, like wearing a uniform for criminals, isn't it, detective constable?'

'It definitely helps us to identify who works for who,' Coop said, nodding. 'Thick as pig shit, like the boss said.'

'Be careful, Babylon,' one of the men warned. 'You're crossing the line.'

'Does that offend you?' DS Alfred asked. 'Some people say, thick as mince but I like mince.'

'He loves mince,' Coop agreed. The men looked confused. 'Can't get enough of it.'

'So, thick as pig shit fits the description better, don't you think?' DS Alfred said. 'Your gang all have the same hairstyle. It's quite possibly one the most idiotic things I've ever heard. It screams, "search me, I'm a fucking drug dealer!" Then you complain when you get searched.' The men became agitated. He waited for a response but none came. 'You get searched because you're all involved in selling drugs and selling drugs is illegal, as you all know. This is a nice place but where did all the money come from? It's ironic really,' he said, looking around. 'Selling drugs paid for all this. It pays your wages; it carried Suzette through her education and then selling drugs got her killed. Ironic, you see.' The men remained silent and the tension in the room became palpable. Coop shuffled from one leg to the other waiting for the situation to explode. 'Drugs are a very lucrative business to be in but it can be dangerous too and Suzette found out the hard way. You couldn't write it, could you?' DS Alfred asked. 'But you know all about it, anyway, don't you?' he added. 'Of course, you do.'

'We don't know nothing about nothing, Babylon.'

'Of course, you don't. Are you sure she isn't here because her Porsche is at the back of the building?'

'She got a taxi home last night,' the older man said. 'Had a few too many and doesn't drive when she's over the limit.'

'She's a law-abiding citizen, just trying to earn a living, innit,' a man with a gold tooth said. His voice was gravelly and his eyes dark and aggressive. He looked like he ate six-inch-nails for breakfast.

'Oh, fuck off, you idiot,' DS Alfred snapped. His jovial demeanour changed. 'Jet Unganu hasn't been law-abiding since she was old enough to suck a dick,' he said. The men were taken aback. They looked at each other. 'She used to suck dicks to get a discount on her gear. That's how she was able to undercut the opposition and that's what got her got started. From sucking a dick to being a millionairess in eighteen months.' He watched their expressions hardening. 'That is a good title for a book and it would sell but she couldn't write it because she's an idiot. Thick as pig shit, like you lot.'

'You need to watch your mouth, Babylon,' gold tooth said.

'Why is that?' Alfred asked, smiling. 'What are you going to do, tough guy?'

Gold tooth moved forward and the older man held up his hand. He stopped but bared his teeth in anger.

'You need to listen to this man because he knows the score. Make one more aggressive move and you'll be eating porridge for the next five years.' Gold tooth was seething. Alfred could see the veins in his neck pulsing. He locked eyes with him, neither man flinching. It was only a matter of time before one of them reacted. DS Alfred pointed at the older man. 'What's your name?'

'People call me Smigger,' he said.

'I didn't ask you what people call you,' Alfred said, approaching him. 'I want your name and if you fuck me about, I'll have a bus load of coppers down here in the blink of an eye and I'll make sure every single one of you gets a finger up your arse every day until we release you. How does that sound, Smigger?' he asked. 'Name?'

'Carlton Smith,' he answered, nodding slowly.

'That wasn't difficult, was it?' Alfred asked.

'Get their ID and run them through the system,' Alfred ordered. Coop pulled back his shoulders and approached gold tooth.

'Show me some ID,' Coop said.

'I don't have to show you fuck all, Babylon,' he said, his voice a growl. 'Come near me, Babylon and see what happens.'

'Call for backup,' Alfred ordered. He walked over to gold tooth and took out his cuffs. 'That was a threat and reinforces my point that you're all as thick as pig shit.' Gold tooth was about to explode. Alfred could smell the testosterone. 'I think he's going to take a swing at me. Get backup here, sharpish.'

Coop took out his mobile and made a call. It was very quick. The four men eyed the detectives nervously, not sure what to do.

'I want to see ID from each one of you, right now,' DS Alfred said. 'I'm not going to ask again.'

'We haven't done anything,' Smigger said, shaking his head.

'Gold tooth here threatened my detective constable, which is a very serious offence.' The sound of boots on the stairs echoed up the stairwell. Loud voices echoed up the stairwell. 'Last chance. I'm not going to ask again.'

'Who the fuck is that?' the barman muttered. He heard the racket in the stairwell. 'They must have backup waiting downstairs. Show them your ID,' the barman said, loudly. The four men looked at him, confused. 'This is a fit up. Show them your ID now!'

The entrance door opened and six detectives rushed in, backed up by six uniformed officers. They approached and the men looked shocked and confused.

'This is a fucking stitch up, Babylon,' gold tooth, shouted. He pointed at the DS. 'You will get yours. Wait and see. I'm going to be there when it happens.'

'Arrest him,' Alfred said. Two detectives approached him. 'Turn around before you get hurt.'

'Fuck you!'

'Do it now. Turn around.' Uniformed officers held him by the elbows and detectives flanked him. 'Arrest him for making threats to kill.'

'I didn't say nothing about killing anyone!'

'You did and all these officers heard you, didn't you?' Alfred said. The officers nodded that they had. 'Are you beginning to understand that our gang is bigger than yours?'

'Okay, okay,' gold tooth said, shaking his head. He took out his wallet. 'There's no need for this.'

'It's too late for that. You had your chance,' Alfred said, taking his wrist and clicking on the cuffs with expert speed. 'I warned you not to fuck me around.' He grinned at the others, who were being searched and their ID checked. His officers found cannabis resin and several wraps of white powder. 'Oh dear me!' Alfred said, shaking his head. 'This isn't going to end well for you.'

The barman made a call on his mobile. 'Put that phone down, sunshine or you'll be joining these boys when they have a rubber glove up their poo-pipe.' The barman ended the call and put the phone down. 'Put it on the bar where I can see it.'

'This is entrapment,' the barman said.

'You can't spell entrapment, never mind understand what it is,' Alfred said, shaking his head. 'Do as you're told and there won't be anything for you to worry about unless you've done something illegal.'

'What the fuck is going on here?' a female voice shouted. DS Alfred turned around to see Jet Unganu walking towards them. She was flanked by two giants, who looked like they were carved from stone. A man in an expensive suit walked from a doorway that had been marked, staff only. 'Who is in charge of this shitshow?'

'That would be me and unfortunately for you, I'm not on your payroll,' Alfred said, smiling. Jet glared at him. 'Nice to see you, Jet but I'm surprised because your man Smigger over there said you weren't here.' He turned to face Smigger. 'You said Jet had gone home in a taxi because she'd had a few drinks. So, Smigger is telling us lies.' He looked back at Jet. Her eyes were piercing, darting everywhere. 'If he had told us the truth, none of this would have been necessary. And now we've found cannabis and white powder on their person. They'll all be arrested.'

'What do you want?' Jet asked.

'We came to talk to you about Dr Kalu Sammi,' Alfred said. Her eyes blinked. She didn't respond. The man in the suit moved next to her and whispered in her ear. She nodded almost imperceptibly. DS Alfred pointed to a tall man, who was being held by two uniformed officers. 'What is his name?'

'Algernon Unganu,' one of the officers said, reading his driver's licence. 'From Camden Town.'

'Algernon Unganu from Camden Town,' Alfred said, frowning. He feigned confusion. 'Is he a relative, by the way?' Jet remained stoic and didn't react. 'It doesn't matter but Algernon said a funny thing earlier.' Alfred studied her face. A nerve twitched in her cheek. There one second and gone the next. She was nervous. He had her attention for sure. 'I mentioned that your niece had pulled a knife and attacked Dr Kalu Sammi and he said, "I heard he got his".' Jet glanced at Algernon for a second. 'Now that is very strange as we haven't released any names from that incident as we can't find one of the victim's relatives.' No reaction. The other men stared at the floor, giving nothing away. 'How do you think he knew that name?'

'If there's a specific line of questioning for my client, I suggest we make an appointment and do it officially,' the suit said. He stepped forward and handed a card to Coop. 'This is my contact number. We have nothing to say here under these circumstances.'

They moved to walk away but DS Alfred wasn't ready to let her off the hook.

'We found the body of Harry Trainor and someone had done a real number on him,' Alfred said. 'It was way beyond what any of your muppets are capable off.' He felt eyes boring into his soul. 'These boys might be juiced up and battle hardened but they're too stupid to be able to plan something on that scale. Thick as pig shit, all of them, especially Algernon over there. He's a whole new level of stupid.'

'Fuck you, motherfucker,' Algernon mumbled.

'Fuck me?' Alfred repeated. 'I don't think so. But I'm going to make it my mission to see every one of you banged up.' He looked around the room; there was no reaction but pulses were raised. He sensed they wanted to kill him, right there. 'We figured Trainor was down to you on a revenge streak for Suzette's death but now, because of what Algernon said, we know it was you that caused the little accident at London Bridge station as well.' Silence. 'It was done on your instruction, wasn't it?'

'I have no idea what you're talking about,' Jet said, shaking her head. She glanced at Algernon and her expression said he was in trouble.

'Algernon does! He knows exactly what I'm talking about,' Alfred said, laughing. 'Don't you Algernon, you gave the game away. What did you call me, a motherfucker? That makes you a stupid motherfucker, doesn't it?' No one spoke. The silence was deafening. 'I heard he got his, that's what he said when I mentioned Dr Sammi.' He paused. 'I heard he got his?' No one spoke. 'What do you think he meant by that?'

'I'm not playing games with you, Babylon,' Jet said, shaking her head.

'Are you actually going to arrest my client for something?' the suit asked.

'The problem is,' Alfred said, ignoring the brief. 'You got the wrong man.' Confusion flashed in her eyes. The other men looked up. Their reaction was genuine surprise. 'I can see just by looking at the expressions on your stupid faces that you don't know.' He chuckled coldly and studied her face. Anger. Deep anger. Confusion. Hatred. It was all there. 'It will be all over the news by now. You took out the wrong Dr Sammi, Jet. You pushed his brother under a tube train.'

Chapter 11

It was turning from dusk to dark and the heat was dropping but only slightly. Day turns to night quickly in Monguno. Oke and Isime had walked around the town for the third time beneath a star-studded sky. The moon was a silver crescent to the south. They knew the streets of Monguno better than most and they could remember them when they were busy, children played and the smells of cooking were everywhere. The town's streets crisscrossed like a grid-map, each block a rectangle, and they covered as many as they could. The town square was at the centre surrounded by buildings which were once occupied by traders and small businesses. The butcher, baker and candlestick maker were all gone now, the windows empty and dark. There wasn't a single light on in any of the buildings. Monguno had expanded to the north, east and west but three bodies of water to the south of the town halted any expansion in that direction. They were deep and dangerous and patrolled by squadrons of mosquitos and crocodiles. The sisters were tired and hungry and had established that people weren't rushing back to Monguno just yet.

'There is no one else here,' Oke said. 'We need to move her tonight while there are no witnesses.'

'Why are there no others here?' Isime asked. 'They can't all be dead.'

'I think anyone from here, who had family living somewhere else in Nigeria, has gone to live with them. People are still scared of Boko returning and any residue of General Basse's chemicals. I heard people in the hospital gossiping about the land being poisoned and how the food and water will be tainted for years,' Oke said. 'Do you think other families will eventually come back?' Oke asked her sister. Isime shrugged. 'I am confident people will come home. I hope the shops will open again, one day and the market square is busy with animals and people,' she added. 'I think it will be soon. Surely, we can't be the only ones here forever?'

'We can't assume that we are the only ones here,' Isime said.

'What do you mean?'

'Just because there are no lights in the windows, doesn't mean there are no people here. We need to be careful moving her body,' Isime said. 'I bet some people are hiding and we can't risk being seen.'

'People are hiding from what?' Oke asked.

'Everything. Even the soldiers think Boko will return,' Isime said. 'We can't risk any witnesses. The old crone lived somewhere nearby to us but we never saw her, did we?'

'No. She must have been close enough to see soldiers at our house,' Oke said, whispering. 'Or I suppose she could have heard the trucks and walked to see what was going on?'

'Maybe,' Isime agreed. 'She should have kept to her own business and left us to ours.'

They saw the lights of the hospital in the distance and the floodlights at the barracks in the opposite direction but the houses between them were in darkness. The sound of millions of insects chirping resonated through the air. It was a comforting noise. Home.

'There is no one else here. We need to move her body right now, tonight,' Oke said, nervously. 'Before she starts to smell.'

'Why are you whispering?' Isime asked.

'Because you hit an old crone over the head with a rolling pin and now we have a dead body in the cellar and I don't want anyone to know, that's why I'm whispering!' Oke explained. 'Why do you think I'm whispering?'

'At least we're not in a jail cell being beaten, raped and who knows what else would have happened to us,' Isime said, frowning. 'I will die before I go back to being enslaved again. It's never happening to us again.' Oke hugged her. She could feel her shaking. 'I couldn't let her leave and inform about us. I had no choice.'

'No. We had no choice. We couldn't have let her leave,' Oke said, hugging her. 'You saved us. I know why you did what you did but now we must dispose of the body and then we can get on with life as normal as it can be.' She linked arms with Isime.

'When has life been normal?'

'Parts of it were normal and the future will be normal,' Oke said, nodding. 'The middle bit has been shite.'

'I hope you're right,' Isime said, agreeing.

'Let's see how much water is in the lake,' Oke whispered.

'Which lake?'

'The big one.'

'What are you thinking?'

'We take her body out of the cellar, roll her up in the mat and use the handcart to move her,' Oke whispered. 'Then we tip the body somewhere she won't be found for a long time, if at all. The creatures in the water will devour the fleshy bits. If she's ever found, there won't be anything left. No one will investigate how she died.'

'That's a good plan,' Isime said, nodding. 'We dump her in the water and forget all about it.'

'Yes. Except I won't be able to completely forget it,' Oke added, smiling. 'I will never forget my little sister becoming a killer.'

'Oh shush!' Isime complained.

The sound of a diesel engine firing up drifted to them. Headlights pierced the night to the north of the town. An air-raid siren began to wail. The droning noise boomed across the town, a foreboding and melancholy tune.

'I remember that sound from being a child,' Oke said, suddenly frightened. 'It was only sounded when something bad was happening.'

'Like what?' Isime asked.

'It was used to practice for an enemy air-raid when there was friction with our neighbours in Chad. They thought we would be at war,' Oke explained.

'But we're not at war, so what is it for?'

'I don't know, sister,' Oke said. 'Whatever it is for, it's not a good thing. We need to get home.'

They walked faster, heading for home. It was about a mile or less but there wasn't much cover. They moved as swiftly as they dared, watching the lights pierce the night sky. The siren droned on, frightening them. After a few minutes, Oke pulled Isime into the doorway of a single-storey building. It had once been a mechanic's bay. The smell of diesel oil still tainted the air.

'Let me catch my breath,' she said, panting. The sound of more engines joined the first. More lights swept the darkness, lighting up the night sky like searchlights and the siren droned on relentlessly. The vehicles were approaching the deserted town at speed. Lots of them. 'Soldiers. They're coming from the barracks,' Oke said. 'Why are they coming out of the barracks after dark?'

'I don't know but they're coming this way,' Isime said. 'This doorway isn't going to hide us. They will see us. We need to hide.'

'We haven't done anything wrong,' Oke said.

'Since when has that mattered?' Isime said. 'We're two young women alone in a deserted town. They're animals and we can't let them find us outside like this.'

'Run,' Oke said, holding her hand. 'We can make it to the alleyway if we're quick.'

The sisters ran as quickly as they could. Oke was breathing heavily; the damage to her lungs was clearly audible. It sounded like she had phlegm on her chest. The vehicles appeared to have split into three columns, each heading for a road parallel to each other, which dissected the residential area of the town. They could hear orders being shouted as the vehicles grew closer. Headlights pierced the darkness at the end of their street. They reached the entrance to the alleyway as the first jeep turned the corner, followed by two trucks.

'I can't run anymore,' Oke said. 'Leave me here.' Oke leaned against the wall, breathless. 'I can't catch my breath.'

'I'm not leaving you anywhere,' Isime whispered, half carrying her into the darkness between two rows of bungalows. Oke tripped over something she couldn't see and stumbled onto one knee.

Isime nearly fell beneath her weight but managed to stay upright. The military vehicles slowed down and came to a halt. They heard soldiers dismounting from the trucks. Orders were shouted but they couldn't make out what they were saying. The sisters crept further up the alleyway, stooping low, moving as quickly as they could in the pitch blackness. Heavy footsteps echoed in the darkness. Raised voices carried on the night air, sounding closer than they were. Each sound made them freeze in fear.

'Just take one step at a time,' Isime whispered. 'We need to find somewhere to hide. I think they're searching for something.'

'Or someone. You lead. I'll follow,' Oke puffed. 'Hold my hand so I don't lose you.'

'You don't think they're looking for us, do you?' Isime asked.

'Why would they send an army to find us?' Oke said. 'Because of a few beds?'

'What if they know I killed that woman?' Isime whispered. 'What if someone was watching and they've reported me?'

Oke couldn't answer but the possibility was real. Her heart was thumping in her chest. Fear gripped her. The sisters crept along the alleyway, stumbling over discarded belongings that they couldn't see in the darkness. Isime was using all her strength to carry her sister and she kicked an empty paint tin. It clattered and rattled and she was sure the soldiers would hear it. They froze for a moment and crouched. Isime squeezed her arm and they set off again slowly, hugging the wall as close as they could. The shadows were deeper there. It felt like it had taken hours to reach the back of a row of houses. The garden walls were intact and overgrown with creeping vines and climbing ivy. They could hear animals scurrying through the undergrowth as they approached.

Oke was struggling. Her breathing was laboured and she had developed a wheeze. The noise threatened to give their position away. They stopped for a second to rest. The sound of more vehicles reached them from the opposite end of the alleyway. They were trapped between two units of troops.

'What if they come down here?' Oke said, whispering. 'They will find us. We need to hide.'

'I'll tell them it was just me that killed the woman and you weren't there,' Isime said.

'You'll do no such thing,' Oke said. 'We'll tell them she attacked us for our food and we had to kill her.'

'I don't want to go to prison. Let's try and get into one of the houses,' Isime said. 'We can hide until they move on.'

'Okay, let's try this one.'

Oke stepped between two gateposts. The gate had long since disintegrated. She tiptoed along a concrete path that was invisible beneath the vegetation, following a straight line and using her instincts to guide them. Her feet were becoming entwined in the brambles. Tiny thorns pricked her and scratched her skin. She felt blood trickling down her left leg.

'Ow!' Isime hissed. She crouched down.

'What is it?' Oke whispered.

'I've stubbed my toe on something!' Isime moaned. 'I think it's broken.'

'Can you walk?'

'Yes. Carry on,' Isime said.

It was painful to move but they couldn't stay still. She pulled her foot from the undergrowth and moved forward tentatively, almost blind in the darkness. The back door was closed and Oke tried the handle. It turned and she nudged the door with her shoulder. It resisted at first but moved with a little encouragement. The hinges creaked, sounding deafening in the blackness.

'Shush,' Isime said. 'They will hear us!'

'Shush yourself,' Oke muttered. 'I can't walk through doors. I have to open them!'

She pushed the door and it opened enough for her to slip inside. Isime followed and closed the door behind them. The sounds of insects and soldiers were dulled. They slid down the wall and sat on the floor, sweat pouring from them. Their breathing was deep and loud but it was slowing. They held hands in the darkness, seeking comfort from their touch. Oke rested her head on Isime's shoulder and Isime stroked her hair, concerned by Oke's breathing.

'How are you feeling?' Isime asked.

'Like my lungs are full of snot,' Oke whispered. 'I'll be okay in a few minutes.'

They listened to what was going on outside.

Engines, voices and boots on the ground. Men running. They were entering the alleyway from both ends. Their voices were becoming louder and more frantic. Oke was waiting for them to kick the door in. There was a cry of anguish. A single gunshot rang out and there were a few seconds of silence before all hell broke loose.

Chapter 12

Kalu made his way to the nurses' station. It was way past the end of his shift and he was comfortable that he had covered his cases with other doctors. He had spoken to each of his patients and their parents, which had taken hours but he had to out of professional courtesy and a sense of responsibility. Some of them were distressed he was leaving for a while and wanted to know for how long but there was no way of knowing when he would be back. The cases had to be transferred for the safety of the children.

It was mid-afternoon and his eyes were burning tired. He had spoken to Beb earlier, from Chad, and he had landed safely and was ten hours drive away from Monguno. Beb sounded cautious about the transport arrangements across the borders but confident they could do it. Kalu felt sick with excitement and fear. His connection to Beb was intense and they talked to each other as if they had never been apart. The child he once knew had grown into a strong man with manners and morals. His years spent being a nomad had shaped his character. Kalu had sent him some cash to oil the wheels at the border checkpoints. All he could think about were Isime and Oke and the fact they were alive or had been when they had watched the news reel. It wasn't broadcast live and they had no idea if they were still in the hospital or even in Monguno anymore. He felt desperate to find them, fearing they may move on and he would never find them again. People had a way of disappearing into thin air in Africa. His need to be there, looking for them, was overwhelming everything else. He ran all the scenarios through his mind. Would they know him? Would they forgive him for thinking they were dead? Could they forgive him for leaving them in Africa as young children, even though he was convinced they were dead? What would he say to them to make things right? How do you greet children you thought were dead years ago? The guilt was crippling. His head was spinning.

'You look tired,' the ward sister said as he approached.

'Someone paged me. Is there a call for me?' he asked her. Her name was Beth and he'd known her for longer than he could remember.

'Yes. It's Kissie on line three,' she said, smiling. Her smile lit up the room. In another life, he would have asked her out but she was married and very happy.

'Kissie?' he answered, yawning. 'I'm sorry I'm late but I got stuck but I'm done now. Is everything okay?'

'No, dad,' Kissie said. 'Everything isn't okay.'

'What has happened?' He snapped awake. 'Is it Beb?'

'No, dad.' Kissie tried not to break on the phone. 'Celia called.'

'Celia?' Kalu said, confused. 'She never calls. What's happened.'

'Uncle Chuk is dead,' Kissie sobbed.

'What are you talking about?' Kalu said, his voice almost a whisper. 'I just saw him last night when he finished his shift.'

'He's dead, dad,' Kissie sniffled.

'What happened?'

'Celia doesn't know all the details but he fell under a train,' she explained. 'Another man was killed too. He was at London Bridge tube station.'

'How does a grown man fall under a tube train?' Kalu asked, squeezing the bridge of his nose between his finger and thumb. He felt tears spilling from his eyes, tickling his cheeks as they fell. His stomach twisted and a desperate sadness filled him. Loss. It was a familiar feeling for him. An emotion he had shared his life with for what felt like forever. He had spent more of his life grieving than any man should. Chuk had been the one constant in his life. His big brother, hero and mentor. Chuk had guided him through his studies and encouraged him when he was at the point of quitting. He felt like he was going to throw up.

'I've been trying to ring you, so you didn't find out from social media or the news. I'm ten minutes away, dad,' Kissie said, sniffling. 'I'll park at the back of the hospital and wait for you.'

'You're driving here now?' Kalu asked.

'Yes. You didn't take your car and I didn't think…'

'I would want to take the tube?' he finished her sentence. 'Thank you, Kissie. I'll meet you there.'

'Okay, see you soon,' Kissie said, ending the call.

'I'm so sorry for your loss,' Beth said. 'I couldn't help but overhear.' She walked over to him and opened her arms. Kalu accepted her into his and rested his chin on her shoulder. 'I heard there had been an accident last night, but I can't believe it was Chuk. I'm so sorry. Everyone loved him, so much.'

'I know they did,' Kalu said. He closed his eyes. 'He thought the world of you,' Kalu said, squeezing her. 'He fell under a train. How can that happen?' he muttered.

'Doctor Sammi,' a familiar voice said from behind him. Kalu turned around to see DS Alfred and his DC. His name was Coop, he remembered. 'Do you mind if we have a word in private, please?'

'I'm not in the right frame of mind,' Kalu said, shaking his head. 'I've just been told my brother died last night. I don't have time for your stupid questions.'

'I don't have any questions, doctor, stupid or otherwise,' Alfred said. 'It's your brother we have come to talk about.'

'What about him?'

'Can we talk in private?' the detective asked.

'The relatives' room is empty,' Beth said. 'Take them in there.'

'Thank you, sister,' Alfred said.

'Can I get you a drink?' she asked.

'Tea please,' Alfred said. 'White with one sugar.'

'Same for me,' Coop said.

'Kalu?' Beth asked.

'Just water for me, please.'

Kalu opened the door and flicked the lights on. He felt numb, like his body was working on autopilot. Emotion and exhaustion had sapped all his strength. The detectives followed him and waited for him to close the door.

'Firstly, I want to offer my sincere condolences,' Alfred said, offering his hand. 'It's terrible news for you to deal with and I know

I'm the last person you want to talk to but we must have this conversation, I'm afraid. I'm truly sorry about your brother.'

'Thank you,' Kalu said. 'I'm tired and confused. I'm not being rude but what has Chuk's accident got to do with you?'

'We don't think his death was an accident,' Alfred said.

'So, what do you think it was?'

'We think he was pushed under that train.'

'Pushed under the train?'

'Yes.'

'Why would anyone want to kill Chuk?' Kalu asked, shocked. 'Everyone loved him.'

'We think he was murdered because the killer thought he was you,' DS Alfred said. Kalu opened his mouth to speak but couldn't think of the right words. It made sense. Grown men didn't fall under trains unless they jumped or were pushed. He was certain that he was to blame for his brother's death, Kalu began to shake. 'The chances are Jet Unganu has ordered a hit on you and they screwed it up.'

'Are you going to arrest her?' Kalu mumbled.

'We're working on a theory here. There's no evidence she is involved,' Alfred said, shaking his head. 'She's probably hired someone to do it, so her hands are clean. But the killer got their research wrong.'

'If you're not going to arrest her, why are you here?'

'Because they will try again,' Alfred said. 'You and your family are in danger.'

'What do I do now?' Kalu asked, shrugging. 'We're leaving for Nigeria tomorrow.'

'Who is?'

'Kissie and me,' Kalu said. 'We're going back to the town we lived in.'

'How long for?'

'I don't know.'

'Does anyone else know you're leaving the country?' DS Alfred asked. Kalu shook his head. 'Keep it that way. I need you to keep in touch with me and let me know when you're coming home. If we have any news, I'll message you. We'll put a vehicle on your address tonight if you want us to?'

'I've booked a hotel at the airport,' Kalu said. 'Thank you for the offer but we'll be fine there, surely.'

'What time do you fly?'

'We need to be at the gate for five in the morning,' Kalu said. 'Kissie is waiting for me in the carpark at the back of the hospital. Everything is packed, so we won't be at home for long.'

'Okay, good,' DS Alfred said. 'Keep your eyes open. Anything or anyone that seems to be out of the ordinary, you find a policeman and ring me.'

Chapter 13

Beb was sitting in the front seat, trying to avoid making eye contact with the beggars and traders outside. Poverty was part and parcel of the African continent but witnessing the misery and desperation was no easier to witness just because he was African. It was still as distressing. It's impossible to become hardened to it. Limbless men, macheted during the civil war kept pace with the traffic, begging for a few coins. Beb watched the passenger in the vehicle in front of them holding out some coins but the beggar had no hands to hold them, his arms chopped off above the elbow. He asked the man to put them into his shirt pocket, which he did. Beb wondered how he would get them out but that was probably the least of his problems. How did he eat or go to the toilet? The poor soul was suffering long after his wounds had healed. Even begging was almost impossible with no arms. It was such a miserable existence, desperate and hopeless. Chopping off their limbs doomed them to a life of never being able to work for a living. Beb had seen it before and thought it was the cruellest of all punishments for fighting on the opposite side. Death was a million times kinder than subjecting a person to such a despairing future, unable to support themselves or their families. He wanted to help them but which ones did he help? He couldn't help them all. There wasn't enough money to help them all.

Omar was nudging the Toyota forward a few feet at a time. The queue to cross the river into Cameroon was chaotic and slow. It had no beginning and no end. The concept of joining the rear of the queue and waiting in line was alien there. People drove as far along the queue as they could and then tried to cut in when they couldn't physically go any further. Some drivers honked their horns in protest but it was pointless. Tempers frayed and slanging matches broke out frequently. Omar seemed very chilled about everything.

Beb turned around and smiled at Amira. She returned his smile and stroked her daughter's hair. Heba was sleeping, tired out by the journey. Beb felt anxious about travelling the route they had to follow. He couldn't have flown direct into Nigeria with Heba and Amira because of their distinctive eye colouring. They were obviously Tuareg and on the Nigerian restricted list. Chad was more flexible and the northern borders of Cameroon appeared to have no rules at all. Crossing into Nigeria would be the biggest hurdle as far as their papers were concerned but the need for paperwork could be bypassed by cold hard cash. Once they crossed into his homeland, travelling from Fotokol to Dikwa through the wilderness would be treacherous and that wasn't lost on him at any point. They were going to need all their wits, the help of other people in the same situation, weapons and a sprinkling of good luck.

His childhood experience of being ripped from his family by pirates and kidnappers had left him traumatised. As a young boy, enslaved in the vastness of the Sahara Desert, he had missed his mother and father so much that he thought his heart would break into pieces. At night, he would stare into the universe and wonder where they were and when they would come to rescue him. Some nights, he cried so hard that he couldn't breathe. The pain he suffered thinking about his family had been unbearable. He prayed for death more times than he could remember. There was no way he could allow the same thing to happen to Amira and Heba. That couldn't happen to such beautiful human beings. He would die before they were taken. His concern for his wife and child was crushing him. He couldn't relax and kept shifting in his seat. Omar sensed his unease.

'Have you been this way before?' Omar asked.

'To Chad?' Beb asked, frowning. 'No. Never. I was a child when we left Nigeria.' Beb tried to push his fear to the back of his mind but it was like a dog barking in the distance, always there, never letting up.

'Where did you go?'

'North,' Beb said. 'We were heading for Tripoli to cross to Europe.'

'Wow,' Omar said, shaking his head. 'Obviously, you didn't make it?'

'That's a long story.' Beb didn't want to talk about it. Amira and Heba were nervous enough as it was. He changed the subject. 'Have you driven this route before?' Beb asked.

'Into Kousseri?' Omar asked, smiling. He nodded enthusiastically. 'My wife is from a village in Cameroon about an hour on from Kousseri. We go there a couple of times a year. My wife is a curvy woman but my mother-in-law is the biggest woman you have ever seen. She has an ass the size of the moon but she makes the best food I've tasted. I swear I go home twice as heavy as I when I arrived.'

'I meant into Nigeria?' Beb said, chuckling. His attention was taken by a woman screaming. He watched as a border guard beat a woman with a whip, which was flexible like a long riding crop. She was running away but he kept pace with her, whipping her continuously. He felt his hand go to the door handle, the urge to intervene powerful.

'What are you doing?' Omar asked, gabbing his arm.

'Look at that soldier beating that woman.'

'Don't even think about opening that door,' Omar warned, shaking his head. 'He's one of the men in charge of the crossing. They're not soldiers. They're border guards and they're criminals in a uniform but they have weapons and they decide who goes and who doesn't.'

'I can't sit and watch that,' Beb said, angrily.

'Then look the other way because those men will shoot you without thinking about it and pull your wife and child from this vehicle in the blink of an eye. They are murderers, rapists and thieves but they are in charge here. Who do you think will look after your wife and daughter if you get yourself shot?' Omar said, calmly. 'Think about your family and nothing else. There is no room for sentiment in this place.' Beb looked away and Amira put a hand on his shoulder. He took it in his and squeezed gently. 'T.I.A. Beb,' Omar said, shaking his head.

'T.I.A?'

'This is Africa. This is a fucked-up continent,' Omar said. 'This was the most fucked up continent on the planet until Putin started firing cruise missiles into Europe. I think we've been demoted to second place for a while but don't worry, we will win the title back.'

'I don't understand why a man would do that,' Beb said, shaking his head.

'What, fire missiles into Europe?' Omar joked.

'No. Beat a woman in the street with a whip,' Beb sighed.

'Power. It is a different scale but amounts to the same thing,' Omar said. 'They do it because it makes them feel powerful. They're arseholes with authority and they wield it however they choose. Bullies and nothing more.'

'What is wrong with people?'

'People are people. Violence is a human trait. It's in our nature,' Omar said, matter-of-factly. 'Survival of the strongest at any cost. Doesn't matter who else dies as long as we live. That's who we are.'

Beb looked back at the spot where the woman was but the crowds had swallowed them up. He spotted the guard walking back towards the barrier, growling at people in his way. His whip was raised as a warning to all. Beb despised him. A man he had never met. Could he have hurt the guard to stop him beating the woman?

In a heartbeat.

Omar had said violence is in our nature, Beb couldn't argue with him about that. He didn't like to admit it but it was true. The traffic moved a car length and Omar was quick to close the gap between them and the vehicle in front to block anyone trying to cut in. They had reached the part of the queue where the road had narrowed and formed a single line. Crowds of people on foot were impatiently waiting to cross the border. It was a hundred metres to the bridge. There were crowds on the opposite side of the bridge waiting to cross into Chad from Cameroon. It was organised chaos.

Border guards stopped each vehicle and checked the occupants' documents. Other guards moved along the queue and searched vehicles at random, opening boots and rifling through people's belongings. If the occupants had no money, valuable items were seized and arguments were breaking out. The guards were brutal and anyone protesting was beaten with their batons and whips. Money was demanded and paid in plain view as if it was common practice. If you wanted to cross, you had to pay their toll. There was no attempt to hide their corruption. Beb looked back at Amira and she looked appalled and terrified.

'They are targeting women,' she said, shaking her head. 'I think it would be best to blend in.'

She covered her head and face with a hijab in an attempt to make herself look less interesting. Men paid her attention, too much most times. Beb didn't say anything but he felt relieved she had covered her face by choice. He watched as two guards pulled a woman out of a vehicle, bent her over the bonnet and frisked her. One of them stuck his hand up the back of her skirt and laughed as he groped her. It was a sexual assault disguised as a legal search but none of the onlookers intervened. A male got out of the vehicle and tried to stop the assault but one of the guards struck him between the eyes with the butt of his baton, splitting the bridge of his nose. He was beaten and kicked to the ground until the other occupants got out of the vehicle, grabbed him and dragged him back inside. One of the passengers reluctantly offered the guards some money. They snatched the notes and pocketed them. The assaulted woman was thrown aside, their amusement complete. She was hysterical as she scrambled back into the vehicle.

'That is so unnecessary,' Beb said. 'They're acting like thugs and for what?'

'Money of course,' Omar said.

The guards shared a joke and lit a cigarette each oblivious to the anguish they were causing. They moved to the next vehicle.

'They didn't give them any money,' Omar explained. 'That's why they searched them and gave them a hard time. It's better to pay them first.'

'I'm shocked they're allowed to do whatever they like,' Beb said. 'Why does the government not stop them?'

'Money. Corruption rises all the way to the top,' Omar said. 'They give the local government officials a cut. It's a tax for crossing the border and they all get richer.'

Beb could feel his blood boiling. If anyone touched Amira, he wouldn't be able to control himself. He began to consider turning around and finding another way but there was no other way. It was this way or no way. They were two cars from the barrier when the first guard knocked on the passenger window. It was the guard who he had seen forcing his hand up the woman's skirt. Beb opened it and the guard looked around inside. The smell of stale sweat and cigarettes drifted in.

'Three adults and one child,' he said, staring at Amira. Beb wanted to punch him in the face until it was mush but controlled himself. Amira avoided his gaze and focused on the windscreen. Eye contact could trigger a reaction. 'Let me see your papers.' Beb handed him their passports and the guard scrutinised them. It was clear he couldn't read. 'Where were these papers issued?'

'They were issued in Morocco.'

'Morocco?'

'Yes,' Beb said.

'Where are you going?'

'Monguno.'

'Nigeria?' the guard asked, handing back the passports. Beb nodded. 'Why are you going there?'

'It's my home,' Beb said.

'You're Nigerian but she isn't.'

'That's right.'

'Is she married?' the guard asked, smirking.

'She's my wife,' Beb said, calmly.

'Lucky man.' He stared at Amira. 'I have seen eyes like hers before,' the guard said, nodding. 'She's Tuareg.'

'Yes, she is,' Beb said, nodding.

'And the child is yours?'

'Yes.'

'Another African mongrel,' the guard said, shaking his head. 'That's what wrong with this country. No one knows who they are or where they're from.' Beb didn't argue but maintained eye contact. 'Is this man driving you all the way?'

'Yes,' Beb said.

'It's a long journey in a taxi. Is it cash?' the guard asked, spotting an opportunity. 'How much are you paying this man to drive you to Nigeria?'

'I'm taking them as a favour,' Omar said.

'No one does anything for nothing,' the guard snorted.

'It is just a favour,' Beb said. He handed a fifty-dollar note to the guard. The note was slipped into his breast pocket with practiced ease. He looked around to see if the other guards had seen him pocket the money.

'Move on,' the guard said, moving away from the window. He put his face to the glass in the rear door. Amira glanced at him, unable to ignore him. He licked the glass with his tongue and glared at her.

'Do not turn around,' Omar said, grabbing Beb's knee.

'I'm fine, Beb,' Amira said, touching his shoulder. 'He's gone now.'

Beb watched him walking away in the wing mirror, taking aim at his head with an imaginary rifle. He didn't look back. When they reached the barrier, the charade wasn't finished. This time it was Omar who had to open the window.

'Where are you going?' the guard asked, looking inside. He had stripes on his sleeve.

'Monguno,' Omar said.

'Nigeria?' the guard asked, frowning.

'Yes.'

'Where are you crossing the border?'

'Fotokol.'

'Don't stop for anything when you pass Fotokol until you reach Dikwa,' the guard warned. 'Make sure you have enough fuel to get you there. There are a lot of bandits in the jungle.'

'We will be careful,' Omar said, smiling.

'Thank you for the advice,' Beb added, handing him a fifty-dollar note. He took it and pocketed it without any acknowledgement at all.

'Let me see your passports.'

'Your colleague has checked the passports,' Beb said.

'Has he indeed?' the sergeant asked. Beb nodded. 'Did you give him any money?' the guard asked, frowning.

'Yes,' Omar said. 'We gave him one hundred. He said the passport check was included in the price.'

'Did he say that?' the sergeant asked, shaking his head. 'On you go. Take care and don't let the women out of your sight,' he added, looking into the back seat. 'Is this your wife and child?'

'Yes,' Beb said.

'Nigeria is a shithole. I don't know why you would take your wife and child to such a place.'

'We're just going home,' Beb said. 'But thank you for your concern.' The guard nodded but wasn't sure how to take it. Omar closed the window and the barrier was raised, so they could pass.

'Welcome to Cameroon,' Beb said as they drove across the bridge over the river Chari.

'You told the sergeant we gave his man one hundred?' Omar said, shaking his head. He smiled. 'He will demand that he hands it over.'

'Did I say that?' Beb said, shrugging. 'Maybe I made a mistake.' He looked out of the window. 'The river looks swollen.'

'That guard will be beaten until he pays up,' Omar said, ignoring the comment. 'You know what you did, don't you?'

'What goes around, comes around,' Beb said. 'The river is very high, isn't it?'

'This time of year, they all are,' Omar said. The river was wide and fast. 'It has been raining heavily for the last few days. One of the bridges upriver was washed away yesterday.'

'Is that why the queue was so slow?' Beb asked.

'Yes. The forecast is more rain so, people are trying to get to wherever they need to be. The roads to the west of the river turn to mud quickly,' Omar explained.

'Really?' Beb asked, concerned. 'We're heading west.'

'Don't worry, it's not raining now. We have four-wheel-drive,' Omar said. 'We'll be fine. This thing will pull like a train if needed.'

Beb nodded and sighed. He felt more anxious now than ever. The weather was another hurdle that they didn't need. It was going to be difficult enough without the roads turning into muddy rivers. He had seen it happen in Monguno. Most of the roads were nothing but compacted dirt. A tropical rainstorm could loosen the dirt in a few hours and roads became rivers. Four-wheel-drive was handy if they became wet and muddy but if they flooded, nothing was getting through. They would be safe while they were moving but no one is truly safe in such remote places. A vehicle bogged down in the mud unable to move would be extremely vulnerable. He closed his eyes and wished he had made the journey alone. Bringing Amira and Heba along was not the best idea although leaving them alone in Marrakesh would not have been much safer. He wondered if the anxiety he felt for their safety would ever subside or was it just part of being a husband and a father. Amira touched his shoulder again and she squeezed him gently as if she could read his thoughts. Her instincts were uncanny. She could read him like a book. There was no point in sugar coating the truth to Amira. She was as sharp as a knife and just as deadly. He sometimes forgot she had been brought up in a community which had survived in the desert for centuries. Amira ruffled his hair and he felt the burning glow of affection in his chest. She was his world and Heba was his moon and stars. Without them there was simply nothing. A dark grey cloud scooted across the sky from the south and the first droplets of rain hit the windscreen.

Chapter 14

Oke put her fingers in her ears as the sound of machinegun fire rattled through the darkness. Muzzle flashes lit up the room for seconds, blinding them, then plunging them back into inky blackness. Another burst came from further away. It sounded like it was in another part of town. A different gun fired from their right, then another long burst from their left. The sounds were deeper, booming, like the high-calibre machineguns they mounted onto the flatbed jeeps. A prolonged burst of fire came directly from the alleyway outside. She could hear men talking between volleys. Stray bullets ripped into the bricks and plaster of the living room wall, punching huge holes through it. The sisters were showered in dust and debris. They held each other in the darkness, afraid to speak, afraid to breathe, afraid to cry out as bullets smashed into the exterior wall. They could feel the vibrations through the floor. More bullets came through the window, pulverising pictures that hung on the opposite wall. The glass and frames disintegrated into deadly shrapnel. Another burst of fire shattered the top of the door they had used to enter the house. The wood splintered into tiny needle-sharp pieces that exploded across the room. A shard pierced Oke's arm and it was all she could do to keep from crying out. She pulled a three-inch splinter from her forearm and threw it across the room. Blood trickled down her wrist. A scream of anguish and pain joined the sound of gunfire. It sounded close.

The door burst open with a deafening crack as it struck the wall and split into three large pieces that clattered onto the floor. A man staggered in, illuminated by the strobing muzzle flashes. He appeared to be moving in slow motion, his hands raised in surrender, terror in his eyes. His focus was on whoever was outside, not even noticing the sisters crouching in the shadows. Machineguns roared and bullets punched through his body, spraying blood and pulverized bone up the walls. His body bent into unnatural shapes as it was pummelled by gunfire and he was catapulted against the far wall. Even as he slid down it, the bullets didn't stop. His left leg was blown off below the knee and landed next to the sisters with a soggy thud. The sound of voices drifted to them. They were close and coming closer.

'Move now!' Oke hissed. She grabbed Isime by the wrist and dragged her, bent double, across the room. They ran through an open doorway into a hallway, which had rooms off either side. The front door was at the far end of the hall. 'There,' Oke said, pointing at the dim light which filtered through a glass panel in the door. 'Run sister!' she whispered, fear in her voice. 'And keep your head down.'

The sound of boots running spurred them on. Oke heard someone enter the room they had left. The sound of cracking wood. A man panting, gasping for breath. Loud voices in the alleyway.

'Don't shoot!' a man cried. 'I surrender!'

A barrage of machinegun fire erupted, so close it was deafening. The man screamed but it was cut short. Bullets punctured the walls, ricocheting through the house. They could hear them whizzing by, close to their heads, smashing into furniture and the doorframes. Debris struck them in the face, coming from all directions.

They ducked low and ran, blind towards the front door. A clatter came from the other room, followed by two more as something heavy hit a wall and then they rolled along the floor. Oke grabbed the door handle and turned it but it was latched. She slid the snip with her thumb and tried again. The door opened and she felt the cold night air touch her skin. There were a few seconds of silence and then three hand grenades exploded in a blinding flash and the blast wave rocketed down the hallway and hit them like a ton of bricks.

Chapter 15

Kalu hung his work coat in his locker. He wondered when he would put it on again but it didn't seem to matter. His work had become insignificant to him. It was getting cold outside and he had his bubble jacket to wear; he struggled into it and zipped it up. He pulled his beanie hat over his ears and slipped on wool gloves. The woollen gloves had been a present. Celia had bought them for his birthday, wrapped them and given them to his brother to take to work with him. Of course, the card was signed by both of them but Chuk never had a clue what Celia had bought him. Whenever Kalu opened a present from them it was as much a surprise to Chuk as it was to him. Chuk was so laid back, he was horizontal. Kalu couldn't compute that he was dead. Dead because someone wanted 'him' dead and they fucked up and killed the wrong man. The police suspected a woman was responsible for the assassination. Her name was Jet Unganu and she was a drug dealer. Apparently, everyone knew she was a major player in Soho's underworld, yet she was free as a bird to buy and sell cocaine and kill people.

How the fuck did that work?

It was all such a cluster-fuck. Beb, who wasn't Beb, had set up a drug deal with her niece, Suzette and she had double-crossed him. She took the money and tried to steal the drugs back and killed the man he thought was his son. He watched him die, after years of believing he was his son. That had shattered his heart into pieces. It was like losing Beb again. The fact was that Suzette Unganu pulled a double-cross, which backfired, and then stabbed a man in cold blood for financial gain and left him bleeding to death on the floor of a public toilet. That made her a danger to society. A bad person. An evil person who had then attacked Kalu in her desperation to find the drugs. She attacked him with a knife. Who was in the wrong here?

Suzette died falling on her own knife during the attack she instigated, yet the aunt wanted him killed and had killed his brother by mistake. Where was the sense in any of it? She murdered a young man and then died because of her own dreadful behaviour and for that, Kalu deserved to be murdered.

How the fuck did any of that work?

He closed his eyes and leaned against his locker, letting the cool metal sooth his forehead. Chuck was dead. Killed beneath a tube train. He couldn't comprehend the fear he must have felt before he died, falling in mid-air, knowing he was going to be hit by it and there was nothing he could do to stop it. How terrified would he have been in his last lucid moments before the catastrophic impact? Kalu felt nauseous thinking about it. Dwelling on his brother's pain and suffering was debilitating. He hoped the impact had killed him before he fell beneath the wheels.

Kalu tried to clear his mind but he couldn't think straight. There seemed to be no release from the mental torture he was feeling. Thinking about it was crippling him. Dwelling on how terrible his last seconds on this earth would have been over and over again was driving him insane. The fear, the pain, the knowing his life was about to end and not knowing why.

Was the why important? Did victims of aneurisms, heart attacks, blood clots or sepsis know why they were dying and if they did, would it make it easier to let go? Would knowing allow them to cross into the endless nothingness without fear or panic? Kalu didn't know the answers or why he was asking them but he knew grief was overwhelming him and he had to wrestle back control.

Kalu felt stinging tears run from his eyes. It was supposed to be him that died, not Chuk. He had dodged death again. His wife had drowned when he hadn't and there were times when he wished she had lived and he had died. Some said he had been blessed but there were times when it felt like a curse.

Kissie and he had thought they were the only survivors for years and now they knew the real Beb was alive and so were his daughters, Oke and Isime. The joy that knowledge had brought to their lives was indescribable. They were so excited to go to Nigeria and find them. To have his family reunited once again would be beyond his wildest dreams. What were the chances of that happening? A million to one, ten million to one, even a hundred million to one couldn't measure it. He had been given his dead children back. They had been brought back from the dead for him to have another chance at a life with them. He couldn't believe it was possible to feel such incredible joy and love for his family.

Then his brother was pushed under a train. A brother he had loved and idolised since the day he was old enough to remember.

Was that the universe balancing things out? Was it too much to ask to be ecstatically happy for a change? Did something shit have to happen to compensate for something so amazing?

How the fuck did that work?

His phone buzzed and he looked at the screen. Kissie. She would be worried about him. He checked his reflection in the mirror and wiped his eyes. They were red from crying but he couldn't do anything about that. He left the staff changing room and headed for the service lift. There was less chance of bumping into anyone if he went that way. The last thing he needed was tea and sympathy, no matter how well meaning it was. Condolences meant nothing right now. He had to focus on getting Kissie and himself to the Raddison at the airport. Despite what had happened, finding his daughters was the priority. The corridors were a blur as he made his way to the lift.

The lift door was closed when he arrived and he pressed the call button. The light showed it was in the basement but as soon as he clicked it, the lift began to climb. He tucked his hands into his pockets and waited. The sound of cables moving and motors whirring came from inside the shaft. The double doors at the end of the corridor opened and a lone female appeared. She was wrapped up against the cold with a scarf covering the lower half of her face. Her dark hair hung loosely at her shoulders. She looked at the floor as she walked oblivious to his presence, lost in her own thoughts like so many others visiting loved ones in hospital. The building was full of sick children, many of them wouldn't leave.

The lift door opened with a ping and Kalu stepped inside. It smelled of disinfectant which was just about masking the smell of vomit but not quite. He pressed the G button and the doors started to close. A hand appeared and grabbed at the lefthand door. They opened slowly and the woman he had seen stepped inside. Kalu nodded and half smiled, but she didn't respond.

'What floor are you going to?' he asked.

'The ground floor,' she said, without turning around.

The doors slid closed and the lift began to descend. Kalu was in a world of his own as they dropped by the fifth floor, fourth and third. His mind was twisting and turning, churning out what ifs faster than he could cope with them. He caught the scent of her perfume and it registered as nice. Attractive even. On a different day, he might have made small talk but not today. The lift stopped on the second floor and a cleaner trundled in with a mop bucket and a smile.

'Afternoon, Dr Sammi. I didn't expect to see you in the service lift,' she said as she entered. 'How are you?'

'I'm fine thank you,' Kalu said, nodding. The other woman stepped out of the lift without turning around. 'This isn't the ground floor,' Kalu called after her but she was gone.

Chapter 16

Beb could feel his eyes becoming tired, his lids heavy, but he fought sleep. His protective instincts wouldn't allow him to take his focus from protecting his family. Mile after mile of tropical wilderness rolled by interspersed by a scattering of humans on foot, a few farms and dozens of burnt-out military vehicles. It was a monotonous drive and he was tired. His brain felt foggy and slow. He felt his chin drop to his chest and woke with a start.

'You're tired,' Omar said, smiling. The wipers clicked back and to. One of the rubbers needed replacing and left a smear with each pass of the windscreen. 'Close your eyes and grab some sleep while you can. We're an hour from Fotokol and we need to refuel there and make sure we don't need to stop once we get the other side.'

'I'm okay,' Beb lied, twisting in his seat to look at Amira. She was sleeping on the backseat, Heba curled in her arms. 'These two can sleep anywhere,' he added. 'I don't know how they do it.'

'I suppose if you have spent most of your life in the desert, riding camels, comfort is a novelty?' Omar asked, smiling.

'You're not wrong,' Beb said, nodding. 'It certainly makes you resilient.'

'Tell me how you met a Tuareg woman?'

'I was one of them from a young age,' Beb explained. 'I was taken from my family and sold to a Tuareg tribe. I became part of their community.'

'Wow!' Omar said, whistling. 'You were a slave?'

'At first, very much. I hated them for taking me from my family,' Beb explained.

'That must have been tough to take as a child.'

'Yes, it was.'

'So, you're going home to where you grew up?'

'Yes.'

'Do you have family still there in Monguno?'

'We think so,' Beb said. He looked out of the window at the El Beid river, which formed the border between Cameroon and Nigeria. They had followed it once they entered Cameroon and they would have to cross it to enter Nigeria. The road followed its course for hundreds of kilometers. Across the river was Nigeria, his homeland. He could see it and he felt it calling him but there were no crossing points and there was nothing but wilderness there. 'We know my sisters were there but we don't know if they're still there.'

'You're a braver man than me,' Omar said. 'I would wait until all the communications were up and running and then call them.'

'Call which number?' Beb asked, laughing. 'I'm not psychic. There are no officials there, no police, no infrastructure that we know of. The inhabitants have been scattered on the winds but we're hoping people are drifting back to where they came from. We have no way of knowing until we get there.'

'True.' Omar shrugged. 'You are going there blind?'

'Pretty much,' Beb agreed. 'But it's home. If they're anywhere, that's where they will be.' He paused. 'I hope.'

'Let's hope they let us into the country,' Omar said. 'I want to get paid.'

'We'll be fine,' Beb said. 'Gamboru is the town on the other side of the river. My father researched the crossing and the troops guarding the border there are mostly there because the government is punishing them. It's the farthest, most remote posting a Nigerian soldier can endure and none of them are there because they want to be, which offers up its own opportunities.'

'Such as?'

'Bribery and corruption on a monumental scale,' Beb said. 'If you have money, you cross. It's simply a matter of how much they want on the day and how much they think you have.'

'I hope you have enough,' Omar said, grinning.

'So do I,' Beb agreed. 'Apparently, they're trigger happy and unruly.'

'That sounds like most of Africa.'

'Unfortunately.' Beb shrugged. 'Apparently, they also have a decent selection of military weapons for sale.'

'Weapons?' Omar stammered, surprised.

'Yes. People forming convoys to travel to Dikwa purchase them to protect themselves.' Beb looked out of the window and shrugged. 'It would be foolish to make that journey unarmed.'

'You are comfortable using firearms?' Omar asked.

'We were taught to shoot as soon as we could pick up a rifle,' Beb replied, nodding. 'In the Sahara, if you can't shoot, you starve to death.'

'So, you're a sharpshooter?'

'I managed to feed us,' Beb said. He gestured to the back seat. 'Amira could hit a viper at a hundred yards. She's as good as the best shooters I've seen, if not better.'

'If you want a weapon, I can sell you one.'

'What?'

'You don't think we drive taxis in Chad with no protection?'

'I hadn't thought about it,' Beb said. 'What do you have?'

'I have a rifle and two revolvers,' Omar boasted. 'I can sell you a revolver for a good price.'

'What do you call a good price?'

'Five hundred dollars.'

'Here we go again,' Beb said, shaking his head. 'When we stop, you can show me what you have and we can talk money. I'm beginning to think I'd be better off dealing with the Nigerians.'

'They're all thieves,' Omar said.

'I'm Nigerian,' Beb said. Omar blushed. 'And I'm not a thief.'

'Yes. I know but you haven't been there for a long time,' Omar backtracked. 'You've lost the urge.' He grinned and winked.

'You're a funny man,' Beb said. He closed his eyes, tiredness creeping through his bones. 'Wake me up when we get to Fotokol.'

Chapter 17

Oke felt like she was being pushed through the door by a hurricane. A blinding light flashed and there was a high-pitched buzzing in her ears. She felt like she was underwater, her senses dull and distorted. Time seemed to slow down, blurred and surreal. She hit the ground with a painful bump, landing with all her weight on her elbows. The shock jarred all the way up to her shoulder sockets and the pain was intense. She felt her knees scrape on the path, the skin scratched and painful. Her sister landed a few yards to her left and Oke could see blood running from her nose. She rolled in the grass a few times and came to a halt on her back, looking up at the stars through wide eyes, unblinking and in shock. The sound of men shouting snapped her back to reality. She crawled on her hands and knees to where Isime was lying.

'Isime!' she whispered in her ear. 'Can you move?'

'What just happened to me?' Isime mumbled.

'There was an explosion,' Oke said. 'We need to move before the soldiers come. Can you move?'

'I think so,' Isime said, trying to sit up. 'My ears are ringing.'

'Mine too,' Oke said. She stood up and grabbed Isime by the elbow, gently helping her up. Isime felt unsteady on her feet. There was a trickle of blood running from her left ear. 'The soldiers are at the back of the house in the alleyway but they will check the house in a minute. Let's get away from here, quickly!'

They linked arms and staggered away from the house into the darkness of the empty streets. Oke wasn't sure what had happened or who the soldiers were hunting but the voices and gunshots indicated the soldiers were concentrated in the streets to their left. If they could keep heading to their right, away from the area, then they could cut north to the street where they lived. There were no headlights in the direction of their home. If they could make it back to their house, they would be safe inside with the doors locked and the lights off. The soldiers weren't kicking in doors looking for people at random. From what they had heard, they were tracking gunmen and assassinating them. They had heard at least two of them and both tried to surrender but were terminated in brutal fashion. It appeared that surrender wasn't an option. They had been shot to pieces and then blown to bits with grenades just to make sure the job was done. Whoever the victims were, killing them in cold blood wasn't just or legal even if they were Boko. They didn't know if the killers were United Nations or Nigerian troops but if they knew there were witnesses to the slaughter, they would realise they could be in serious trouble. Oke had no intention of becoming a witness. In Africa, witnesses disappear.

They reached the end of the block and hid behind a garden wall, peering up the next street before risking crossing it. The intersection was clear. The sound of gunfire burst out from behind them. It was a few blocks away to the south. It spurred them into action.

'Are you ready to move?' Oke asked. Isime nodded. 'We'll cross the street here and keep going until we reach the Mosque.'

'Is it only a block to the Mosque?' Isime asked, dazed.

'Yes,' Oke said. 'We're nearly home. Come on.'

The sisters crossed the road, bent over as low as they could. They were breathing heavily, sweating, exhausted and bruised. The block of houses to their left were burnt out shells. Their roofs were collapsed into the buildings; only the odd charred beam protruded. The windows were empty and darker than the ruins around them like eyeless sockets in blackened skulls. A charcoal aroma tainted the air in this section of town, a hangover from the battle which drove Boko away. The gunfire was intensifying and spreading to the west, towards the hospital, the hunt for intruders in full swing.

Suddenly, headlights pierced the night ahead of them and they climbed over a low garden wall and crouched down to hide. The vehicle turned the corner at the top of the street and screeched to a halt. A searchlight mounted on the roof was switched on and they heard orders being barked. A soldier aimed the powerful beam into the ruins, scanning it slowly, searching every window, crack and crevice for signs of life. The vehicle crept forward slowly as they searched the darkness for the enemy. Oke could hear the engine ticking over, coming closer to where they were hiding. The searchlight combed the burnt-out structures and the undergrowth which surrounded them. Rubble and debris were strewn everywhere. The sisters held hands and waited with bated breath as the vehicle crept along the road to the intersection. It stopped and some of the soldiers jumped out.

'Oh, no,' Isime whispered. 'Have they seen us?'

'Shush,' Oke said, squeezing her hand. 'Stay down.'

The soldiers chatted as they climbed over the wall, just metres from where they were hiding. Oke didn't dare look up. She heard the sound of the men urinating. It seemed to go on forever and the odour of piss drifted to her. One of them was wearing cologne and she could smell that too; they were so close. They held their breath as the men zipped up and scrambled back over the wall. The soldiers climbed into the vehicles and the doors slammed. Oke peered over the wall, as it slowly moved away and turned right. As it straightened up, the searchlight was extinguished. The engine revved and the vehicle accelerated and disappeared into the next street.

'Oke,' Isime whispered.

'What sister?' Oke said.

'If we don't get home quickly, I'm going to piss myself.'

Chapter 18

Kalu walked out of the lift and headed down a service corridor, which led to the kitchens and the car parks at the rear of the hospital. A fire exit was wedged open with an extinguisher and two porters were smoking outside, staring at their phones and oblivious to his presence.

'Hey guys are you asking for trouble?' The men looked up, shocked. 'Do you have any idea how many rules you're breaking right now?' Kalu asked, as he stepped outside. The porters looked worried and embarrassed. 'You could lose your jobs for smoking anywhere on hospital property.'

'Sorry, doctor, but it's been a long shift. We were just grabbing a few minutes break,' one of them said. He stubbed out his cigarette and blushed. 'Please don't tell anyone. I need this job.'

'I'm not going to tell anyone but don't wedge the fire exit open with a fire extinguisher and don't smoke in the grounds,' Kalu said over his shoulder as he walked towards Kissie's BMW. 'HR will have no choice but to fire you for either of those things. Be sensible for your own sake.'

'We will,' the other man said, standing on his cigarette stub.

'Better still, stop smoking altogether!' Kalu added, opening the passenger door. 'That will solve all your problems.' He slumped into the passenger seat and Kissie hugged him. They cried in each other's arms for a while. 'Are you okay to travel?' Kalu asked. 'I completely understand if you want to delay your flight for a few days.'

'What?' Kissie said, shaking her head and wiping her eyes. 'And have you wandering around Nigeria on your own? I'd be out of my mind.'

'Good. I'm glad. We need to stick together right now. Let's go home and grab our bags and we need to keep an eye out for anything that looks out of place,' Kalu said. Kissie looked confused. 'The police came to see me earlier. They think Chuk was killed by mistake.'

'What do you mean, mistake?' Kissie asked. 'Are you saying it wasn't an accident?'

'Yes,' Kalu nodded. 'They think Chuk was pushed and the real target was me.'

'That's unbelievable,' Kissie said. 'Who would want you dead?'

'Jet Unganu,' Kalu said. 'Apparently, she blames for me for her niece's death and there's a price on my head.'

'What the actual fuck!' Kissie whispered. 'Why don't they arrest her?'

'She hasn't done anything wrong herself.' Kalu shrugged. 'They think she may have hired someone to kill me but they screwed up and thought Chuk was me.'

'I don't believe this is happening to us,' Kissie said, banging the steering wheel with her hand. 'Just when everything was beginning to make sense and all the pieces were coming together.'

'We can't let this stop us, Kissie,' Kalu said, kissing her forehead. 'We need to focus on meeting up with Beb in Monguno and finding your sisters. Let's get home, grab our bags and get to the hotel. Whoever is trying to hurt me has no idea that we are leaving the country,' Kalu said. 'Once we're at the airport, we'll be safe. Are you okay to drive?'

'Yes,' Kissie said, starting the engine.

As the vehicle pulled out of the car park and slid into the traffic, a lone female watched them from a dark Volvo. She followed at a safe distance and checked her mirror, looking for any sign of a police presence. Jet had told her that detectives were pointing the finger of blame right at her. They would be watching the doctor with or without his permission. She couldn't identify any police but she noticed a van that was two vehicles behind her, occupied by two black men wearing shades; their hair was in bangs. They were so obvious; it was almost laughable. She shook her head in frustration. It appeared that Jet was making sure she got the job done properly this time but her efforts were as subtle as bricks in the teeth. She was risking the entire operation by sending her goons to follow the doctor.

Chapter 19

Nazia was sitting on a thin mattress, chatting to Najma and Rida. They were asking when their mother would come to take them to their new home. Karcem was already asleep which was nothing new. That boy could go to sleep on a roundabout and not be disturbed. His gentle snoring was rhythmical, reassuring and peaceful. It had been a difficult time for them, waiting for their mother to become well enough to be released from hospital. For a long time, their aunt Isime had cared for them and she constantly told them their mother was very sick and may not come home but there was always hope. Oke was a strong woman. Hope there was and she had made it through when so many had died. Nazia told them they were the luckiest children in Monguno to have a mother and aunt, who cared for them so much. Of course, no matter what she said, they asked where she was and what her and their aunt were doing that took so long. She had explained that they were going to their family home in the town and they had no idea what they would find or what would need to be done to make it liveable. Once the house was organised, clean and safe, they would come for them.

While they were chatting, the sound of gunfire reached them. It was intermittent at first and a few miles away but it was moving closer. They tried to ignore it but the girls were frightened. Their experience of gunfire was still fresh in their memory and it wasn't good. There had been a bloodbath when Boko were driven out of the town. The girls were whispering and frightened but Kareem remained asleep, which was a blessing. He was woken by loud banging on the backdoor.

'Who is there?' Nazia asked, nervously approaching the door. She hadn't locked it as she thought they were safe. There were no people in the town yet.

'Open the door, woman!' a voice growled. Nazia put her shoulder to the door and turned the key. It clicked as the lock slid home. She felt the door rattle and the handle turned both directions.

'Come here,' she whispered to the children. They were frozen with fear. 'Move now!' she insisted. The children crept to her. 'Take your brother and sister and climb down into the food cellar. Do it now. quickly,' she said calmy to Najma. Najma shuffled into the kitchen with her siblings. They were whispering their objections but she encouraged them with a gentle shove.

'Open the door!' the voice boomed. The door threatened to break in two. 'I can see the lights on in there!'

'What do you want?' Nazia asked, stalling for time. 'I'm just a woman minding my business.' Najma lifted the hatch and Rida and Kareem climbed into the cellar reluctantly. She followed them and lowered the hatch as she climbed down. Nazia pulled the mat over it and stood on the hatch to force it closed. The wood had swollen but it could be forced closed with her weight.

'Open the door before I break it down!'

'Okay, okay,' Nazia said, turning the key. The handle turned before she could open it and the door burst open. She was thrown backwards against the wall. 'Please don't hurt me,' Nazia pleaded. 'I'm just a widow trying to survive.'

'You are alone in this house?' the man asked, his eyes darting everywhere. He walked into the kitchen and looked around. Nazia could tell from his uniform that he wasn't a soldier. Not a government soldier. He wasn't Boko either. Maybe he belonged to one of the many rebel groups. 'Are you alone? Answer me, woman!'

'Yes. I'm alone,' Nazia said, cowering. She refused to make eye contact with him. He was young and frightened. She could see the fear in his eyes. His weapon was slung from one shoulder and a bullet belt hung from the other. He was standing directly above the hatch. If one of the children coughed or started crying, he would hear them. She could hear the floorboards creaking as he shifted his weight. It would be terrifying for the children beneath him. Kareem would be traumatised. He was so sensitive.

'What are you doing here alone?' he asked, eyeing her suspiciously. 'Are you hiding from the authorities?'

'No. I'm not hiding. This was my family home before the war. All my family are dead. It's just me here. You can look around the other rooms if you like,' she said, trying to coax him from the kitchen. 'There are two bedrooms down the hall but they're empty. Take a look.'

He stepped towards the sink and the floorboards creaked again. Nazia felt her heart stop. He looked down and shifted his weight. The board creaked again. There were long seconds as he shifted his weight again and again, looking down at the floor. She imagined the children huddled together in the darkness of the cellar looking up at the hatch, wondering what was going on. If one of them panicked, he would hear them and they would be kidnapped, no doubt about it.

‘I think I can hear someone outside,’ Nazia lied. ‘Are you alone or running away from someone?’

‘I am not alone but I’m separated from my group,’ he answered, ducking low. ‘What did you hear?’ he asked, peering through the window into the night. ‘Tell me what you heard!’

‘I’m not sure but it was definitely outside.’ Nazia gestured to the front window. He ran out of the kitchen into the living room and Nazia sighed with relief.

‘What did you hear, woman?’

‘I thought I heard voices,’ she said, kneeling. ‘I might be hearing things but I’m sure it came from outside at the front of the house. They were male and they were Nigerian, I think.’

‘Get up!’ the man said. Nazia hesitated but he looked spooked and unpredictable, so she did as he asked. ‘Do you have any money?’

‘No,’ Nazia said, shaking her head. ‘There is nothing to buy here in Monguno,’ she added. ‘It’s a ghost town. I have no need for money.’

‘How are you living if you have nothing?’ he asked, angrily. ‘What do you eat, or are you a witch?’

‘I live from the kindness of others and from the land,’ Nazia said. ‘There are plenty of fruits and berries growing locally. I pick them daily.’

'A woman your age has children. Where are your children?' he asked, suspicion in his eyes. Sweat ran from his forehead. He was running from something, she guessed.

'They are all dead,' she said.

'Husband?'

'Dead.'

'How did he die?' he asked.

'He was shot by UN soldiers at the school,' Nazia said. 'He wasn't a good man.'

'The UN killed many Boko at the school. He was Boko?' Nazia didn't reply. 'I asked you if you were you married to a Boko?'

'Yes,' she whispered. 'I was forced to marry him. I am not Boko. I was taken as a young girl and enslaved by them but I am not one of them. Please leave me alone.'

'Shut up, bitch!' he snapped. He took a length of rope from his belt and tied her hands together. 'Boko are regathering and they're paying a reward for their women to be returned. Especially a pretty one like you,' he added. 'I might even have a go myself before I sell you,' he said grinning. 'You're coming with me!'

'I can't go back to that life,' Nazia struggled. 'I would rather you killed me than take me back to them.'

'Shut up, woman!' he said, striking her with the back of his hand. She felt her lip split and tasted blood in her mouth. She had tasted her own blood many times before and it triggered terrible memories of her marriage. Nazia felt her heart breaking and a crippling fear engulfed her. What about the children? Panic gripped her. She glanced to where the children were hiding and wondered if they would be found in time. What if Oke didn't come back for a few days and they had no water? The heat would kill them. She felt sick to the bone.

'Please don't do this to me,' she begged. He grabbed her hair and dragged her roughly to the door and looked around outside. The light from the inside was limiting his view. The dark shadows outside seemed to blur and swirl so that he couldn't see much further than the garden gate. He leaned out of the door to look up the street but it was pitch black. 'Please just leave me here in peace,' she sobbed. 'You have no idea what it's like to be forced to marry one of them. It's literally a hell on earth. Let me go please. I can't go back to that life.'

Nazia grabbed his wrist to take the pressure from her scalp but he twisted her hair with his hand and pulled harder. The pain was blinding and he was too strong to resist.

'Move before I lose my temper!' he screamed in her face.

'Get off me!' Nazia fought against him but it was useless.

He stood in the doorway, silhouetted by the lights inside. A burst of gunfire exploded from across the street and the man's jaw disintegrated. Nazia felt blood and brains splatter her face. A powerful thump hit her abdomen. She struggled to breathe and felt like she was winded. Confusion and pain spread through her. She looked down and put her hand over a hole in her robe. She felt warm blood spreading from a bullet wound below her navel and she fell to the ground. Her breath was shallow and she couldn't think straight. She stared up at the ceiling as a dark cloud descended over her entire being.

Chapter 20

It was dark when Beb awoke and he felt like he needed to sleep for a week. He yawned and stretched. Amira put her hand on his shoulder and squeezed gently. A sign she was anxious without saying it. The vehicle hit a pothole and rocked violently, sending a jolt up his spine.

'Sorry, my headlights aren't great,' Omar said. 'That was unavoidable.'

Beb sat up and looked around. Omar glanced at him, looking nervous. Beb sensed something was wrong and became alert.

'Where are we?' he asked.

'The outskirts of Fotokol,' Omar replied. 'There has been some trouble up ahead.'

'What makes you say that?'

'Because everyone is heading in the opposite direction,' he said. He pointed to an armoured vehicle trundling across their path. Beb took in the scene. 'We have passed two petrol stations that are closed up and guarded by soldiers.'

Beb could see smoke rising from beyond the town and military vehicles were parked on each intersection. There was a constant stream of people heading away from the town.

'What is happening?' Beb asked, dozily. His senses were returning slowly.

'I don't know but there are soldiers everywhere,' Omar said. 'Cameroon must have a big army and it's all here.'

'They do have a big army but those soldiers are from Chad, not Cameroon,' Beb noted.

'How do you know?' Amira asked.

'I recognise their uniforms from being a boy,' Beb said. 'When Boko first started attacking towns in the Borno region, where I lived, they would cross the borders to raid and then retreat into Chad or Cameroon. Our soldiers could not cross the borders, so they got away every time. Eventually, the neighbouring governments cooperated to try to drive them out. Chad, Cameroon and Nigeria chased them across the borders many times. There were often soldiers of different nationality around when I was boy.'

'Did it work?' Omar asked.

'Did what work?'

'The cooperation,' Omar said.

'For a while, yes,' Beb said. 'I remember father telling us the Nigerian army was useless on its own and if the neighbouring armies went home, we would be in trouble. They needed help from Chad and Cameroon to keep Boko at bay but eventually the other countries asked for money to pay for their armies and our government said no. The help was withdrawn and Boko advanced. The government just gave up. That's when we had to leave Monguno.'

'But why are the soldiers here now?' Amira asked.

'Boko must be back,' Beb said, shrugging. He looked at Omar and he nodded, concern on his face. 'I can't see any other reason.'

'This situation changes everything,' Omar said. 'I didn't figure on driving through a warzone to take you home.'

'Don't panic, Omar,' Beb said. 'Let's get across the border and away from here,' he added. He saw a crowd further down the road. 'There is a petrol station.'

'Where are all these people going?' Amira asked. Dozens of men, women and children were walking in the opposite direction. Most of the women were wearing burkas and the men flowing overshirts and pants. There were bikes and trikes loaded with belongings but the most popular modes of transport were donkey and carts. A line of vehicles queued impatiently, trying to leave the town, their headlights illuminated the chaos.

'They're getting away from here,' Beb said. 'This reminds me of being a boy.'

'It must have been frightening,' Amira said. 'I'm frightened looking at it.'

Omar navigated the Toyota through the crowds against the tide of humans. It appeared that people had packed up whatever they could take and were leaving in a hurry. He pulled the vehicle onto the forecourt of a petrol station, which had two pumps; both were covered with orange material, which said empty. Heavily-armed soldiers guarded the pumps. A crowd of angry men and women were banging on the windows, holding jerry cans, buckets and bottles. Soldiers were monitoring the crowds and holding them back as best they could but their need for fuel was unquenchable. Desperation overruled their fear of the soldiers. The fragile standoff was holding for now.

'It looks like there's no fuel to be had,' Omar said. 'This is a fucking nightmare,' he muttered. 'There's no way we can get to Dikwa without filling up.'

'We're not going to get any here any time soon,' Beb said, sighing. 'Let's find some Nigerian troops and ask them what the situation is at the border. We need to cross that bridge today.'

'What about fuel?' Omar said. 'We can't risk it!'

'Calm down. Let's not panic,' Beb said. 'There may be more stations in town, if not, there will be some across the bridge in Gamboru.'

'How do you know that?' Omar asked, frowning.

'Because there are cars and trucks in Nigeria and they need fuel in Nigeria too. There will be petrol stations. We're not going to the moon,' Beb said, shaking his head. 'There will be as many stations over there as there are here and they may not be affected. The trouble may be just this side of the border.'

'May be, may not be, may be, may not be, may be?' Omar said, flapping. 'May be is no good to me. I need to know what is happening before we cross the border.'

'This is how the government operates. The army will commandeer fuel supplies for themselves if they think an attack is coming. They can't fight without fuel.' Beb shrugged. 'It's standard procedure and nothing to worry about.'

'How do you know this?' Omar asked.

'I read and listen to the news,' Beb said. 'There is no need to panic.'

'Okay,' Omar said, reluctantly. 'We'll find some Nigerians, ask them what's going on and then we will make a decision. I can't function on may be. May be is no good to me.'

'Okay, Omar,' Beb said, nodding. He sensed Omar was thinking of aborting the journey. That couldn't happen. 'Drive on and let's see what is going on.'

'These people look so frightened,' Amira said as Omar drove slowly through the fleeing hoard. Women and children were crying, the men looked hopeless and desperate. The soldiers looked menacing and nervous. A few hundred yards further on, they spotted the lights on the bridge to Gamboru in the distance; smoke was rising from it. Omar indicated and nudged the Toyota through the crowds towards it. Progress was slow and they passed dozens of military vehicles but they were all from Cameroon and Chad.

'There doesn't seem to be any Nigerian troops on this side,' Beb said, shaking his head.

'Why would that be?' Omar asked.

'They won't cross the border,' Beb said. Something caught his attention. 'The government is so stubborn; it cuts its nose off to spite its face.' He sighed and looked around. 'Over there,' Beb said, pointing. 'There are Nigerian police officers.'

A group of uniformed men were smoking in an open top jeep, watching the people flowing around them. It was clearly marked as a police vehicle. They were laughing and joking and appeared unaffected by the plight of the fleeing people.

'Pull up next to them,' Beb said, winding down the window. The officers looked on angrily at their approach as if it was rude to approach them and interrupt their smoke break. 'Hello,' Beb said. The policemen eyed him suspiciously. 'How are you today?'

'What do you want?' the sergeant asked. The men looked into the Toyota and focused on Amira. She kept her head down.

'I am Nigerian, from Monguno and we're trying to cross the border to reach home.'

'Monguno?'

'Yes.' Beb asked.

'You must have left there a long time ago,' the sergeant said, inhaling his cigarette.

'My family left there when Boko invaded,' Beb said.

'You're actually from Monguno and now you want to go back?' a sergeant asked, surprised.

'Yes. I was born there.'

'Where have you travelled from?'

'We came from the airport in Chad,' Beb said.

'And you're taking a taxi all the way to Monguno?' the sergeant asked, frowning. 'This is a good job for your driver,' he said, stooping low to see Omar. 'How much is he paying you, driver?'

'I'm a friend of the family,' Omar lied. 'This is a favour.'

'You must be a good friend,' the sergeant said, turning his attention back to Beb. 'If you're from Monguno, what family are you?'

'Why do you ask?' Beb asked.

'I'm also from Monguno.'

'My family name is Sammi,' Beb said, nodding. 'My father is Kalu and my uncle Chuk Sammi. Their father was Ganu.'

'That name rings a bell. Remind me about them?' the sergeant said.

'They were academics,' Beb said.

'They were teachers, right?' the sergeant said, smiling.

'Yes. At the school next to the hospital.'

'Ah, yes. I remember it well.'

'Good to meet someone from Monguno,' Beb said, reaching out of the window to shake his hand. 'What family are you?'

'Abara,' the policeman replied.

'I remember a policeman called Gebril Abara,' Beb said.

'My uncle. I have his name,' the police officer said, proudly.

'Gebril?'

'Yes.'

'Good to meet you, Gebril. I remember him coming to our school,' Beb said. 'He used to frighten the life out of us and tell us he would put us in prison if we misbehaved.'

'That's him. He used to say the same to me and my cousins,' Gebril said, nodding. 'So, you need to cross the border if you're going to Monguno.'

'We're trying to.' Beb gestured to the bridge. The smoke rising from beneath it was thick and black. 'What has happened?'

'A suicide bomber attacked the bridge last night,' Gebril said. 'It was a coordinated attack as troops attacked civilians in Gamboru. They killed them in their houses and even in the mosque,' Gebril said. 'Hundreds have lost their lives.'

'That's terrible news.' Beb shook his head. 'Why have they attacked the bridge?'

'There is a market on the bridge at night when it gets cooler,' the policeman explained. 'People from both sides of the border go there to buy food and meet family. The bomber walked into the centre of the bridge and detonated his device. There are over thirty dead from the blast and hundreds killed on the other side.'

'Hundreds, you say?'

'Yes, hundreds. They're still counting the dead. It was a twelve-hour massacre. Most of the victims were slaughtered in their own homes,' Gebril said, shrugging. 'The victims all had their throats cut.'

'That's not the work of rebels. Rebels use bullets. That is the work of Boko,' Beb said. The policemen nodded. 'They made a similar attack here a few years ago, didn't they?'

'You know a lot about it,' Gebril said, grinning. 'Are you a journalist?'

'No but I follow the news,' Beb said.

'It was twenty-fifteen,' Gebril said. 'They killed over three-hundred that time.' He gestured to the people scurrying down the street. 'That's why people are leaving. They think last night was a prequel to a bigger attack on this side of the border.'

'I can understand why they're running. What do you think is happening?' Beb asked.

'I don't know but I think going to Monguno today would be foolish,' Gebril said. 'The bridge is damaged. Part of it has been blown away and there is structural damage underneath and we have no idea where the attackers went to. They could be in Nigeria or they could still be in Cameroon. You might find out the hard way if you cross over.'

'How did you cross?'

'We crossed upriver but it's very remote up there and we think some of the attackers headed north.'

'Is Gamboru secured?' Beb asked.

'It depends on what you mean by secure,' the sergeant said, wryly. 'They thought they were secure yesterday before this happened.'

'I mean is it safe; are there troops in Gamboru?' Beb asked.

'It's under control but there are only Nigerian forces over there,' Gebril said, nodding. 'Our government isn't keen on letting neighbouring forces across the border.'

'That is why Boko stay here,' Beb said. The policemen all nodded in agreement. 'We need fuel. Can you help us?' Beb asked. The sergeant looked at his officers. They smiled and nodded.

'We might be able to acquire enough to fill your tank for the right price,' Gebril said, grinning. He patted his pocket. 'The soldiers have confiscated the petrol stations and their stocks, so it would have to be from Gamboru and it's expensive today,' he added shrugging. 'You know how it works.'

'Obviously, we need to cross the bridge,' Beb said.

'We can get you over but it's at your own risk,' Gebril said. 'If it collapses, we warned you.'

'And we'll need some weapons,' Beb added. The policemen stopped smiling. 'An automatic pistol and a decent rifle.'

'How much money do you have?'

'It depends on how much you're going to ask us to pay to get across that bridge,' Beb said.

'One thousand American dollars,' Gebril said, his smile gone now. Beb shook his head and frowned.

'That's crazy money,' Beb said.

'The woman and child are not Nigerian. I'm guessing they're Tuareg and they're not welcome without special visas,' the sergeant said, looking serious. 'Do you have special visas for them?'

'No,' Beb said. 'That's why we're travelling by land.'

'I suspected as much. Letting them cross the border could get me thrown into jail. Look around you at this chaos.' Gebril gestured to the crowds of people. 'Getting you across the bridge will be expensive today and if you want fuel too, you will have to pay.'

'I don't mind paying,' Beb said. 'But we aren't carrying that amount of money. We're poor people. My wife and child are Tuareg and have nothing but the clothes they're wearing.' The policemen looked deflated. 'We have nothing of value to trade.'

'Stop, please,' Gebril said, shaking his head, wiping imaginary tears from his eyes. 'You're breaking my heart. I will need some tissues if you carry on.'

'There is no need to mock me,' Beb said. 'A fair price is three-hundred dollars.'

'You're insulting us,' Gebril snarled.

'It's not meant as an insult,' Beb said. 'It's what we can afford.'

'I wouldn't risk it for that amount.'

'Three hundred US dollars is over a month's pay, isn't it?' Beb asked.

'Give me eight hundred and we have a deal,' Gebril argued.

'We only have three hundred.'

'Five hundred is my last offer,' Gebril said, angrily.

'I'm not in a position to bargain with you,' Beb said, sighing. 'We have three hundred dollars.'

'Then drive on and try and get across on your own!' Gebril spat into the sand.

'I didn't mean any offence,' Beb said. 'We are poor people, trying to get home.'

'Go and be poor somewhere else and stop wasting my time.'

'Okay. We'll do that,' Beb said. 'Good luck to you. I wish you well.' Beb smiled politely and closed the window. 'Drive, Omar.'

'Are you sure?' Omar asked, putting the Toyota in gear. He pulled away from the policemen. 'You want me to drive away from them?'

'Yes,' Beb said. 'Head for the bridge.'

'But he said it was damaged.'

'He doesn't know how badly,' Beb said. 'With all this chaos going on, I don't think there will be any border guards there and if there are, they will let us cross over for a lot less than five hundred dollars.' Beb checked the mirror and the policemen were arguing amongst themselves. 'He was testing me to see how much money we have on us.'

'What makes you say that?' Amira asked. 'Wasn't he just haggling?'

'He's a liar,' Beb said.

'What do you mean?'

'Monguno is a small town. Everyone knows the Sammis are doctors, not teachers, and the school is on the opposite side of town to the hospital.' Beb shrugged. 'And I made up the name of the policeman, Gebril, but it turns out it was his uncle.'

'Wow,' Amira said, shaking her head.

'He's a shark and we need to stay clear of him.'

'I did wonder why you said that,' Amira said, impressed. 'You are very good at lying. I will have to keep an eye on you.'

'He was befriending me to get me to let my guard down,' Beb said, smiling. 'If he thought we had over a thousand dollars on us, they would lure us somewhere with the promise of fuel and weapons and rob us.'

'It's sad we can't trust the police,' Amira said. Omar and Beb turned around simultaneously and laughed. 'Why is that funny?'

'There were no policemen in the desert,' Beb said, chuckling. 'You're not to know.'

'You're making fun of me,' Amira said, with a sulky expression which turned to a smile seconds later. 'I don't think it's funny.'

'It shouldn't be funny,' Omar said, 'But it is.'

They made slow progress through the town until they reached the bridge. It was a scene of devastation. There were a few vehicles dotted about, their occupants standing around, some chatting, others staring at the damaged structure as a troop carrier crawled across, weaving between the smoking debris.

'What is happening?' Beb shouted to a group of men.

'They are testing the bridge,' one of them shouted back to him. 'Nothing has crossed since the explosion.'

'They're braver than me,' Omar said.

'Brave or stupid,' Beb added. He watched as the truck progressed. The remains of market stalls and tables were still in place and a burned-out van was still smouldering on the apex. The safety rails and part of the road had been blown away from one section, leaving a ten-metre crescent-shaped hole in the north edge of the bridge. Bodies lay crumpled in the road.

'Why haven't they moved the dead?' Amira asked.

'In case they're boobytrapped,' Beb said, watching the truck. 'I can't see any guards. We should follow that truck and stay in its tracks.'

'Are you mad?' Omar said. 'I'm not crossing that bridge.'

'We have to cross the bridge while there are no guards,' Beb said.

'There are no guards because there has been a massacre on the other side.' Omar shook his head. 'For one thing, we don't know what is going on over there now but we do know hundreds have been macheted in their homes and secondly, if I cross that bridge, I have to know that I can get back safely at some point.'

'We have to cross that bridge and get to Monguno, Omar,' Beb said, turning towards him. 'If Boko are back and attacking border towns, they may be planning to attack Monguno and my sisters are there. They could be massacred or they could be forced to flee again and we may never find them.' Beb stared at Omar. Omar couldn't hold his gaze and looked away. 'I have this one opportunity to find them again. The clock is already ticking and I have to get there as soon as I can. Do you understand how important it is for me to get there?'

'Yes,' Omar said. He turned off the engine and undid his seatbelt. He faced Beb. 'But I have a family too.' He looked at Beb eye to eye. 'I have a wife and three children at home and I need to get back to them safely. My family is just as important as yours is. Do you understand how important it is to me to get home?'

A loud rumble and the squealing of metal split the air. They looked at the bridge in time to see the mid-section begin to shiver and shake. Steel girders buckled and snapped and concrete crumbled and cracked. Huge sections of the bridge disappeared into the deep ravine beneath it. A deafening crack pierced the silence and the troop carrier toppled into the abys.

Chapter 21

Oke was about to stand up when something caught her eye. She grabbed Isime and held her tightly to stop her moving. Isime was bruised and confused and just wanted to get up run home as fast as she could.

'What's wrong?' Isime asked.

'Stay still!' Oke whispered. 'Over there.' She gestured with her eyes. There was movement to their right. They watched as two figures rose from the debris. It was difficult to see them in the dark but Oke caught a glint of steel. Their faces were hidden but she could see they were small. Very small. They slowly made their way towards where the sisters were hiding, one tentative step after another. The machineguns that they had looked too heavy for them to carry, almost as tall as they were. One of them was sniffling and sobbing. The other was trying to reassure him that everything was okay. He told him that the soldiers had gone and they were safe. Listening to their voices, Oke could tell they were children. Boy soldiers.

'They're boys,' Isime said. 'What are they doing here?'

'Shush,' Oke said, pressing a finger to her lips. Isime was going to speak but changed her mind.

The boys looked almost comical in their uniforms, that hung from skinny shoulders. They were wearing green berets and the patches on their arms bore the symbols of Boko Haram. The sense of sympathy Oke felt was replaced with fear. It didn't matter what age they were; they were indoctrinated by hate. A hatred of anything that wasn't Boko. The age of the finger on the trigger didn't matter; the bullets were just as deadly.

Oke tried to melt into the wall behind her as the boy soldiers neared. They were almost upon them when the sound of a diesel engine reached them. The boys froze and looked around.

'They're coming back!' one of them said.

'Which way is it coming from?' the other asked.

'I can't tell, but I don't want to fight them. I just want to go home. Let's surrender.'

'Shut up and run!' the other one said. They turned and ran towards the burnt-out houses, stumbling and tripping on the bricks and timbers that were strewn across the area. A jeep appeared from the east and its headlights picked out the fleeing child soldiers. The searchlight was switched on and aimed at them.

'Stop where you are!' a voice boomed.

One of the boys stopped and turned towards the lights. He held up his hands in surrender. The other boy ran into the ruins, his footsteps clearly audible.

'Drop your weapon!' the voice ordered. The boy slipped the strap from his shoulder and the machinegun clattered onto the floor. His bottom lip started to quiver and he was blinking rapidly against the glare of the lights. A single shot rang out and a dark hole appeared in his forehead. The back of his skull exploded as the high-velocity round exited. There was a look of surprise on his face as his knees buckled and he slumped forward, face down in the ashes.

'Oh no!' Isime whispered, covering her mouth.

Oke tapped Isime and pointed to a gap in the wall about a hundred metres to their right. Isime nodded and began to crawl on hands and knees, trying desperately not to make a sound. A burst of machinegun fire exploded from the ruins, the muzzle flash bright orange against the charred structure. The boy had obviously decided to fight it out. Bullets pinged off the armoured vehicle and catapulted dirt and concrete from the ground around it. The men in the jeep dismounted and took up defensive positions.

'Light him up,' a voice shouted and multiple weapons began spewing bullets into the building. The muzzle flash was their target.

'Move as fast as you can,' Oke said, scrabbling over the rubble. The gunfire was deafening and they used it to cover their escape from the ruined plot. An RPG whooshed towards the spot where the child soldier had opened fire from and it exploded with catastrophic results. The remaining structure was blown to smithereens and the charred rafters collapsed into the ruin, crushing everything beneath it. The machinegun fire continued until their magazines were empty and they fired another RPG into the smouldering mess for good measure.

'They killed those boys,' Isime said, horrified. 'I bet they weren't even in their teens.'

'They killed two Boko,' Oke said. 'No one cares how old they are.'

'But those soldiers are supposed to be the good guys,' Isime argued.

'There are no good guys anymore,' Oke said. They slipped through the gap in the wall and ran, stooping low where they couldn't be seen. A few minutes of scrabbling along the road and they reached the old mosque. It was shot full of shell holes and the dome above it looked like an apple with a bite out of it. The doors were hanging off and the windows were no longer rectangles, just blackened maws. An unwholesome smell wafted from inside and they both recognised the stale scent of death. They had been close to the building before but not close enough to experience the odour. Their pace increased as they neared home and the sound of gunfire became muffled and far away. They didn't speak until they reached their home. Oke put the key in the back door and unlocked it. They stepped inside and closed it behind them, leaning their backs against the wall. The relief was incredible. And then they noticed the smell and the fact that the front door was open. A warm breeze blew into the house.

'Why is that door open?' Oke asked. 'I locked it from the inside.'

'Put the light on,' Isime said.

'No,' Oke said. 'No lights until everything is closed.'

She went towards the front door and looked up and down the street. She closed it, locking it quietly, and then she closed the blinds on all the windows.

'Okay, put the light on,' Oke said. Isime switched it on and they let their eyes adjust. 'I don't believe this,' Oke said. The cellar hatch was open and a trail of blood led from the kitchen to the front door. Oke walked into the kitchen and looked down into the cellar. 'She's gone!'

'How can she be gone?' Isime asked, shocked. She joined Oke at the hatch. 'She was dead!'

'Obviously, she wasn't,' Oke said, shaking her head. The odours of urine and excrement were strong. 'She climbed out of here, so she wasn't dead at all!'

'Should we follow her?' Isime asked, running to the front door.

'Have you forgotten what is going on out there?' Oke reminded her. 'We're going nowhere. We need to clean up this mess, eat something and rest. Now she's gone, we can go and fetch the children in the morning. They will be terrified by the gunfire.'

'But what about her?' Isime asked. 'What if she informs about us?'

'I think the soldiers have more important things to worry about than a few beds and some vegetables,' Oke said. 'She must be badly injured and she might not make it very far.'

'What if she tells them I hit her over the head?'

'We'll deny ever seeing her but we need to clean up any trace of her and we need to do it quickly.'

'I'll make it look like she was never here,' Isime said, moving into the kitchen with purpose.

'Good,' Oke said. 'Don't hit anyone else on the head.'

Chapter 22

Sean Trainor opened the back of the van and took out a five-litre tin of petrol. He took it to the centre of the old warehouse and placed it on the floor next to a metal chair. Sitting in the chair was Jude Unganu, a slightly-built black man with a glass eye and his hair in bangs. He lost his eye in a bar fight over a game of pool when he was in his teens. Finding trouble had been one of his greatest talents but this time he had surpassed himself. His mouth was duct taped closed and his nose was bleeding. Sean had taped his arms and legs to the chair and stripped him to his boxer shorts. A thick gold belcher chain hung from his scrawny neck and he wondered if his captor would steal it. Jude was shivering with fear and the cold. He could see his breath coming from his nostrils and his feet were numb. The man who was holding him captive was quiet and focused and went about his work without a word. Jude had no idea who he was or why he had kidnapped him. Obviously, being related to Jet was his best guess. She was always telling him to be careful and most of the time, he was but the man had got the drop on him. The first blow to the back of his head had stunned him and by the time he had regained his faculties, he was trussed up. He was terrified and wanted the opportunity to communicate with his captor and negotiate an exit from the situation. The introduction of a can of petrol was very concerning and he had no intentions of testing his attacker's willingness to use it. Whatever the man wanted, he could have. Simple.

Sean was searching for something in the van for a few minutes. When he returned, he ripped the duct tape from his captive's mouth in one tug. It ripped the top layer of skin and some lip tissue with it. Blood trickled down Jude's chin.

'What the fuck is this about?' Jude asked. 'Whatever the problem is, we can work it out.'

'This is your mobile.' Sean held up the mobile phone he had taken from Jude's jeans. 'What's the code to unlock the screen?'

'Listen to me, mate,' Jude said. 'Whatever you want, you can have it. I don't want to cause any problems. Tell me what you want and I'll sort it out for you.'

'I'm not your mate on any level and all I want is the access code to your phone.'

'Is this about money? How much do you want?' Jude asked. 'Jet will pay you whatever you want. Has she pissed you off? This is about her, isn't it?'

'What is the code?' Sean asked again.

'Come on man,' Jude pleaded. 'What do you want?'

'Okay, you had your chance,' Sean said, angrily. 'Enough is enough.'

'Wait a minute!' Jude protested. 'I'll tell you!'

Sean opened the petrol canister and tipped it over Jude. The stinging liquid ran into his nose and mouth and his eyes were burning.

'Wait, wait, wait,' Jude spluttered. 'Two, four, six, eight.' He coughed and nearly choked. 'The code is two, four, six, eight. Whatever you need, man. You can have it. Don't hurt me.'

'What is Jet's number stored as?' Sean asked.

'Jet. It's stored as Jet,' Jude said. 'Just tell her what you want. She'll pay you whatever you want. I'm her uncle, you see.'

'I know who you are,' Sean said.

Sean scrolled to the number and pressed the call button. It rang a few times before she answered.

'Yo, Jude,' Jet answered, sounding happy. 'What's up?' Sean switched on the camera and focused on Jude. It took her a few seconds to realise what was happening. 'What the fuck, Jude?' she shouted. 'Who has done this to you?'

'Talk to this fucking nut case,' Jude said, crying. 'Just pay him what he wants. He's covered me in petrol for fuck's sake!'

'Hey, hey, hey,' she shouted. 'Asshole! Do you have any idea who you're fucking with?'

'I know who I'm fucking with, Jet. You're a little fish in a big pond. Soho is a dot on a map and outside of that shithole, no one knows your name.' He paused and zoomed in on Jude. 'The question you should ask yourself, is do you know who you are fucking with, Jet?' Sean asked, calmly.

'Why don't you tell me?' Jet said. 'Point that camera at your face and let me see you. Who am I fucking with, asshole?'

'You set your attack dogs on the wrong family and now you will watch as I show you what happens to anyone who hurts my family. Your uncle Jude is the first of many.'

Sean lit a match and flicked it. Jude ignited and his screams were memorable. Jet got a box office view of her uncle burning to death.

Chapter 23

Kalu and Kissie made their way across London in a weird silence. It wasn't uncomfortable but it was necessary. There was so much to say but neither of them could find the words. Emotions were raw and conflicted. They were about to cross continents to find their family, long thought of as dead people and yet their focus was on the attempted murder of Kalu and the death of his brother. The police thought they were in danger and had offered protection but Kalu had turned it down because their belongings were packed and ready to take to the airport hotel. He didn't intend to be around long enough to become a victim but in the cold light of London in the winter, he had become anxious. They were two people in a metropolis of millions, insignificant to anyone but themselves.

When they arrived at their home, they parked their car in the underground car park.

'How long do you think we'll be gone?' Kissie asked.

'I don't have a clue. I haven't booked a taxi yet,' Kalu said. 'I feel terrible planning to leave here when Chuk has been murdered.' He shrugged. 'But what can we do?'

'Chuk would want you to go and find your children,' Kissie said. 'He was so excited when we told him we had seen Isime and Oke.'

'He really wanted to meet them,' Kalu said. 'We talked about going back to Monguno to spend time with them. He said they would have children of their own.'

'They probably have,' Kissie said. 'We will soon find out. We must stick to our plan.'

'I know all the reasons why we should go but I still feel like I'm deserting him,' Kalu said.

'You're not deserting him,' Kissie said. 'He'll be with us every step of the way.'

'I know,' Kalu agreed. 'Let's get out of here.'

They climbed out of the vehicle, locked it and headed for the lift. The car park made Kalu nervous; he felt vulnerable there. The attack by Suzette had traumatised him and he was sure he could still see a stain where she had bled to death on the concrete. Kissie told him it was all in his mind but he wasn't so sure. Concrete is porous and all the bleach they had used had failed to reach the deeper pits. It couldn't be cleaned away, not ever.

The underground space had a low ceiling and was poorly lit and felt claustrophobic. It smelled of diesel and puddles of water formed in the winter. Fuel floated on the surface, the iridescent hues of blue, green and amber reflected the light. He pressed the call button and waited impatiently. He heard the sound of an engine and looked around to see a vehicle coming down the ramp. A dark Audi pulled into the lot and parked at the far end. It belonged to a solicitor who lived on the top floor. She was an attractive lady, who seemed to have a new boyfriend every week. Her social media posts were filtered to the point that he had to look twice sometimes as the images didn't look like she did in reality. He waved as she got out of her car and headed for the stairs, her briefcase tucked under her arm. Her lips were becoming duck-like, more swollen each time he saw her.

The lift arrived and they stepped inside, turning quickly to face the doors as they closed. Kalu imagined hands grabbing the doors just as they met in the middle, but that was Hollywood and this was London. His heart was beating quickly as the lift began to ascend. He took a deep breath and relaxed a little. Kissie hooked her arm into his and put her head on his shoulder.

The lift arrived on their floor and the door opened with a ping. Kalu looked both ways before stepping out into the dimly-lit corridor, something he had never done before. The ends of the corridor were in darkness and the brooding shadows seemed to shift as he looked into them. His nerves were shattered. He wished he had taken up DS Alfred's offer of protection. It felt like ages before the lights in the corridor flickered on, triggered by a motion sensor. Their apartment was at the end of the landing on the left and they walked towards it arm in arm, nervous and afraid. They sensed each other's fear.

'Are you okay?' Kalu asked her.

'No. I'm not okay,' Kissie said. 'Everything feels weird.'

'Everything is weird,' Kalu said.

'Can you smell weed?' Kissie asked, frowning. 'Weed and Creed?' she giggled nervously. 'That rhymes, Creed and weed.'

'My old nose isn't as sensitive as yours,' Kalu said.

'I feel like I'm looking for things to be afraid of. This feels so weird,' Kissie said, squeezing his arm. 'I have never been afraid of living here, until now.'

'It's only natural,' Kalu said. 'We've had a terrible shock. Being afraid is part of our self-preservation mode.'

They reached the door and Kalu stopped in his tracks.

'What is it?' Kissie asked.

'Look,' Kalu said, pointing.

The door was open an inch.

'That is not good and I can smell Creed aftershave but it's not the real thing,' Kissie whispered. 'It's the copy and it's nasty.' She squeezed his arm again. 'I've never smelled it in our building before.'

'I don't like this,' Kalu said. 'I'm calling the police.'

Chapter 24

Beb watched a tower of dust climbing into the sky. His stomach knotted as another huge section of the bridge collapsed into the torrent below. There was a gap over a hundred metres wide and the remaining structure looked fragile. The bridge was completely impassable and the river was too swollen to consider a crossing by boat. The plans he had made to reach Monguno were going up in smoke, literally. He opened his door and climbed out, walking towards the riverbank and the sound of the river thundering by smothered everything else. Omar followed him and Amira climbed out, carrying Heba. They watched as smaller sections of the bridge tumbled into the water, washed away by the force of the water.

A group of men were gathered by their vehicles, talking in panicked voices. Beb listened to what they were saying. They were all desperate to reach the other side and were discussing what the options were. He approached the group to hear exactly what they were suggesting.

'What are you doing?' Omar asked.

'These people wanted to cross into Nigeria,' Beb said. 'I'm listening to their ideas.'

'I can't believe the bridge has gone. I'm sorry for you,' Omar said, shaking his head. 'This is terrible. I know how badly you need to cross this river.' Omar took out his phone.

'Don't be sorry,' Beb said. 'We would have been on that bridge if you had listened to me. I wasn't thinking straight.'

'What are we going to do?' Amira asked.

'We need to weigh up our options,' Beb said.

'What are the options?'

'There's another bridge about ten miles north of here at a place called Post Tango,' Omar said, looking at his phone.

'How do you know?' Amira asked.

'I have OS maps on my device,' Omar said. Beb smiled and shook his head. 'I'm a taxi driver. I have to have an alternative route in case of a disaster.'

'You're full of surprises,' Beb said.

'Post Tango is a very old crossing and I wouldn't advise going north to that bridge alone,' a voice said from behind them. A group of men approached. One of them clapped his hands to gain the attention of the crowd. 'Listen to me, people,' he said. 'Whoever blew up the bridge, blew it for a reason.'

'We were told it was a suicide bomber,' Beb said.

'Yes. There was a suicide bomber but that bomb couldn't have caused so much damage to the structure of the bridge.'

'What do you mean?' Beb asked.

'The suicide bomber was carrying a device designed to kill humans in close proximity, not take down a structure like this bridge,' the man said. 'The bridge was blown on purpose with demolition charges.'

'How do you know this?'

'Why would anyone do this?'

'What is the point of destroying the bridge?'

The small crowd shouted questions at him. He held up his hands to quieten them. 'It is the truth. I was in the army for a long time. The explosion which damaged this bridge was set by demolition experts. I have training in this. Trust me, I know this for a fact.'

'Why would anyone blow up the bridge?'

'To stop people crossing into Nigeria or to stop Boko crossing the border to attack Fotokol. Both sides have motive to blow it up, you can take your pick who it was, but that was a military operation,' the man said. 'Whoever is responsible can defend the smaller bridge at Post Tango with ease. It's much narrower and would not take heavy vehicles. I think they will move their forces there very quickly.'

'We're not soldiers,' Beb said. 'Surely, they will allow civilians to cross?'

'The army will be nervous because of the attacks. Going north to cross the border could be suicide,' the man added.

'I have to cross the river today,' a tall man said. 'My family are in Nigeria. I have no choice but to try the other crossing.'

'Me too. I must cross the river,' a woman shouted.

'It should be a safe passage to the town. Post Tango is deserted and almost derelict,' someone said. 'My family used to live there but the rebels raided it all the time. It became too dangerous to live there but the houses are still there.'

'I heard that Boko may have headed north. It would be a good place for them to hide. What if they're there?'

'The soldiers told me they attacked Gomboru, so they were on the other side of the river,' a man argued. 'I have to cross the river today. If we go together in a convoy, we can protect each other.'

'I have to be in Nigeria today. I'm going to cross with you,' someone shouted from the back of the crowd.

'We will join you too,' another said.

'Us too,' someone else said.

'It sounds like a lot of people want to cross the river. We should ask if anyone can take us,' Amira said.

'What?' Beb said, confused.

'There will be a convoy. It's the only thing that we can do. We need to go north with them,' Amira said, nodding. 'If Omar can't take us any further, we'll need to go with them and then find transport when we get across the river.'

'It's too dangerous,' Beb said. 'I can't take you and Heba.' Beb shook his head. 'I will go on alone and you should go back with Omar. I'll come and get you in a few days.'

'You're not leaving us, Beb,' Amira said. 'If you think we can split up and not go mad with worry, think again. We're staying together, no matter what. I'm not made from rice paper. I won't break in the breeze.' She frowned and looked annoyed. 'If you go, we go.'

'We cannot risk it. You must go back with Omar,' Beb argued, shaking his head. 'I will get a ride with someone going that way.'

'Don't you argue with me,' Amira said, becoming impatient. 'This is not a debate. You go, we go, full stop.'

'I don't see how we can do that, safely,' Beb said.

'This journey was always risky,' Amira said. 'We knew that from the start.'

'I'll take you over the river,' Omar said.

'What?'

'I can't leave you here.'

'You need to go back to your family,' Beb said, shaking his head.

'Go home, Omar,' Amira said, touching his shoulder. 'Go and see your children.'

'You didn't fly into Nigeria because you don't have the papers, right?' Omar said. Beb and Amira nodded. 'I don't have that problem,' he added. 'I'll get you to Monguno but you have to agree to get me home.'

'What are you saying, exactly?' Beb asked.

'We drive across the bridge to the north and drive to Monguno as planned but we assume that I can't drive back this way,' Omar said. Beb looked confused. 'You need to buy my Toyota and put me on a plane home.'

'Ah, I see.' Beb exhaled and rubbed his chin.

'I can't just leave you here stranded,' Omar said. 'But I want to go home safely to my family.'

'My father is meeting us in Monguno.' Beb and Amira exchanged glances. 'We will honour your terms and get you a flight home. I promise you.'

'And you will buy my Toyota,' Omar said, shrugging. 'I can't take it with me.'

'Deal,' Beb said, offering his hand.

'You haven't asked me how much it is,' Omar said, grinning.

'Let's negotiate when we get there,' Beb said.

'I don't think I can cope with that conversation just now,' Amira said, shaking her head. 'Let's just get out of here and into Nigeria. Whatever happens after that is out of our hands.'

'Are you crossing with us, friend?' a man called over to them.

'How many vehicles are going with you?' Beb asked.

'Six,' the man said. 'That's over twenty people, some with weapons.' The man walked closer to them. 'I'm Mata.'

'I'm Beb.'

'You're Nigerian?'

'Yes.'

'Do you have weapons?'

'No. We don't carry weapons,' Beb lied.

'Where are you heading to?' Mata asked.

'Dikwa,' Beb said.

'That's a long drive through dangerous territory,' Mata said. 'Maybe we could help each other.' He eyed Amira and Heba. 'You need to keep your family safe. Let's get across the border and then we can see where the other people are going. We can all help each other.'

'That sounds like a plan,' Beb said, nodding.

'We may need to pay the soldiers to cross the bridge,' Mata said. 'If we do, do you have money?'

'If we do, we have some,' Beb said, nodding.

'We're going to lead the way,' Mata said, pointing to a battered old pickup truck. 'Follow us. The bridge is an hour drive away.'

'No problem.'

The group went back to their respective vehicles and waited for Mata and his two friends to set off north towards Post Tango. Omar fell in at the rear.

'I don't like this,' Omar said. 'Something doesn't feel right.'

'I agree,' Beb said, nodding. 'Some of those people are desperate to cross the river. Desperation makes people vulnerable. There's always someone who will take advantage of vulnerable people.'

'Especially vulnerable people carrying cash.'

'What do you think we should do?' Omar asked.

'Follow the convoy but stay far enough back to be able to change direction if we need to,' Beb said. 'Keep your eyes peeled for anything that looks odd.'

'This is Africa,' Omar said. 'Everything is odd.'

Chapter 25

Nazia was drifting in and out of semi-consciousness, never quite waking up but aware. She heard voices through the haze and the pain, sometimes clear, sometimes a jumble of sounds. The pain was so excruciating that she couldn't breathe properly. Her abdomen felt like it was on fire and she couldn't move a muscle. She was aware of her surroundings but unable to interact. The voices that she could hear were loud and angry, arguing and swearing. Lots of swearing. They used words that she had never used. Words she had only heard on the television in films. American films.

'Trigger happy motherfucker.'

'Fucking squirely asshole.'

'Scared of your own motherfucking shadow.'

'You shit-for-brains stupid motherfucker.'

There was a lot of motherfucking going on and she had never heard the like of it. There were several men there, shouting at each other. One of them was saying that the woman was a civilian and that there would be hell to pay when their senior officer arrived. He said that opening fire when a civilian was in the firing line was irresponsible and they would have to explain how the woman had been shot by a motherfucking peacekeeping force. Nazia listened to them arguing and wondered who the woman was. Her mind was in turmoil. She was panicking about the children. The children were in the cellar and she wanted them to scream for help so that they could be rescued. She wanted to tell the soldiers but she was incapable of speech.

Surely, they would help her soon. It was obvious that she was injured. She was worried that the soldiers would take her to hospital shortly and there would be no one to get the children out of the motherfucking cellar. It hurt so badly. At first, she'd thought that she'd been punched in the stomach but there was too much blood for it to be a punch. So much blood. If she lost much more, she would die. She knew that much. The soldiers would stop the bleeding soon but they seemed preoccupied by the woman who had been shot because she was a civilian. There would be hell to pay, apparently. One of the men kept on repeating it.

'You shot this poor woman and she's a civilian!' he shouted. 'There will be hell to pay, you stupid motherfucker,' she heard him say again. 'We're a motherfucking peacekeeping force, not murderers.'

'We're here to protect the civilians, you fucking idiot,' another man said, angrily. 'Not shoot them.'

'I didn't see her until it was too late,' a third man said. 'We can say the rebel shot her and we shot the motherfucker. No one will know any difference'

'And what about when she comes around and tells the truth?'

'Then we'll all be investigated and you know what that means. We'll be confined to barracks and made to clean the latrines all day and there will be no bonus pay for us. Our lives will be shit until they ship us out of here.'

'They won't ship us out of here if they don't know anything. There were skirmishes all over town last night. Anything could have happened to her,' one of them said. 'We need to keep our story straight and we'll be fine.'

'But what about her?' another man asked. 'She knows what happened.'

'She can't say anything if she's dead,' one of the men argued. She heard footsteps approaching her but she didn't hear the motherfucking bullet that blew the top of her head off.

****

In the kitchen cellar, Najma put her hand over her brother's mouth. He was crying in fear of the sound of gunshots and the men shouting and swearing. The latest gunshot was the final straw and had sent him over the edge. He was shaking with terror and sobbing uncontrollably. She could feel his skinny body quivering and she held him tightly and whispered softly in his ear.

'Everything will be okay,' she said. 'Don't be frightened. We're safe down here until mother comes for us.'

'When is she coming?' Rida whispered. 'I need to go to the toilet, so badly!'

'You can't go to the toilet, sister,' Najma said. They couldn't see each other in the darkness. It made their terror even more intense. 'Crawl into the corner near the shelves and do it.'

'I need to poo,' Rida whispered. 'I can't hold it anymore.'

'Go and do what you need to do,' Najma said, stroking her hair. 'We can't leave here while the bad men are up there. They might shoot us.'

'When is mother going to come?' Kareem asked, choking back a sob. 'I want my mother.'

'She will come for us,' Najma said, feeling tears running from her eyes, running down her cheeks. 'Don't be frightened, brother. Everything will be okay.'

Chapter 26

Kalu grabbed Kissie by the arm and walked backwards down the corridor. He put his forefinger to his lips and they tiptoed towards the lift. Their eyes never moved from the apartment door, expecting it to open at any second. Kalu took out his mobile and scrolled through it for DS Alfred's number; his fingers felt like lifeless sausages bumping against the screen. The fear was debilitating. They were almost at the lift when his mobile rang. He was so shocked, he almost dropped it. In the stifling silence of his mind, the sound was deafening. He held his breath and looked at the apartment door, expecting whoever was in there to burst out, guns blazing. The screen showed it was DS Alfred calling him. Kalu answered it and they scampered to the lift doors and pressed the call button.

'I was trying to call you,' Kalu whispered.

'What's the matter?'

'You need to send someone quickly! Someone is in my apartment,' Kalu whispered. 'It must be them…'

'How do you know someone is in there?' Alfred asked.

'The fucking door is open!'

'You are sure you locked it?'

'Yes. I'm positive!'

'Get out of there quickly,' DS Alfred said. 'Where are you now?'

'Getting into the lift…' Kalu said, as the doors opened. Two men in balaclavas were standing inside pointing sawn-off shotguns at them.

'Drop the phone, doctor,' one of them said, stepping out. He snatched the phone from Kalu. 'Get in the lift,' he ordered, grabbing Kissie by the hair. 'Any trouble and she gets it first, understand?'

Chapter 27

Oke was so exhausted that she slept reasonably well in her comfortable new bed, woken only a few times by sporadic gunfire. Each time she awoke, she was covered in sweat, her heart was pounding with fear and she took a while to drop off again but when she awoke, she felt refreshed. Some sleep was better than none. Isime hardly slept at all and she tossed and turned for hours but eventually she drifted off into a troubled slumber. Her dreams were haunted by visions of the old woman pointing a bony finger, accusing her of being a murderer, even though she had climbed out of the cellar. She was paranoid that she had died somewhere else. The entire incident had unsettled her and the old crone was giving her nightmares. She dreamt that the woman came back to the house to get her and her imagination warped her into a monster. Her nails were long and crooked and her teeth were pointed and sharp like a comic book vampire. In the twilight zone between sleep and consciousness, she knew it was nonsense but was terrified, nonetheless. The hours of darkness felt like weeks as she dwelled on her fears. Every shadow was a ghost, each sound a ghoulie.

Her anxiety only faded as the darkness receded and night turned to morning and the ghouls and ghosts faded to distant memories that would be forgotten before lunchtime. The sun warmed the house and Oke woke her with a cup of green tea and sat on her bed.

'How did you sleep?' Oke asked, handing her the tea. Isime sat up and sipped it.

'That's nice. Thank you. I had crazy nightmares,' Isime said. 'That old woman was chasing me around town.'

'You need to dream of having a rolling pin,' Oke teased. 'That would scare her away.'

'In my dream, she had claws and big teeth.'

'She does have claws and big teeth.'

'Oh, shush!'

'Was she mad at you?' Oke joked.

'She was really mad,' Isime said, sipping her tea.

'She's probably got a headache.'

'Stop it, Oke.'

'You did hit her over the head,' Oke said. 'So, she is allowed to be mad at you in your dream.'

'Shut up!' Isime said, grinning and shaking her head. 'You tease me too much.'

'There is no such thing as too much teasing,' Oke said.

'I'm not arguing with you,' Isime said. 'Anyway, are we going to get the children this morning?'

'Yes,' Oke said. 'I'm so excited. I can't wait to see them and bring them home. They will be so happy here.'

'Nazia won't know what to do with herself when they come home,' Isime said, drinking her tea. 'She will be lost without them to look after.'

'She can visit whenever she likes,' Oke said. 'The children adore her. She will always be welcome here.' She stood up and looked through the blinds. 'I haven't heard any shots this morning. We should be safe to cross town.'

'Last night was frightening. What do you think happened?' Isime asked.

'I don't know. Those boys we saw were Boko soldiers, probably sent to see what is happening here and if there's anything worth stealing,' Oke said, shrugging. 'If they were raiding or attacking the barracks, they wouldn't just send children.'

'They never attack barracks. They're cowards,' Isime said. 'They prefer to attack civilians and kidnap children.'

'Luckily for us, there are no civilians here,' Oke said. 'They'll realise Monguno is a ghost town and move onto somewhere else.'

'I hope you're right,' Isime said. 'I feel safer knowing there are soldiers just down the road.' Just as she spoke, an army jeep turned into their street. Isime watched it slow down and pull up next to the kerb outside their home. Two officers checked their paperwork and climbed out of the vehicle. 'I think I spoke too soon,' Isime said, biting her lip. 'Two officers are here.'

'Army or police?' Oke asked.

'Army.'

'Oh shit,' Oke said, panicking. 'Just deny everything. Don't admit to anything. Let me answer and you agree with everything, okay?'

'Okay,' Isime said, nodding. 'It's the old woman. I know it is. She's told them about us.'

'We don't know anything, yet,' Oke said.

A loud knock on the door echoed through the house. Oke went to the front door and opened it. The soldiers looked at her and exchanged glances. The sisters were attractive women in a town with no women in it.

'How can I help?' Oke asked.

'We need to ask you some questions,' one of the officers said. 'I'm Captain Ahmed and this is Lieutenant Gant.'

'Come in,' Oke said, opening the door. 'We have some tea made. This is my sister, Isime and I'm Oke.' Isime gave them some tea and smiled too much.

'Thank you for the tea,' the captain said. 'You're sisters?'

'Yes.'

'I can tell,' he said. 'You look alike.'

'I'm the younger sister,' Isime said, smiling.

'And this is your property?' the captain asked.

'By default, yes,' Oke said. The captain looked blankly at her. 'This is our family home. Our family name is Sammi. Dr Kalu Sammi was our father and he bought the house in the early nineties. We were forced to leave when Boko invaded the town. Boko used it until they were driven out and we have returned, so the answer is yes. It is our property as it was never sold to anyone, our family still own it.'

'I see. We have heard similar stories in neighbouring towns and villages,' the captain said, nodding. 'What happened to your father?'

'He died during the invasion,' Oke lied. 'All our family were killed except us.'

‘So, you survived and what happened to you?’

‘We were captured and enslaved as small girls,’ Oke said.

‘Did you become Boko wives?’ he asked, examining their response. The question hit Oke like a bus. ‘There’s no shame in it but we have to ask.’

‘No. We didn’t marry Boko men,’ Oke lied again. Isime shuffled uncomfortably. ‘We were smuggled away by a kind neighbour and taken to Lagos and placed with extended family. We went to school there until we were sixteen. I married a tailor and we had three children.’

‘Boys or girls?’

‘Two girls and a boy.’

‘Perfectly balanced,’ the captain said. He was analysing Oke as they spoke. She could feel his eyes boring into her mind. ‘Where are your children?’

‘With a friend,’ Oke said. ‘Across town.’

‘And your husband?’

‘He died from a heart attack. And so, we decided to come back home.’

‘What about you?’ the captain asked Isime.

‘What about me?’ She blushed before she replied and looked as guilty as sin.

‘She didn’t marry,’ Oke said, interrupting. ‘She’s not all there in her head,’ she added, tapping her forefinger to her temple. ‘A few men tried to have relationships with her but she’s a handful.’ Isime looked dumbstruck. ‘You wouldn’t know to look at her, would you?’

The captain shook his head. ‘Not at all.’

'She's pretty enough but daft as a brush, I'm afraid.' Isime glared at her sister. 'I don't think I'll find another husband willing to take us both on, and the children. It's been a struggle but I've looked after her all my life.'

'I see,' the captain said, nodding. He looked deflated. 'Did you hear the gunfire last night?'

'Yes. Of course,' Oke said. 'You would have to be deaf not to hear it. What happened?'

'There was an incursion into the town and the surrounding area, mostly young Boko and a few rebels,' he explained. 'We captured one of the rebels, who said Boko has put a reward on any Boko women and children who are returned to them. Hence, we're out and about checking on the few people who have returned.'

'I see,' Oke said, nodding. 'They do have a bad reputation for abducting young girls and boys. They will be disappointed with the meagre pickings in Monguno. We haven't seen any other families here yet.' The soldiers exchanged glances and nodded. 'Are there many Boko wives left in the area?' Oke asked.

'There are quite a few, surprisingly, but they keep a low profile for obvious reasons,' the captain said. 'A lot of the Boko men died when a nerve agent was mishandled, leaving their wives widowed.' He studied the sisters, looking for a reaction. Oke tried to look surprised and interested. 'We've set up a camp for them next to the barracks. It will take a while to process them all.'

'You've put Boko women into a camp?' Oke asked, shocked but trying not to show it.

'Yes,' the captain said. 'They're from all over Africa and we need to process them before we repatriate them.' Oke could feel her blood pressure rising and the veins in her neck pulsing. 'You look shocked.'

'I am,' Oke said. 'What happened to compassion?'

'I'm sorry, the captain said, frowning. 'I don't follow.'

'My family were driven from here and died in their attempt to escape and Boko were allowed to establish themselves in this region because our government did nothing.'

'Mistakes have been made but they're doing something now,' the captain said, straight-faced. 'We're trying to clean up the mess they have left behind, which is significant.'

'By putting innocent woman, who have been traumatised, into a camp?' Oke said, shaking her head. 'Most of them will have been kidnapped as children and forced into marriages they didn't want to be in and held captive while they were raped and impregnated time and again,' Oke said. 'And the best we can do for them is to put them into a prison camp while we decide where we can dump them?'

'It's not a prison camp,' the captain said politely, finishing his tea.

'Does it have barbed wire around it and armed guards?' Oke asked. The captain didn't reply but his eyes said, yes. 'Because if it does, then it's a prison camp.'

'Thank you for your time and the tea,' the captain said. 'We have a lot to do today. We'll leave you in peace.'

'Thank you for coming to check on us. Best of luck to you,' Oke said, closing the door behind them. 'Why can't I keep my big mouth shut?' she muttered to herself.

'I often ask myself that question,' Isime answered. The officers got into their jeep and drove away. 'I can't believe you told them that I'm not right in the head,' Isime said.

'You were about to answer his question without engaging your brain,' Oke said. 'You would have dropped us in the mire.'

'You did that for your own amusement.'

'They're acting as if they're doing us a favour by coming here to check up on us but all they wanted to know was if we were Boko wives,' Oke said. 'It's like a witch hunt.'

'You could have come up with a better lie than I'm daft as a brush,' Isime argued.

'That's not a lie,' Oke said. 'Anyway, as the younger sister, you should respect my decision to tell lies, so that we're not imprisoned as Boko wives,'

'Your answer was so good that I believed it,' Isime said.

'I practiced it in my head,' Oke said.

'How did you know they would ask that?' Isime asked.

'I didn't but it has been on my mind since the old woman came knocking,' Oke said. 'We will be pigeon-holed as Boko if we're not careful. You heard what he said, they're putting Boko widows into a prison camp. There is no one left to say any different than what I told them today. If we don't tell anyone, no one will know. We never speak of being Boko wives, not ever.'

'Okay, sister,' Isime said. 'I don't feel safe,' she added. 'If they suspect we're lying, they could search the house and they will find the Boko weapon and we could be in trouble. I think we should get rid of the gun and go and get the children.'

'Yes,' Oke said. 'So do I. Let's go and get the children.'

Chapter 28

Kalu was shaking with fear as the elevator descended to the car park. His attackers were sweating, aggressive and twitchy. Twitchy wasn't good while they were holding guns. He could smell their perspiration, a sickly-sweet odour, made more potent by the confined space of the lift. Their eyes were darting here and there and as intimidating as they were, they didn't look comfortable. They didn't look comfortable at all. Not one bit. Kissie was crying and very distressed. One of the men had her hair twisted around his hand, holding her tightly. She was struggling against his grip and making it more painful for herself but Kalu couldn't think straight enough to tell her to stop struggling. He could see her nails scratching deep into the man's skin, drawing blood in rivulets. The grimace on his face told Kalu he was struggling. She was using the C-word, which wasn't like her but under the circumstances, he could sympathise. His brain was racing through the different scenarios. The murder of his brother meant that he was in no doubt that their intention was to murder him and killing his daughter in front of him would be a bonus for the psycho-bitch who was calling the shots. They were there to kill him, in which case they could have done it upstairs but they didn't. That meant that they planned to take them somewhere else to kill them. Somewhere they wouldn't be disturbed and the sound of their weapons being discharged wouldn't alert dozens of people to their murder. Witnesses are to be avoided at all costs. Everyone has a camera in their pocket. His brain searched for answers. He had watched a documentary about a close protection bodyguard and his advice to his clients was that if you think an attacker is going to kill you, never go easily, no matter what. Fight with every ounce of strength you have and there's always a chance you can escape. Make as much noise as you can and other people may rescue you. If you die, you die fighting. You're going to die anyway, don't make it easy for them. The advice was irrelevant at the time but it came back to him in an instant.

'Kissie, they're going to kill us,' Kalu said, becoming lucid.

'Shut up!'

'I think they're going to kidnap us to kill us elsewhere,' Kalu said. 'Whatever happens, don't get into their vehicle.'

'Shut up!' one of the attackers snarled. He punched Kalu in the side of the head. It was a stinging blow but not concussive. 'One more word out of you and you're dead.'

'Fuck you,' Kalu said. His attacker grabbed the back of his neck and squeezed but Kalu was a big fit man and strong too. The squeeze did little to silence him. 'Make yourself a dead weight,' Kalu said. Kissie looked at him and her eyes focused. 'Listen to me. Fall to the floor and no matter what they say or do, don't stand up.'

'I told you…' the attacker began. Kalu ended his sentence with a headbutt to his nose. He felt the cartilage and bone crack beneath the crushing blow. His head snapped backwards. Kalu hit him below the chin with the palm of his hand, driving it upwards. His skull crashed into the mirror on the wall, shattering it with a deafening crash. The man cried out in pain and shock. Kalu brought his knee up into his midriff and he folded, the wind knocked out of him. Kissie made her body floppy and fell to the floor. Her attacker was still holding her hair tightly and the weight of her body pulled him off balance.

'What the fuck are you playing at?' he stammered. He tried to swing at Kalu with the gun in his hand but missed. 'Get the fuck up, stupid bitch!'

Kalu turned his attention to Kissie's attacker and kicked him in the testicles. He exhaled air like an elephant blowing its trunk. As the lift doors opened, Kalu grabbed at the gun. He twisted it as far as he could, bending the attacker's fingers painfully in the wrong direction. He heard the bones crack. Kissie was released and Kalu dragged her clear of the lift.

'Get down on the floor!' a voice ordered. Kalu could see three men aiming pistols into the lift. He dropped to his stomach and held Kissie. 'Drop the weapons!'

'Don't shoot!'

'Drop the weapons, now!'

Kalu was looking at his attackers in the lift. One of them tossed his gun onto the concrete but the other was still stunned and tried to stand up, gun in hand. A volley of nine-millimetre bullets smashed into him and he slid down the wall, leaving a bloody smear.

'Don't shoot me!' the other man begged, kneeling, hands in the air. 'Don't shoot me, please…'

'Drop onto your front, face down, hands behind your head,' an officer shouted.

A stain spread across his attacker's groin and Kalu took some satisfaction that he was so frightened, he pissed himself before lying on the floor.

'Are you okay, Dr Sammi?' an officer asked.

'Yes, I'm okay. Thanks to you.'

'Are you hurt?'

'No.'

'Was there a scuffle in the lift?' the officer asked, smiling.

'My dad headbutted one of them,' Kissie said, shaking her head. 'And he kicked the other one in the balls. Where the fuck did that come from?'

'We need to talk about your swearing,' Kalu said, smiling.

'Fuck no,' Kissie said.

'Are you okay, Kissie?' the officer asked, helping them up. The surviving attacker was being handcuffed. Kissie nodded. 'DS Alfred deployed us to protect you when you left the hospital. He had a feeling they might try again,' he said. 'Good job we were here,' he added.

Chapter 29

Omar followed the small convoy of vehicles through the town towards the outskirts, navigating a never-ending stream of humans heading in the opposite direction. Some had torches, most didn't. It was devastating to see such anguish and grief on their faces as they trudged away from their homes in the darkness. Their headlights illuminated vehicles which had been abandoned here and there and they saw several groups of men trying to syphon fuel from parked cars. One man was beaten around the head with a baseball bat, when the owner of the vehicle that he was trying to syphon from ran out of his house to protect what fuel he had left. People were desperate to leave by any means possible. Beb had seen it all before and it was no easier the second time around.

'Do you know which way they're heading?' Beb asked. 'There are no lights and I can't see where we are.'

'According to the map, once we turn north, the road is a single track until we get to Post Tango,' Omar said. 'Then it splits into a grid pattern through the town's housing. It's a small village of thirty or so homes, not really a town and the bridge is on the other side of the estate. If we need to break from the convoy, that's where we can do it.'

'Someone said it's derelict,' Beb said. 'That means the roads through the town could be blocked by wrecks or roadblocks. We can't take it for granted that all the roads are accessible. The last thing we want is to break away and drive into a dead end in the dark.'

'I'm not going to take anything for granted. If the bridge is open and there are no troops, we're crossing it regardless of the convoy,' Omar said. 'I've got a feeling Mata and his friends are going to try something. I'm not stopping for them or anyone else.'

'I agree,' Beb said. 'We're vulnerable if we stop.'

'I agree too,' Amira said. 'If something does happen, where are the weapons?' Omar looked at her in the mirror and smiled. 'I assume they're in the boot behind me, so if we're not stopping, I will have to get them. It will save time if I know where they are.'

'I forget that you're comfortable with firearms,' Omar said, smiling. 'I bet you're a better shot than me.'

'I was shooting snakes as soon as I could hold a rifle,' Amira said. 'When you live in a tribe, if you can't shoot, you starve.' She shrugged and smiled. 'There's no doubt that I'm the best shot in this vehicle.'

'I can second that,' Beb said, nodding. 'If we have to arm ourselves, Amira takes the rifle.'

'That's fine by me,' Omar said. 'You shoot, I'll drive. The rifle is in the wheel well and the pistols are in the lockbox above the driver's side wheel. The ammunition is with the rifle.'

'Pass me one of the pistols and some ammunition,' Beb said. 'I'll put it in the glovebox. If I need it, I'll need it quickly.'

'I'm going to set up the rifle and put it under the backseat,' Amira said, looking at Omar in the mirror. 'If that's okay.'

'That's fine by me. I was hoping we wouldn't need them but I think we are better safe than sorry,' Omar said. 'Pass me the other pistol. Just to be on the safe side.'

Amira climbed over the backseat and retrieved the three firearms. The rifle was an Enfield 303. Both the pistols were Colt revolvers. She shared out what ammunition they had.

'That rifle is older than you,' Omar said.

'The British Army used them here against the Germans in both World Wars,' Amira said. Omar looked surprised. 'They gave hundreds of them to the Tuareg. My ancestors hated the Nazis although some of the other tribes sided with Hitler. We shot thousands of them in the desert,' she added. Omar looked at Beb and shook his head. 'Does that surprise you?' Amira asked, smiling.

'Nothing surprises me anymore,' Omar said.

'At night, when the sun goes down, the desert is a void,' Beb said. 'The nomads sit around fires and tell stories about their ancestors. There isn't much else to do.'

'Ah, so they tell war stories about their war heroes?'

'Absolutely,' Beb said.

'The Enfield is one of my favourite rifles,' Amira said. 'They fire straight and true. Even if they are old.' She patted the rifle and slid the bolt to-and-fro, looking inside the barrel at the rifling. 'It's well-oiled and the rifling is still intact. You've looked after this one.'

'Youtube is my teacher,' Omar said, smiling. 'There is nothing you can't learn how to do on the internet!'

'It will fire straight and hit the target as long as the aim is true,' Amira said, nodding.

'Let's hope we don't have to test that out,' Omar said. No one replied and the atmosphere in the vehicle was filled with nervous tension. Heba was wide-eyed and listening to everything, not really understanding the gravity of their situation but sensing her parents were on edge.

The convoy rolled on and their speed increased as they reached the outskirts, where the road was empty of pedestrians. The north of the town was sparsely inhabited. Rows of houses were replaced by detached dwellings and then there was nothing but jungle and bushland and the odd smallholdings, which were mostly owned by goat herders. The smallholdings appeared to be occupied and the animals roamed free, scattering from the road as the convoy approached, its headlights startling them. The jungle was to their right and the bush to their left, between the road and the river. Beb caught glimpses of the water through the bush. It appeared to be as black as tar, the lights of the town across the river reflected from the surface. As they progressed, the road became a bumpy track pitted with deep potholes and exposed bedrock. It was impossible to maintain their speed without damaging their vehicle. The Toyota lurched and rocked and the ride became uncomfortable. They had to slow down to navigate the increasing number of potholes. Some of the exposed rocks jutted up through the compacted road, threatening to rip the bottom from the Toyota. The slower the convoy advanced, the more vulnerable they felt. Omar dropped a gear to steer around a large rock in the road. The vehicles in front of them zigzagged as the condition of the road deteriorated, their red taillights glimmering in the darkness. A suitcase tumbled from the roof rack of a Volvo and burst open on the road, spilling its contents. The following vehicles rolled over it and scattered the garments into the bushes and trees either side of the road but the vehicles kept moving, increasing speed where they could.

'Someone is going to need new clothes,' Omar said. He swerved to miss the suitcase and a deep pothole. The convoy increased speed and pulled away from them. Omar was reluctant to accelerate and damage his vehicle. His visibility was limited and keeping up wasn't a priority. He watched a Ford pickup-truck lurch to the side, almost rolling over. It crashed back onto the road, showering dirt and dust into the air. The convoy was creating a cloud of sand in its wake, making it difficult to see what was ahead. Omar accelerated and pushed the speed to as fast as he dared. 'This road is getting worse. Some of those smaller vehicles are going to get banged up pretty badly if they hit those rocks at speed.'

'I can't see more than fifty metres ahead,' Beb said. 'Don't try to keep up if you can't drive safely,' he added. 'We can catch them nearer to the bridge.'

'Don't worry. I won't push it. We have a long way to go and I want to keep this machine in one piece before you buy it from me,' Omar joked. 'I don't want you knocking the price down.'

No sooner had he spoken, out of the dust cloud, when a wheel came into view, bouncing down the road towards them. It was travelling at speed. Omar didn't have time to break and couldn't take the Toyota off the road to avoid the imminent impact. There were deep ditches either side and thick jungle to their right. They watched as the wheel bounced again. It landed and appeared to pick up speed as it bounced again on a bedrock. It lurched up, spinning, and smashed into the windscreen, showering the occupants with shattered glass. Omar tried to slow the vehicle as much as possible but the impact was catastrophic. The noise was a deafening crunch. Beb ducked low and covered his face with his arms but he felt the tiny shards piercing his exposed skin. Amira screamed as she smothered Heba with her body, instinctively protecting her child. The wheel penetrated the Toyota, shattering the windscreen before hitting Omar directly in the face with incredible force. His head was ripped from his body and catapulted through the back window, where it rolled along the road for a while before dropping into a deep pothole. The Toyota trundled forward and Beb grabbed the steering wheel and pulled on the handbrake as he stared at his headless driver. Blood spurted upwards, hitting the roof before dripping back down like red rain.

Chapter 30

Oke picked up the Kalashnikov and wrapped it in an old mat. It felt heavier than she remembered. Everything felt heavier these days and she was becoming breathless quickly. The doctors had told her that the damage done to her lungs was considerable and they had no way of knowing the long-term prognosis. Her recovery had been long and painful but she had felt significant improvements at first. Recently though, her condition had gone into decline. Any exertion made her breathless. She heaved the machinegun and wondered who could carry it for a long way and then fight; men and women much younger and stronger than her. People without lung damage. She couldn't imagine aiming it at another human and pulling the trigger, feeling it recoil as it spat death. They had hidden it with best intentions, to use it as a last resort to protect themselves and her children from Boko. She wasn't sure if she could use it but having it there had given them some comfort but right now, it was a liability. If it was found on their property, they would have to explain why they were in possession of a Boko weapon.

'What are we going to do with it?' Isime asked from behind her. Oke flinched and took a sharp intake of breath.

'You nearly gave me a heart attack!' Oke said, covering her mouth with her hand. 'Don't sneak up on me like that.'

'I wasn't sneaking,' Isime said, laughing. 'I came to see if you needed some help, that's all.' Oke sighed and shook her head in mock despair. 'Where are we going to put it?'

'We can't carry it far,' Oke said. 'It's too heavy and we can't risk being seen by the soldiers.' She gestured with her head. 'Next door has an outhouse too. We can put it in there and if it's ever found, we can deny ever seeing it.' She shrugged. 'But if we need it, it's not far away.'

'That's a good idea,' Isime said. 'Wait here and I'll go around there and see if it's locked. I might have a look through the windows too and see if there's anything interesting inside.' Isime walked down the path to the road. 'I'll shout you in a minute.'

'Don't shout!' Oke said but Isime was already gone. 'That girl will be the end of me, she will,' Oke muttered. She leaned the gun against the wall, tiring of the weight. It seemed like an age as she waited for Isime to return. As the minutes began to tick by, she became concerned what was taking so long. 'Isime,' she hissed. There was no reply. 'Isime! What are you doing?'

'I'm trying to get the lock off the door,' Isime said. Oke heard a loud crack and the sound of something heavy thud on the floor. Hinges creaked and squealed. 'Oh, my word!'

'What is it?' Oke asked.

'You need to come and see this,' Isime called a little too loudly.

'I don't want to see it,' Oke whispered. 'What is it?'

'Come and see.'

'Can we hide the gun or not?'

'Yes,' Isime said. 'Hurry up before someone comes.'

'Why can't she just tell me what she's found?' Oke muttered to herself as she walked down the path. She looked in each direction before stepping onto the road and walking the short distance to the house next door. The gate was weathered but still hanging. She walked up the overgrown path to the outhouse, which was built as an afterthought and attacked to the gable end. Vines had grown up the walls and covered the roof. They had a sweet smell and attracted the biggest wasps in Monguno. Oke ignored them and tried to pretend they weren't there. The door was open and a rusty padlock was swinging from a broken clasp. 'Where are you, sister?'

'In here,' Isime said. 'You need to see this.'

Oke was reluctant to step inside the small brick structure. The experience of unlocking their family home was still fresh in her mind. There was no stench of decay coming from the doorway yet she envisaged skeletal young women shackled to the walls, their eye sockets empty and their skin leathery and torn. She placed the machinegun against the wall and stepped into the outhouse. It took a while for her eyes to adjust to the darkness inside. The daylight only penetrated a few metres. She focused on wall to ceiling shelves that were crammed with tins. They were out of place and the sheer number of them was mind-boggling. It made no sense to her.

'What is this place? Where are you?' Oke whispered.

'Over here,' Isime said, excited. 'Why are you whispering?'

'Because we're breaking into a property we don't own, in possession of a Boko Kalashnikov machinegun surrounded by hundreds of tins of tuna fish,' Oke said. 'What is all this?'

'There's tuna fish, beans, vegetables, tinned fruit and meat stew,' Isime said. 'Over here are tins of Pepsi, Fanta and Sprite. Whoever used this house must have been the quartermaster. This must be one of their storage units for their supplies. We need to move it all to our house,' she added.

'No, sister,' Oke said. 'This is a Boko hoard. If we get found with it, we'll be branded Boko and locked up in the prison camp.' Oke stepped outside and picked up the gun. She scurried inside and leaned it against one of the shelves. 'We need to leave everything here where we found it. Come on. We need to close the door and get away from it.'

'You need to calm down,' Isime said, shaking her head. 'Stop stressing and have a Pepsi.'

'Stop stressing?' Oke said, shocked. 'Have a Pepsi?'

'Yes. Have a Pepsi. When was the last time you had a Pepsi?' Isime opened a can and handed it to her. Oke looked at it as if it might explode in her face. Isime grinned. 'How long has all this stuff been here?' she asked. 'Years and years and no one has found it yet. Why would they find it now?' Isime sipped her drink and clinked tins with Oke. Oke sipped it and closed her eyes as she swallowed. 'Good, yes?'

'Oh, that's so good,' Oke said. 'Okay, we can use some of it but we must hide everything we use,' Oke said. 'If we use a tin, we must dispose of them far away from our house.'

'Shush,' Isime said, smiling. 'Stop worrying and drink it. We have enough food here to feed us and the children for years.'

'Don't tell me to shush,' Oke said, smiling, but behind the smile, she didn't think she had years. The overwhelming sense of foreboding which descended on her took her by surprise. She felt her eyes welling up. 'We need to go and fetch the children,' she added, sipping from her can. 'Bring that can with you.'

'We can leave the empties in here,' Isime said, shrugging. 'What's the big deal about hiding the empties?'

'Because this is clearly a Boko stash and for the tenth time…' Oke began.

'Okay, okay, okay,' Isime interrupted. 'We don't want to end up in a prison camp for Boko women. I get it.'

'Close the door behind us,' Oke said, stepping out of the outhouse. 'I have a bad feeling about this.'

'Don't over think it, sister,' Isime said, following. She closed the door and picked up the broken clasp, pushing the screws back into the rotten holes she had pulled them from. 'No one has found this before. I bet there are more of them across the town. I bet there are all kinds of treasures hidden here, all just waiting to be discovered.' They walked back to the road and closed the gate behind them. 'I bet there are treasure chests overflowing with gold and silver coins and rooms full of stolen art and antique furniture.'

'In Monguno?' Oke said, shaking her head. 'How many masterpieces do you think were here in the first place and who had gold coins?' She snorted. 'Your mind is a puzzle, sister,' Oke said. Isime looked hurt. 'That's not a bad thing,' she added. Isime smiled. 'Your imagination is a gift. Never change.'

'Why are you being nice?' Isime asked. 'What are you after?'

'Nothing, sister,' Oke said, smiling. She linked arms with her. 'Let's go and get the children.'

A military vehicle turned the corner at the top of the street. 'Hide that can!' Oke said. The sisters put their heads down and walked towards their house. A troop carrier trundled by; the soldiers hardly noticed them. Oke could feel her heart pounding in her chest, waiting for them to stop and bundle them into the truck. The sound of the engine faded as it continued without slowing. She relaxed a little.

'Are you okay?' Isime asked.

'Yes. But I'm sick and tired of being frightened.'

Chapter 31

Sean Trainor watched the back exit of the pool hall for hours. He was picking up chatter on the radio about the shooting of two suspected gang members in a car park beneath an apartment block across the river. Armed police had taken them down in some kind of undercover operation but the details were sketchy. The flurry of activity at the pool hall indicated that they were probably affiliated to Jet Unganu. Vehicles were coming and going, which was amateurish. The police monitored chatter between gangs and the best way to identify which gang a suspect belonged to was listen to who was shouting the loudest. Jet and her minions were agitated and scurrying around the area like ants when their nest is disturbed. They had guilty written all over them. Amateur hour indeed. She was an unlikely adversary for an outfit as big as the Trainors and their associates but she had stepped up into their world and once you step in, you don't step out. You get carried out. Unganu hadn't done her homework about Harry and who he was. If she had, she wouldn't have attempted to seek revenge by having Harry kidnapped, tortured and killed. What she had done was only fit for the worst of the worst criminals. Paedophiles, rapists, child killers and the like, deserved to be mutilated, skinned and removed from their mortal coil but Harry wasn't in that category. Harry was a class act. He was smart, dressed smart, talked smart and was well-liked in the circles they moved in. Sean and Harry were cousins and were brought up together. They were close, like brothers. He didn't deserve to go out like that and Sean intended to wreak havoc against Jet Unganu. She would wish that she had never heard the name Trainor before she begged for death and when that time came, there would be no release for her. It would be prolonged and agonising. Her heart would give up before Sean did. This one was personal.

A police interceptor arrived at the rear entrance followed by several unmarked vehicles and a Trojan Unit. They were armed and wearing tactical gear. The police had sent in the heavy mob. They must be convinced her men were involved in the shooting to get the go ahead for such a high-profile arrest. She would be taken away for questioning, which meant she was safe for now. He could wait for the right time. It would be simpler to pay one of their foot soldiers to put a bullet in her head but that wasn't fitting payback for what she had done to Harry. She would die screaming when the opportunity arrived. He could wait until she was bailed, then she would wish that she had never been born.

****

Kalu tried to call Beb for the hundredth time but got nothing. There appeared to be no connection available wherever he was, which was worrying. He was sure that Beb would be across the border into Nigeria by now but there was no way of being sure. Google was publishing the news of a suicide bomber on the border and that a bridge between the two countries had been demolished. More concerning was a coordinated and sustained attack on the civilians of Gamboru. The attackers had moved from house to house, raping the females and slaughtering the men. The news was sickening. Boko were reportedly raiding along the borders again, probing Chad, Nigeria and Cameroon, looking for weak spots and there were plenty of them. Innocent civilians were being slaughtered because they were soft targets. At the first sign of military intervention, Boko became vapour, scurrying for the hills. It was all so depressingly familiar. All the reasons why he had put his family into a truck and left their home were staring him in the face again. They all hoped Oke and Isime were in Monguno but it was an educated guess, nothing more. Beb had been certain they could get there before Kalu could but they would have to travel overland. It had seemed like a good idea at the time but things were reasonably stable then. With hindsight, maybe it was too perilous to consider. The fear was that Oke and Isime would flee Monguno and fade into the monstrous void of displaced African people. Wars, corrupt governments and extreme poverty drove millions from their homes to look for something better. No one was more acutely aware of the devastation that dwelled in that space than Kalu. There was danger at every turn and his daughters would be sucked into the maelstrom of desperation, hate and violence, and probably never seen again. It was an unsolvable conundrum with no right or wrong answers. Only time would tell if they had made the correct decisions which would keep them all alive. All he could do now was hope that his children were safe.

'They are boarding,' Kissie said, checking her phone. 'Any news from Beb?'

'No, nothing,' Kalu said. 'He most probably hasn't got a signal.' Kalu had no faith in his own words. 'I hope they're not anywhere near the trouble at the border.'

'Don't say that. I can't bear to think of them stuck in that terrible mess. They're reporting hundreds killed in the attack on Gamboru. Some reports are saying it was rebels, but most are saying Boko are responsible,' Kissie said, reading her phone. 'What's the difference between rebels and Boko?'

'The spelling,' Kalu said. 'They're all just pirates preying on the vulnerable.'

'He has to cross the border near there, doesn't he?'

'That was the plan before all this trouble broke out,' Kalu said. 'Let's hope he has made alternative arrangements to cross the river.'

'Will they be safe?' Kissie asked.

'He's survived against all the odds, so far.' Kalu took out his boarding pass and passport. 'Let's get there and make sure they are all safe.'

Chapter 32

Beb climbed out of the Toyota and hurried to open the rear passenger door. Amira was checking Heba for cuts and scratches.

‘Is she okay?’ Beb asked. He felt strangely calm.

‘Yes. She’s fine,’ Amira said. She turned to him and felt a trickle of blood running down her forehead. She wiped it away with the back of her hand. Beb looked worried. ‘It’s just a scratch on my scalp. We’re covered in glass,’ she said. ‘Get us out of here before she realises what has happened.’

‘Climb down and I’ll grab her,’ Beb said.

‘You’re covered in blood,’ Amira whispered. ‘Are you hurt?’

‘A few cuts here and there but the blood isn’t mine,’ Beb said, wiping his face. ‘I can’t believe what just happened.’

‘What are we going to do?’ Amira asked.

‘I’m going to take his body out of there and put him at the side of the road,’ Beb said.

‘We can’t just leave him,’ Amira said. ‘Can we bury him?’

‘Not a chance without digging tools,’ Beb said, shaking his head. ‘I’ll cover him in rocks and leave his ID on him.’ He paused to think. ‘When we get to Monguno, I’ll contact his family and tell them where he is and arrange for a local undertaker to recover his body and take him home. It’s the least we can do.’

‘Can we still use the truck?’ Amira asked. ‘I mean, is it drivable?’

'Yes. I think so.' Beb looked inside the Toyota. 'Everything is fine apart from the windscreen and rear window being smashed. I'll use some of the clothes on the road to mop up the blood and broken glass, then we stick to the plan.' Amira nodded and wiped a tear from her eye. 'He wanted to get us across that river and that's what we'll do. We can't turn back now. There's nowhere to turn back to.'

'What about the convoy?' Amira asked. 'Do you think they'll wait for us?'

'They're a little way ahead but someone is minus a wheel,' Beb said. 'It must have come off a moving vehicle. It was travelling so fast. So I don't think they're going anywhere fast.' He kissed Heba. 'Keep her happy and I'll move Omar.'

'Beb, if the vehicle that lost the wheel was driving away from us, how did the wheel come this way?' Amira asked. 'How could that happen?'

'I don't know, unless it bounced off a tree or rock?' Beb said, shaking his head.

'What if the vehicle had turned around and was driving back this way?' Amira said.

'Maybe they did,' Beb said. 'They may have been spooked by something or changed their mind. I guess we'll find out eventually.'

Beb walked around the vehicle to the driver's door and opened it. The coppery smell of blood was thick in the air and it dripped from the roof with a plopping sound.

Plop, plop, plop.

It was a surreal moment. Looking at the headless corpse of a man he liked, no matter how brief their encounter, he believed he was a good man. He watched the blood dripping from the ceiling and waited for the right moment to touch Omar. Undoing his seatbelt, he reached over and grabbed his waistband, pulling the body from the seat. Omar was a slightly-built man and didn't weigh more than ten stones. There was a squelching sound as he lifted his back from the seat and out of the vehicle. Beb carried him as far into the bush as he could before the urge to drop him became overwhelming. His hands were covered in warm sticky blood. He placed him down gently in the long grass and turned away to find his head. Beb searched the backseat of the Toyota and then the boot but there was no sign of Omar's head.

He grabbed a torch and walked away from the Toyota, sweeping the beam of light from side to side. The wheel was lying in the centre of the track about fifty yards away. He walked towards it, scouring the ditches on either side. They were overgrown with thick vegetation and deep water flowed along them. There was no way of knowing how deep they were but the chances of finding his head in one of them was zero. He trudged on a few yards past the wheel and was about to give up when he caught a glimpse of hair in the light. Omar's head was floating in a pothole, facedown. Beb didn't have a clue how to pick it out and carry it back to the body. He couldn't carry it by the hair or the ear, it didn't seem right.

Some of the clothes from the suitcase were strewn around and he picked up a cotton shirt and two t-shirts. He stooped next to the pothole and pushed Omar's head to the shallowest side. The face was unrecognisable, which made it a little easier to pick up. He wrapped it in the shirt and carried it like a bag of shopping to where he had left his body.

'Are you okay?' Amira shouted.

'Yes,' Beb said, lying. 'I'm as okay as I can be carrying a head,' he mumbled. 'Are you two okay?'

'Yes,' Amira said. 'I've been watching the lights from the convoy. Some of the vehicles turned around and came back this way. They must have realised someone had an accident.'

'Maybe,' Beb said.

He placed the head on the body and began to search Omar's pockets. His wallet was in his jeans and Beb used the torch to go through it. There was the money Beb had paid him in advance and about fifty dollars more. Beb took the driving licence out of the wallet and placed it on Omar's chest. In the unlikely event that someone needed to identify the body before he had it recovered, it would clarify who it had been. He put the wallet into his pocket and began piling rocks onto his body. The ground was covered in smooth stones that were once part of the riverbed. There were millions of them. Fifteen minutes later, he was happy with the makeshift burial. It was the best he could do under the circumstances. The sound of gunshots ahead pierced the night. Four shots in total. Crack, crack, crack, a few seconds and then a fourth crack. There were a few minutes of silence then another two shots. The sound of an engine being revved drifted to him then another shot. It was a pistol of some sort, nothing bigger.

'That sounds like it's just up ahead,' Amira called. 'Are you okay?'

'Yes. I'm done here,' Beb shouted. 'I'll mop the inside quickly and then we can get moving.'

'Moving in which direction?' Amira asked. 'That way doesn't sound good.'

'No. There's a lot of shooting going on.'

'Who is shooting?' Amira asked. 'I don't think it's soldiers. It sounds like a pistol, not a military weapon.'

'I guess we'll find out soon,' Beb said. He felt a shiver run through him. Danger was approaching, in fact, it was all around them.

Headlights swept the trees to his right and he could see a vehicle driving towards them, bumping and bouncing along. It stopped on the driver's side of the Toyota, its lights illuminated Beb. The driver and passenger doors opened and two men climbed out. He couldn't see who it was because of the headlights dazzling him.

'What happened here?' a voice shouted.

'Turn off the lights,' Beb shouted back to them. One of the men reached into their vehicle and put the lights on dip. Beb could see it was Mata and one of his sidekicks. 'What happened up ahead?' Beb asked.

'The car in front of you ended up in the ditch,' Mata said. Beb began to walk towards them. They were thirty yards away. Mata looked inside the Toyota and grimaced. 'What the fuck happened here?'

'A stray wheel came through the windscreen,' Beb said. 'It killed the driver. I have buried his body.'

'Wow, that's unlucky,' Mata's sidekick said.

'That's one way of looking at it,' Beb said.

'That's too bad,' Mata said. He lit a cigarette. 'Did he have money on him?'

'He had some money. The money I paid him and a little bit more. He wasn't a wealthy man,' Beb said, nodding. 'I'll send it to his family when we get to where we're going. It might cover his funeral.'

'No, no, no. You need to share it with us,' Mata said, shaking his head.

'And why is that?'

'This is our convoy and any windfalls must be shared.' Mata shrugged and blew smoke into the air. 'It's only fair.'

'It's not a windfall. It's his money. His money will go to his family,' Beb said. 'He has a wife and three children.'

'What about the taxi?'

'I own the Toyota now and I'll be sending his wife the money we agreed to pay for it too.'

'You bought it before he died?' Mata snorted. 'How convenient. You need to share the money you paid for that too.'

'Nothing is being shared with you or anybody else,' Beb said, shaking his head.

Mata pulled out a pistol from his waistband. He pointed it at Beb. 'This is not a negotiation,' he said. 'Let me see the money. Take it out slowly and hold it up so we can see it's not a weapon. We don't want any misunderstandings, do we?'

'Is that what the gunshots were about?' Beb asked. 'Was there a misunderstanding up ahead?' Mata grinned. A gold tooth glinted in the light. 'Did someone else refuse to share with you?'

'Don't push your luck. I'm offering you our protection to get you across the bridge safely,' Mata said. 'Don't be so ungrateful. It's dangerous out here and your pretty wife and daughter would fetch a handsome price, if anything happened to you.'

'Don't mention my wife and daughter,' Beb warned. 'You are the one pushing his luck,' They locked eyes. 'You threaten me, you'd better be prepared to back it up.'

'I'm stating the facts. Females bring a decent price.'

'They do,' Mata's sidekick added, grinning. 'Especially the pretty ones.'

'He's right. The pretty ones fetch more cash. I might be interested myself if anything should happen to you.' Mata grinned. 'What would happen to them without you isn't worth thinking about. I'm offering you protection at a fair price.'

'We don't need your protection,' Beb said. 'And at no point in this lifetime am I giving you any money.'

'Really?'

'Yes. Really,' Beb said, nodding. 'Put your gun down and go on your way, and we'll go ours. That way everyone gets to go home safely. No one needs to get hurt.'

'You don't listen well,' Mata said, cocking the weapon. The metallic click was audible over the noise of a million insects chirping. 'You can give me the money or I'm going to shoot you and take it. The decision is yours, make it quickly because I'm losing…'

His sentence was cut short by a rifle shot. A dark hole appeared in the centre of his forehead and the back of his skull exploded. His eyes were wide with surprise as he toppled like a felled tree. He hit the ground with a thump. His sidekick stared in disbelief, his mouth wide open, eyes darting everywhere. He couldn't understand where the shot had come from. His reaction was delayed but predictable. He made a grab for the pistol and two rifle shots rang out. The first took the side of his face off, ripping the teeth from the jaw and the second smashed into his chest, dropping him in an instant.

'Are you okay?' Amira shouted.

'I'm fine thanks to you. Nice shooting,' Beb said. He jogged back to the truck. 'You took your time, though.'

'I was making sure there was no other option,' Amira said, reloading the Enfield. 'That wasn't the vehicle they were driving,' she added, pointing to a four-wheel-drive Mercedes.

'It's not, you're right,' Beb said, looking inside the G-Class. It was a square jeep-type vehicle and reasonably new. He looked at the fuel gauge and clapped his hands. The engine was running and the smart key was on the dashboard. 'It's got a full tank of diesel and all the windows are intact. They don't need it anymore, so I think we load our gear into it and try again, don't you?'

'Definitely,' Amira said. 'We would never be able to clean the Toyota properly. It will be daylight soon and I don't want Heba to see all that blood.'

'Let's move quickly,' Beb said, opening the back of the Toyota. 'There are two more of Mata's men somewhere.'

'What about them?' Amira asked, nodding towards the bodies. 'Should we move them?'

'No. They can lie where they dropped,' Beb said. 'They had no respect for anyone else, they'll get none from us. We leave them as they dropped with whatever they have on them and no one can say we robbed them.'

'I'll put Heba into the backseat and then help you,' Amira said.

'I'll manage,' Beb said. 'Get Heba settled and keep that rifle handy. Keep an eye on anything coming down the track. If you're not sure, shoot it.'

Amira put Heba under one arm and the Enfield under the other and walked to the Mercedes. She put the rifle down while she opened the rear passenger door. The handle was sticky and she saw that her fingers were stained red with blood. She wondered which poor souls had been lost while their vehicle had been stolen. A full tank of fuel made it worth killing for, especially to the likes of Mata and his associates. They were pirates just like all the other pirates in Africa. Nothing and nowhere was safe. Her nomadic upbringing had taught her to trust no one outside of the tribe, or in her case, inside the tribe either. Whatever they had, which wasn't much, could only be protected at the risk to their own lives. Heba and Beb were her tribe now and nothing would hurt them while she had breath in her body and a rifle in her hand. She belted Heba into the seat and opened the window, shouldering the rifle. She could see taillights in the distance but they weren't moving. The convoy had ground to a halt and she could only think that Mata and his men were to blame for that. They had probably stopped their pickup truck at the narrowest point, blocking the road so that no one could overtake, and then proceeded to tax the occupants of the other vehicles. Those who resisted were probably shot.

Beb opened the boot of the Mercedes and took two trips to load their belongings inside. He closed it and climbed into the driver's seat, closing the door with a sigh of relief.

'I can see taillights but they're not moving. I think the road is blocked,' Amira said, lowering the Enfield. 'They must have stopped the convoy to rob it. We can't go that way.'

'I think you're right. There must be another way to reach the bridge,' Beb said. 'Omar used an App on his phone,' he added, checking his Samsung. 'I haven't got a signal here but we need to head in the other direction.' He manoeuvred the Mercedes through a five-point turn and headed back the way they had come. 'The road is too narrow where the convoy is. We'll have to go around it.'

'I think I saw another road back where the goats were,' Amira said. 'It must lead towards the bridge.'

'I saw it too,' Beb said. 'We'll try it. If we can cross that bridge, we have enough fuel to get us to Monguno.'

'What about all the other people in the convoy?' Amira said. 'They must be terrified.'

'We can't help them, Amira,' Beb said. 'We have to help ourselves first.'

Chapter 33

Oke and Isime made their way through the deserted streets of Monguno. It was surreal to see the houses and buildings from their childhood memories empty and the gardens overgrown. It was a post-apocalyptic reality and it felt eerie to wander through it. They saw a couple of stray goats and a mongrel dog but they kept their distance from humans and scurried away. There were several plumes of smoke on the horizon, the hangover from the fighting the previous night. They listened for the sound of engines, keen to avoid the soldiers. The news of the Boko prison camp was fresh and raw and terrifying and they did not want to be identified as Boko widows. There was no one living in the town who could identify them; not yet anyway. The fear of being discovered was real, nonetheless. They had been enslaved and abused for all of their adult lives. The freedom they were enjoying now was so precious, the chance of losing it was terrifying. Men with guns were once again making their lives unpredictable and fragile. That had been a constant throughout their struggle to survive. Men with guns haunted them while other men with guns said they were there to protect them from men with guns. The cycle was never ending and they could never completely trust either side. Every day was like walking a tightrope without a safety net and there was no end of the wire in sight. They had to keep walking without falling off, there was no way back and the fall was bottomless. If things went wrong, the end result would be catastrophic.

'Nazia will be surprised to see us,' Isime said, trying to lighten the mood. 'And the children will be so giddy. I bet Kareem will be grinning from ear to ear. He has such a cute smile, your boy. I could eat him all up for dinner,' she added. 'He will cling to you like a limpet for days. You know how he gets when he hasn't seen you for a while.'

'He's a mummy's boy, that's for sure,' Oke said, smiling. She noticed the sadness in her sister's eyes. The loss of her son still burned brightly, although she rarely mentioned it. Not talking about him was her way of dealing with his loss. Oke knew it and respected her strength. Grief was a terrible thing and broke those it touched in many cases and they had suffered more than their fair share. Isime had found a way to cope and that's what they had always done through all the dreadful days. They coped. 'He loves his auntie Issy too,' Oke said, kissing her cheek. 'You're his favourite aunty.'

'I'm his only aunty,' Isime said, smiling.

'Favourite, nonetheless,' Oke said. 'Don't knock it. He clings to your leg when he thinks I'm going to tell him off.'

'He does,' Isime said, laughing. 'Kareem cling on, I call him sometimes.'

'He's way too young to know what a Klingon is,' Oke said. 'Can you remember Star Trek?'

'A little,' Isime said. 'It was too scary for me. I'm much younger than you,' she added with a nudge in the ribs.

'So, you keep saying. He is clingy. In fact, clingy is an understatement,' Oke agreed. 'He's been traumatised these last few years. It's no wonder he's a bit emotionally fragile.'

They walked along a dirt road, baked red by the sun. The road was lined with single storey houses of higgledy-piggledy design. No two were the same. The gardens, once well-tended and planted with vegetables, herbs and spices and tropical flowers were now overgrown with vines and thorny bushes. All except one. They looked at the property and exchanged glances. The garden was tidy and organised and the window shutters were open. It was rundown and needed painting but it was occupied. They crossed the street to see if the occupants were there. The sisters stopped suddenly when they saw a woman lying prone near the front door.

'Look,' Isime said. 'Someone has fallen.' She walked up the path towards the woman. Oke followed and stared at the woman. Her eyelids were flickering and her lips were moving but there was no sound coming from her. 'Oh no!' Isime gasped.

'I don't believe this,' Oke said, whispering. 'It's her.'

'It is her,' Isime said, kneeling next to her. A pool of blood had formed on the dirt path and coagulated beneath her head. 'What shall we do?'

'Go and get her some water,' Oke said. Isime opened her mouth in surprise. 'Close your mouth before the flies land in there,' Oke said. 'Pull yourself together and go and get her some water.'

'From inside this house?' Isime asked, frightened. 'I can't go in there. What if there's someone in there?'

'If there was anyone in there, she wouldn't be out here on the floor in a puddle of her own blood,' Oke said, calmly. 'She's no threat to us anymore and I think she's dying. Giving her some water might ease her passing. Please go and fetch some water.' Isime stood up and walked towards the door. She twisted the handle and stepped inside. It was gloomy and a stale smell drifted out. Isime was gone a few minutes before she returned with a glass of water. She handed it to Oke. Oke put the glass to the woman's lips but her eyes didn't focus. Her lids fluttered wildly. She sipped a minute amount of water and licked her lips. 'Do you want some more?' Oke asked. The woman nodded almost imperceptibly and Oke gave her some more. She swallowed and tried to speak but it was just a rasping sound. 'Take your time. What are you saying?' Oke asked. She leaned closer to her lips.

'I know who you are, bitch. I curse you two bitches to burn in hell,' the woman whispered. 'You and your devil's spawn children. I curse you all to burn in hell.'

Oke felt the woman go limp and her eyes became still. She was gone but her dying words struck fear into her heart.

'Is she dead?' Isime asked. She covered her mouth with her hand. 'Oh, no. I killed her,' she whispered through her fingers.

'You were protecting us,' Oke said. 'We would be in that prison camp if she had talked to the soldiers. Don't torture yourself. You had no choice and we were both responsible for this, okay?'

'Okay,' Isime said, wiping a tear from her cheek. 'What did she say before she died?' Isime asked.

'Do you really want to know?' Oke asked.

'Yes.'

'She said we are bitches and our children are the devil's spawn and that we'll burn in hell,' Oke said.

'Oh no,' Isime said. 'She's cursed us?'

'She is too late to put a curse on us, sister,' Oke said. 'We were cursed a long, long, long time ago.'

'It sure feels like that, sometimes. What are we going to do?' Isime asked.

'We're going to forget this woman ever existed and get the children as planned,' Oke said, standing. She straightened her clothing and composed herself. 'What is that?' she muttered, as a black plume of smoke climbed skywards. 'That one looks new. I don't think it was there before or maybe the fire has grown bigger.'

'I can't tell one from another,' Isime said. 'Which way are we heading?'

'You have no sense of direction,' Oke said. 'That's on the hospital side of town.'

'That's where we're going, isn't it?' Isime said, staring at the smoke. Oke nodded but didn't answer, a look of concern on her face. She grabbed Oke by the arm and they walked quickly back to the road. They weaved through the empty streets that were littered with burnt out vehicles and rusting military trucks, all the time watching the smoke climbing higher, becoming darker and thicker. 'That looks like it's out of control.'

'Do you think it's safe?' Oke asked, shaking her head. Isime shrugged. 'I'm beginning to think nowhere is safe.'

For half an hour, they didn't speak; neither wanted to speculate but their sense of dread deepened, the closer they got to the fire.

'I think the fire is close to Nazia's street,' Oke said.

'I hope it's not too close,' Isime said.

As they neared, it became obvious that the fire was substantial and definitely nearby to Nazia's home. When they reached the street where Nazia lived, their worst fears were realised. Soldiers were blocking both ends of the street. Nigerian troops and United Nations personnel were huddled in groups. Jeeps and personal carriers were blocking the road. A couple of civilians were standing together across the road but they didn't recognise any off them. Oke broke into a jog and ran towards the end of the street to get a better view. She could see the flames leaping and jumping into the air; black smoke was billowing skyward and wood crackled loudly. As she reached the junction, she could see that three houses were ablaze. The middle one belonged to Nazia.

'Oh no, please no!' Oke screamed. 'Nazia!' she bellowed with all her might. She ran as fast as her lungs would allow. Several soldiers ran to intercept her. Isime tried to keep pace but was stunned and her legs felt like they were full of cement. 'Nazia! My children!'

'You can't go in there,' one of the soldiers shouted, blocking her path. 'Can't you see the fire, woman?'

'My children are in that house!' Oke said, pointing. 'No, no, no. Please no!' Her lips were quivering. She grabbed the soldier by his arms. 'Tell me where my children are. Did they get out of the house?'

'There were no children in there,' the soldier said.

'But they were staying with Nazia in the middle house,' Isime said. 'What happened here?' Isime asked, supporting Oke. She was shaking, tears streaming down her face.

'A woman and a rebel soldier were shot and killed and the fire started when we were waiting for the bodies to be examined,' the soldier said. 'The fire started at the back of the house. We think it was started on purpose. It was out of control quickly and spread to the neighbouring properties, so it's way too dangerous to go in there right now. No one can go into the street.'

'What was the woman's name?' Oke asked.

'We don't know,' the soldier said, shaking his head.

'Which house was she in?' Oke asked. 'Which house was it?' she screamed at the soldier. 'My children are in that house!'

'The middle one,' he said. 'We didn't see any children.'

'You're not listening to me. My children were staying with my friend in that house,' Oke was hysterical. 'No, no, no, please no!' she screamed. 'Tell me they got out before the fire started. Two little girls and a little boy. Najma, Rida and Kareem. They must have got out. Did you not see any children?'

'No. There was a dead woman and the body of the rebel who shot her. The UN soldiers told us that the rebel shot the woman and they shot the rebel,' the soldier said. 'I saw the bodies but there were no children's bodies in there. Just two adults.'

'There was a lot of shooting last night,' Oke said, jabbering. She was confused and distraught and trying to make sense of the situation. 'We heard the shooting last night. Was it here?'

'Yes, there was shooting in this area,' the soldier, said wrestling her away from the street. Oke was struggling to get past him. 'You can't go near that fire. You will kill yourself.'

'Don't you see what must have happened? She must have heard the gunfire and hidden the children,' Oke said, collapsing. She was breathing heavily. 'If she heard gunfire nearby, she would have hidden the girls, so that Boko couldn't take them. Don't you see what's happened?'

'We didn't see any children,' he argued.

'She must have hidden them,' Oke shouted. 'There are storage cellars dug beneath the kitchens in all these houses. Don't you see, my children are in that house!'

The sound of glass shattering and wood crackling grew louder as the house where Nazia lived collapsed and imploded. The roof disintegrated with a huge crack and fell into the house. Oke screamed like a banshee and the sound would have broken even the coldest of hearts. Panic gripped her and her chest became constricted, like a giant hand squeezing her tightly, crushing her to death. Her breathing became shallow and frantic. She let out another strangled scream as the flames spiralled high into the air and Oke couldn't breathe any longer.

'No, no, no, no, no, no, please God no!' she begged a god that didn't exist anymore. Not here anyway. 'God please, no, no, no!'

She lay on her back and watched the smoke and ash flicker and dance in the air and slipped into unconsciousness.

Chapter 34

Beb drove the Mercedes as quickly as he could, without feeling anxious that they would end up in a ditch. It was further than he thought to reach the goat farm and the night was turning to day. The sun's rays were shining between the leaves on the trees. The daylight lifted their spirits and the sunrise was beautiful. Eventually, the smallholding came into view and they saw the farmer, who was already pouring water into a trough for the goats; he ignored them as they passed but eyed the vehicle suspiciously. Beb beeped the horn to move a few stubborn animals from the road before turning onto the track they hoped would lead to the bridge. It took them up an incline which had been carved through the jungle and it was obvious the jungle was trying to claim it back; parts of it were overgrown and the branches pinged off the bodywork. There was no room to manoeuvre and no passing points but it was deserted and headed in the right direction. They drove on for what seemed like an age before the trees thinned out and were replaced by a rocky landscape covered with bushes and grasses. From that elevation, they could see the river and his homeland beyond; so near and yet so far. Beb stopped the vehicle so they could look down on the lower road, where the stationary convoy was parked. They could see some of the vehicles but some of them were obscured by ramshackle old buildings. Beyond that, they could see the derelict houses of Post Tango and the rickety bridge that they would have to cross to reach Nigeria.

Beb looked down at the stricken convoy and felt sick. The road and surrounding bushes were strewn with clothing and belongings as if the vehicles had been ransacked. There were several bodies lying on the road. The body of a young woman was sprawled on the bonnet of a Ford, her clothing stripped from her, legs open and face bruised and bloody. The angle of her neck told them she was dead. Amira was staring at the young woman and shaking her head.

'Shoot me before that happens to me,' she said, squeezing his hand.

'That will not happen in this lifetime or beyond,' Beb said. 'I'll see to that. Look down there,' he said pointing. 'This road leads behind the houses and comes out close to the bridge. We were right.'

'I can't see anyone on the bridge,' Amira said. 'Or on the other side.'

'I expected there to be soldiers on both sides of the river,' Beb said. 'I can't see any vehicles.'

'Could they be hiding?'

'Who from?' Beb asked, shaking his head. 'I don't think they would be hiding. I think they probably have their hands full clearing up after the attacks on the town. We might be in luck. If we can get across that bridge, we have a five-hour drive to Monguno. We could be there this afternoon.'

'What are we waiting for? Let's go,' Amira said. She gestured to the convoy. 'I've seen enough of this shit to last me a lifetime.'

'You and me both,' Beb said.

He put the Mercedes into drive and steered it along the narrow track, trying his best to avoid the rocks and potholes. It was worse than the lower road, which had been dreadful. The vehicle bounced and rocked and the wheels were precariously close to the edge and threatened to tip off the road. on occasions. They were a few hundred metres further on when the road began to descend towards the small, deserted township. Amira had a clear view of the lower road and the buildings along it.

'Stop the car,' Amira said.

'What's the matter?'

'Look down there. They have a young girl. Stop it now!'

'What is going on?' Beb asked, slowing to a halt.

'Back up a little,' Amira said. Beb reversed and turned in his seat to look through the rear window. 'There look,' she said.

Beb stopped the vehicle and leaned across to look down at whatever Amira had seen. Two men were dragging a teenage girl along the road by her hair, while an older woman walked beside them, hysterical and begging for them to stop. She had her hands together in prayer. One of the men turned and slapped the older woman with the back of his hand. She fell to the floor and he hit her again.

'She's a baby. Do you want to guess where they're taking her?' Amira asked. Beb shook his head but didn't speak. The men dragged the girl towards one of the abandoned vehicles and forced her onto the bonnet. She was kicking and screaming but the men were too strong. One of them punched her in the face and she went limp. He grabbed at her top, ripping it from her. Her bra was greyed with age and he tore it from her. 'We saw what they did to that poor woman further back,'

Amira said, looking at Beb in his eyes. 'I can't let it happen again, not if I can stop it.'

'Do it.' Beb nodded.

Amira opened the window and shouldered the Enfield. Amira closed one eye and aimed. A few seconds later, a shot rang out. One of the men lurched forward as if he'd been hit in the back with a sledgehammer. He fell facedown onto the bonnet and rolled off into the dirt. The second man turned to look for where the shooter was, his eyes wide and darting everywhere. He prodded his friend with his foot, giving the teenager the chance to break free. She ran to her mother, covering her breasts with her hands, and they were both hysterical as they bolted towards the house, out of sight of Beb. Amira fired again and the bullet hit the second man square in the chest. He collapsed onto his back and dug his heels into the dirt, trying to move. They heard an engine start up and Mata's pickup truck came into view from the head of the convoy. It didn't slow as it ploughed over the two men. Beb saw the brake lights come on and then the reversing lights illuminated. The truck lurched back and reversed over the men again. Then the driver repeated the process several times, squashing them to a bloody mess.

'Someone is pissed off with Mata's men,' Amira said. 'Whoever is driving that truck wants to be sure they're dead.'

'I think they're probably dead now,' Beb said. He started the engine and drove slowly down the incline towards the empty buildings. 'I've seen enough, let's get out of here,' he sighed. 'Good shooting, again,' he added.

'I was aiming for the head,' Amira said, shaking her head.

'Which shot?' Beb asked.

'Both,' Amira said, climbing between the seats to comfort Heba. The gunfire had startled her. She didn't cry but she was clearly anxious. 'Don't be frightened,' Amira said, hugging her. 'Mother was just shooting snakes. You remember mother shooting snakes, don't you?' Heba nodded and smiled. 'They're dead now. There's no need to worry. We're going to drive over that river and go to see the place where your father was born. That will be nice, won't it?' Heba nodded despite not having a clue what she was talking about. Amira caught Beb glancing at her in the mirror. 'What is that look for?' she asked, hugging Heba.

'I'm just thinking what a lucky man I am,' Beb said. 'I used to think I was the unluckiest man on the planet but if all the bad shit hadn't happened, we wouldn't be here together.'

'That's sweet and don't take this the wrong way but I would rather be together somewhere safe, not in this shithole,' Amira said. She smiled. 'Stop being all moony and get us across that bridge, please.'

'Yes, ma'am,' Beb said.

Beb put his foot down and steered the Mercedes down the slope. The road led behind the houses and they caught glimpses of vehicles travelling on the lower road, driving parallel to them. She saw row after row of broken-down houses, once home to dozens of families. Sadness seemed to drift over the town like a fog. The town had an unwholesome atmosphere around it as if bad things had happened there and they were still echoing through time and space, lingering, warning, hating.

'I wonder what made all these people leave their homes?' Amira said. The windowless houses were nothing more than wooden shacks, raised from the dirt on bricks and blocks. Broken furniture littered the gardens; settees, fridges, baby's cots and broken toys were strewn everywhere. Mother Nature was reclaiming it and vegetation was returning and swamped the narrow snickets between the buildings. Beb shrugged and glanced at her. 'You know what it feels like, don't you?'

'Of course,' Beb said. 'It's burned into my mind as if it was yesterday.'

'I know you've told me before but it's hard to imagine how so many people can just up and leave their homes in an instant,' Amira said.

'Leave or die,' Beb said. 'Monguno was a big town with schools, a hospital, a market, even a barracks, and it was emptied within twenty-four hours. It was much bigger than this place. Those who didn't move quickly enough were murdered. It looks like the same thing happened here. This town is exposed and remote and the people were vulnerable and unarmed. That's all the pirates need for a reason to attack. They target the vulnerable.'

'Isn't it the same everywhere?' she asked, gazing out of the window. She stroked Heba's hair as she spoke. 'People hating other people, the strong trampling on the weak, the rich stealing from the poor, it seems never ending to me. My life in the desert was simple when I was a child but as you grow up, you realise the most dangerous things on this planet are other people. Even my own family turned on each other.'

'I can see why it feels that way but I'm sure there must be peaceful places to live, where people are good,' Beb said. 'My father and sister like it in London. We just need to find a safe place to bring up our little one far away from this madness.'

'I feel like wherever there are other humans, we're in danger, and always will be.' Amira looked thoughtful. 'I mean, I fear that my daughter and I could be kidnapped and sold into slavery, raped and beaten because we're female,' Amira said. 'Surely, that can't be right?' Beb nodded in agreement. 'Do women live in fear of being raped in other countries?' she mused. 'Maybe Monguno will be different.'

Beb didn't answer her because he couldn't in all honesty, say it would be different. He had been driven from his home by violent extremism, which still proliferated in the area, and they were heading right back into it. Were they going to rescue Isime and Oke and take them away from the danger and if they were, where would they take them to? Was he putting his wife and child in peril? Yes.

Could he live with himself if he lost them? Not for one second.

His hands began to shake on the wheel. He had to concentrate to control his anxiety and focus on driving. Amira looked lost in her thoughts, a mother trying to protect her child from the horrors of this world but having no idea how to or if it was even possible. Beb wanted to hold them both at that moment and promise them he would protect them but it was a promise he couldn't keep. There were no guarantees.

He couldn't put them in a bubble where they could never be hurt because there was no such thing. There was only this life, which is fraught with danger at every turn. He looked into the rear-view mirror at his world sitting in the backseat of a stolen Mercedes and the fragility of their situation hit him like a ton of bricks.

When they reached the end of the trail, they joined the lower road and turned right, heading for the bridge. They could see three vehicles in the distance heading towards them, a dust cloud behind them. Anyone watching the bridge would be able to see them coming from miles away. Beb didn't think about waiting for them. They needed to cross the bridge, regardless of what had happened. The lower road was in better condition than the other sections and he weaved the Mercedes between discarded fridges and cookers and a couple of rusted cars that were on bricks, the wheels long since stolen. The signposts were unreadable, weathered and warped by the scorching sun and torrential rainstorms. He drove on until he reached the ramp which led onto the bridge. It was two vehicles wide and made from textured steel plates, welded together in squares. The metal was warped and pitted with rust and one large section was missing and a tree had grown through it. The bridge structure was made from wood and looked ancient. He could see floor struts missing and a section of the handrail on the lefthand side had collapsed and was hanging above the raging water. The entire bridge looked like it could be swept away any minute. As he straightened the Mercedes up, he saw a thick rusted chain hanging across the entrance and a battered sign hung from the chain. He could make out a skull and crossbones logo.

DANGEROUS BRIDGE. NO VEHICLES ALLOWED. PEDESTRIANS ONLY. ALL ACCESS IS AT YOUR OWN RISK.

'That's not good,' Amira said, shaking her head. 'It's no wonder there's no one guarding the bridge. You would have to be a complete idiot to try and drive across that.' Beb looked at her in the mirror and opened his mouth to speak. 'Please don't tell me you're considering trying to drive across?' Amira interrupted him. 'I am not taking our daughter over that. Not while I have breath in my lungs.'

'I'm just thinking of how we could try to get across, safely,' Beb said, trying to convince himself.

'Helicopter?' Amira said.

'Maybe we could walk across and see where the weak points are and we might be able to strengthen them.' Beb shrugged.

'You're going to strengthen the weak points of that bridge?' Amira said, shaking her head. Her face darkened. 'Come on, Beb. You tried to hang a picture in our flat in Marrakesh and what happened?'

'I used the wrong screws,' Beb said.

'Yes, and what happened to the picture?'

'It fell off and smashed,' Beb mumbled.

'It did fall off and the frame was cracked and the glass smashed, and what do you know about bridge building?'

'Nothing,' Beb said. 'I have to have a look up close and then we can make a decision.'

'I have made my decision,' Amira said. 'We're not driving across that bridge.' She pointed through the windscreen. 'Look at it. Someone closed the bridge a very long time ago. The entire structure looks rotten to me. Look at the age of the sign,' Amira said, pointing. 'It must have been hanging there a decade at least, so it was dangerous when they put the sign up. What would you call it now, absolutely fucked?'

'We won't know until I take a look. It could be a ploy to deter people crossing here,' Beb said. 'I'm going to walk across for a few hundred yards to get a good look at it.'

'A ploy by who?' Amira asked.

'The government,' Beb shrugged. 'I'm trying to be positive.'

'It's good that you're trying to find the positives while I'm trying not to drown our daughter.' Amira shook her head and glared at him in the mirror. 'You're still going to walk across that bridge, aren't you?' she sighed. Beb nodded. 'Wow. My husband is a crazy man,' Amira said. She looked at Heba, who smiled and chuckled. 'Your daddy is a complete crazy man,' she said. Heba smiled and nodded as if she agreed. 'Do you seriously think that bridge will take the weight of this vehicle?'

'Probably not but I don't know for sure,' Beb said. 'That's why I'm going to look.'

'You're crazy to even walk on it,' Amira said.

'I'll be ten minutes. You can see me from here and if it's too dangerous, I will turn back but we have to know if we can cross the river here or not.'

'I already know without leaving the car,' Amira insisted. 'That bridge is not safe.'

'I'm going to take a look or we'll never know.' Beb turned off the engine and climbed out of the vehicle. He could see the remainder of the convoy approaching and it spurred him on. Multiple vehicles loaded with families and all their belongings would never make it. 'The other vehicles are coming. I won't be long.'

'Be careful, Beb.'

'I will, don't worry.'

He jogged to the bridge and ducked beneath the chain. The pedestrian walkway was on the right and looked to be reinforced as it had been built on top of the road structure. The road was fashioned from railway sleepers which were sitting on top of a wooden lattice, which was designed to carry horses and carts, donkeys, bicycles and humans. It was never meant to take the weight of cars, lorries and trucks. The protective layer of paint and varnish was long since blistered and peeled and the exposed timbers were grey and rotting. Small bushes and saplings were growing from between the sleepers here and there adding to the feeling of dereliction. He stepped over a gaping hole in the walkway and stared at the frothing river below, which roared over a rocky weir a few metres upstream. It thundered over the rocks and caused spray to fall like rain on the bridge. He was drenched by the mist in seconds. The volume of water was terrifying and the timbers vibrated beneath the force of the water below. He looked over the edge into the seething, swirling water and wondered how the bridge could withstand such power. The floodwater had turned the river into a torrent.

He walked on for another few hundred yards but things got worse, not better. Long sections of the opposite siderails were missing and dozens of the railway sleepers had fallen, leaving dangerous gaps in the road. Amira was right, it was impassable for a motor vehicle and there was no quick way to fix it. The gaps between the sleepers were too wide to bridge them. The wheels would buckle and tyres would burst as they banged against the sleepers that remained in place. It wasn't drivable even by the sturdiest of vehicles. The entire structure didn't look fit to walk on, let alone drive. Beb looked up at the sky and silently cursed the run of luck they were having. It was beyond bad. This was their last hope of driving into Nigeria and their hopes were dashed.

Beb began walking back along the walkway, wondering what they were going to do next when he saw Mata's pickup truck accelerating towards the bridge in reverse. It sped past the Mercedes and crashed into the chain, ripping the rusty bolts from decaying wood with ease. Whoever the driver was, he used the truck bed as a battering ram to clear the entrance.

'Hey!' Beb shouted. 'It's not driveable. Don't try to cross the bridge.' His voice was lost beneath the thundering sound of the river.

Beb could only watch in amazement as the pickup reversed off the bridge, dragging the chain with it. The driver jumped out of it and climbed into his Ford, which was parked across the road. The Ford contained his wife and four children. Beb heard the engine being gunned and the Ford climbed the ramp and drove along the ramshackle road. Beb waved his arms above his head to warn them but the driver ignored him and the Ford accelerated along fifty metres of uneven wooden road and the far handrail rattled violently. The vibration and weight of the vehicle was dislodging rotten joints and rusty screws. It approached a large gap in the road and the driver didn't slow as he bumped over the missing sleepers and the front driver's side tyre burst with a loud pop. The vehicle lurched violently to the right, heading straight for the pedestrian walkway where Beb was watching in fascinated horror. Beb froze in fear and couldn't move. The oncoming vehicle was travelling at speed but his legs had turned to concrete. The Ford reached a missing section of bridge and the driver didn't see it in time to stop. He braked too late and the front end dropped into the gaping hole. The other front tyre burst and the spoiler shattered into pieces. He could see the bonnet had buckled and only the engine sump held it from falling into the seething river below. Beb heard a loud crack as the sleepers beneath the rear of the car snapped, unable to bear the weight, and the Ford dropped a few feet. The rear bumper and wings were jammed and kept it from falling. Beb could see the driver shouting at his family, telling them to keep still. The vehicle was balanced precariously, wedged into the gap in the road.

Beb ran to the stricken Ford to help and approached the rear passenger door. The children were hysterical, banging on the glass and trying to open the doors but they were wedged against the railway sleepers. There was no way to open them. Beb tapped on the window and gestured for them to open the windows but the driver shook his head and closed his eyes. He wound down his window. The children and his wife were shouting. Their pleas for help were heart-breaking.

'Be quiet for a moment!' the father shouted. 'I can't hear myself speak.'

'Don't the windows open?' Beb asked.

'I disabled the fuses to stop the kids from opening the windows when I'm driving with the aircon on,' the man said. 'You know what it's like. They drive me insane. I didn't think anything like this could happen. Can you find something to break the windows, please?'

'Of course. Don't panic, kids,' Beb said through the window. 'We'll get you out of there. What's your name?' Beb asked the father.

'People call me Mo,' he said.

'Sit tight, Mo. I'm going to find something to smash the windows,' Beb said. Mo nodded and tried to quieten the children. Beb looked around for something to break the glass with and walked across a single plank, balancing like a tightrope artist to the broken siderail on the opposite side of the bridge. The sound of the water beneath him was deafening and he tried to ignore the fact that if he fell, he was dead. He pulled at a thick wooden baton, which had a rusty bolt protruding from one end but it wouldn't budge. He twisted it and shoved it as hard as he could but it resisted his efforts. Beb tried twisting it the opposite way but it was fastened to the bridge and wouldn't move. 'Come on!' Beb groaned as he twisted it again. 'Give me a break,' he hissed as he pushed with all his strength.

'I'm going to try to climb out. Help me,' the father shouted through the window. Beb ran back towards the vehicle across the single railway sleeper. He had to ignore the raging water beneath him to even attempt crossing the void. 'I'm blocking the way out.' Mo was struggling to get his bulk through the window. 'If you can help me out of the window, my family can climb out after me,' he shouted. He was struggling to squeeze anymore of his body into the gap.

Beb was balancing on the plank and focusing on Mo. He was overweight and Beb didn't think he would squeeze through the window and he didn't want to try pulling him in case the movement dislodged the vehicle.

'Try and open the boot,' Beb shouted over the noise of the water. 'Do you have a tyre iron in there?'

Beb didn't see a rusty nail sticking up from the sleeper he was walking on and he stood on it with all his weight. It pierced his sandal, the sole of his foot and drove through the muscle and tendons before piercing his skin on the way out. He screamed in pain and tried to pull his foot away from it but the nail held him; the pain was excruciating. Beb tried to pull his foot upwards away from the nail but the pain was so intense, he cried out again. He lost his balance and fell backwards, hanging upside down from the sleeper, his weight held by the nail in his foot. His body swung from side to side and he felt a tendon in his foot snap. A scream of pain echoed over the bridge and Amira heard it. She looked for Beb but couldn't see him. He managed to grip the edge of the sleeper with one hand and that steadied him for a moment.

'Help me!' Mo shouted. His head and shoulders were out of the window but he was stuck. His chest and stomach were too big to fit through the gap. He was struggling to breathe and panic was setting in. The Ford was rocking as he tried to free his frame. 'Please, help me!'

'Don't rock the car!' Beb shouted.

Beb was still upside down and he could feel the blood running to his head as he tried to grip something with his free hand. He felt the nail ripping through his flesh towards his toes. A scream came from deep within him and he twisted in thin air to reach up and grab anything that could support him. He knew if the nail ripped free from his foot, he would fall into the torrent below him. His hand closed over a stanchion and his fingers clawed at it, trying to find purchase. Blood was running down his leg and dripping into his face. He strained with every sinew in his body and managed to hook his free leg over the railway sleeper. It supported his weight momentarily but he was becoming dizzy as the blood flooded his brain. He tried to keep still for a few seconds to recover his strength.

A deafening snap echoed across the bridge as a beam cracked in half and the back end of the car dropped six feet with a bang; the rear bumper and wings were ripped off and tumbled into the torrent below. The Ford was wedged against a bridge leg, the occupants pinned in their seats by gravity at forty-five degrees. He could hear the children screaming in terror. The mother was hysterical and Mo's cries for help were like daggers in his heart but he couldn't move.

'Keep still, Mo!' Beb shouted. Beb held his breath and pulled at the beam with his right hand and used his leg to help lift his weight; he managed to right himself and sat on the beam, breathing heavily; he waited for the dizziness to pass and his head to clear. The nail had torn a three-inch rent in his foot, which allowed him to lift it upwards and he cried out as he pulled free of the rusty metal. Blood pumped from the wound and he grabbed it with one hand to apply pressure to it but the blood flowed through his fingers. He tried to stand up but his legs were shaking; adrenalin coursed through his veins making his senses ultra-aware. The pain and exertion had exhausted him.

'Help me, please!' Mo shouted. The car was wedged below him. It was at least three metres down.

'I'm coming now, Mo,' Beb said. He looked for a way to climb down to help them but it looked precarious at best. There was a groaning noise as metal strained against wood. Beb locked eyes with Mo as the front end of the car slipped from the road sleeper and it rolled backwards, jamming Mo between the car and the bridge. His upper body carried the entire weight of the Ford, crushing the life out of him. His lips moved but he didn't speak. Blood sprayed from his mouth. Beb saw the life draining from his eyes as his body was ripped in half at the chest. The head and shoulders fell into the river and disappeared and his body tumbled into the vehicle, spraying blood like a red fountain. The Ford fell another few feet with a loud bang and a wooden stanchion snapped beneath the weight. The vehicle tumbled nose first into the foaming waters with an enormous splash. It floated for a few seconds, long enough for Beb to see the four children through the rear window, scratching at the glass, screaming for help as it filled with water. Then it slipped beneath the surface and was washed away like a twig in a giant game of Pooh-sticks.

Beb was stunned for what felt like an age and he stared at the spot where the vehicle had sunk. As the shock subsided, he stood on trembling legs and looked towards the entrance of the bridge. A second vehicle had tried to drive onto it and was stuck. The occupants were trying to push it from behind and the driver was revving the engine to no avail. Beb hobbled to the walkway and saw Amira running onto the bridge. She was alone. Beb felt sick.

'What are you thinking? Go back!' he screamed. Amira kept running. His voice was lost beneath the sound of the river. 'Go back!' he screamed. She was closer now. 'Where is Heba?' he bellowed at the top of his voice. 'Don't leave her in the car!'

'What?' she cried.

'Go back!'

'But I heard you cry out. I thought you'd fallen,' Amira shouted. 'I was coming to help you!'

'Go back!' Beb screamed. 'After everything that happened to me! How could you leave her?' he cried. Tears streamed down his face. 'Go back!'

Amira realised what he was saying. She shook her head and turned around, running back towards the entrance of the bridge. They both heard the Mercedes engine being started and gunned and could only watch in horror as it turned in a circle, tyres screeching against the metal ramp. It drove away from the access ramp before speeding off down the lower road towards Fotokol with a dust cloud behind it. Beb's life flashed before his eyes as he hobbled along the walkway. Everything he had experienced, the pain, the loneliness, the eternal emptiness of being enslaved, would now fall on his baby girl and he was helpless.

Chapter 35

Kalu and Kissie had been sharing the driving from Abuja airport. Google maps said it was a fifteen-hour drive but they were approaching Monguno in less than thirteen. It was late afternoon and the temperature was soaring, a heat haze shimmered above the road and Monguno was clearly visible. The sight of plumes of smoke rising across the town had dulled their excitement and peaked their anxiety. Finding Isime and Oke was all that mattered but they had hoped Monguno would be a peaceful place when they arrived. The local news on the radio mentioned some probing raids by rebels that had been squashed by Nigerian soldiers, who were stationed in the barracks to the north of the town, supported by United Nations peacekeepers. The newsreader was bigging up the military power that was protecting Monguno and the outlying areas. He also mentioned that the number of civilians returning to the town was increasing. Kalu was driving as they approached the town from the east and he slowed the hire car as they reached the outskirts. They had plumped for a Mitsibushi Pajero for its size, comfort and hardiness. The only thing it couldn't cross was a lake. It had proved to be a good choice for such a long journey.

'Look at this place,' he said, gesturing to the empty properties they were passing. The gardens were overgrown and fences missing and broken. Some of the roofs had collapsed. 'It's like a ghost town.' Kissie nodded and was trying to take it all in. She was searching her memory banks for something she remembered but it was all alien.

'I don't recognise any of it,' she said, shaking her head. 'I thought it might come back but there's nothing, so far.'

'You were very young when we left here, Kissie. You might recognise things as we get closer,' he added. 'If you don't, it doesn't matter.'

'I feel like I'm betraying mother by not remembering,' Kissie said.

'You're not betraying her. I struggle to remember my early years. I think my first memories are school. It's odd the way our memories work. Sometimes, I try to remember your mother's voice and it's as clear as a bell and she looks so young but other times I can't hear her at all, her face is fuzzy like an old photograph and I can't focus on her features. That really sucks when I can't see her face properly.'

'I try to remember her but I can't,' Kissie said. 'I wish we had some photographs of her and us when we were young.'

'I wish we did too,' Kalu said. They drove on through the deserted streets. Burnt-out cars and military vehicles littered the roads but their journey was unhindered and progress was steady. They saw a handful of civilians, some carrying cases and others pushing handcarts stacked with furniture and belongings. Kalu was naming the families who had lived in some of the houses and what their connections and life stories were. His house calls as a doctor had taken him all over the town a thousand times. His life in Monguno was flooding back to him in waves and it saddened him. He wished he could wind back the clock to the time when his family was alive and well, healthy and happy, but time-machines were in short supply and dwelling on the past solved nothing. He had to focus on the now and make the best of tomorrow if there was one. 'Do you recognise anything yet?'

'I think I know this street,' Kissie said. She looked at her father and a tear rolled from her eye as the vehicle slowed. 'Of course, I know this street. Oh, this is such a head-fuck.'

'Language, Timothy,' Kalu frowned and then smiled. 'This is where we lived,' Kalu said, pulling the vehicle to the kerb outside a row of single storey houses. 'Can you remember which one?'

'That one,' she said pointing. The tears flowed freely now. She felt like she had arrived home, the circle complete. 'The windows are open.' They looked at each other and smiled. 'Someone lives here.'

'Shall we go and say hello to whoever is in our house?' Kalu said, shrugging.

'Oh, my word,' Kissie whispered, staring at the house. 'I don't think my legs will move.' She bit her bottom lip. 'Isime and Oke could be inside there. Head-fuck. What if it's not them?'

'If they're not here, we will knock on every house until we find someone who has seen them,' Kalu said. 'Come on. Let's knock on the door and see who lives here.' He turned off the engine and climbed out of the Mitsibushi. His legs were stiff and he stretched his back and closed the door. Kissie climbed out of the passenger side and they walked to the front door. Kalu paused for a second before knocking. 'Are you ready?' he asked, knocking.

'Yes, I'm ready,' Kissie whispered. There was no reply.

'Knock louder,' Kissie said.

'Give them a minute,' Kalu said. Kissie ignored him and knocked three times.

There was a delay before they heard footsteps approaching. The door opened and Isime opened it. Her eyes were puffy from crying. She looked bewildered and agitated.

'Yes?' she said, looking from one to the other. 'What do you want?'

'Isime,' Kalu said, smiling. Tears formed in his eyes. Isime looked at them again, and her eyes focused on their faces. 'I would recognise you anywhere,' he added. She shook her head. Her eyes were drawn back to Kalu. She put her hands to her mouth and stepped backwards.

'Oke,' she called but it came out as a croak. 'Oke, come here!' Isime couldn't move. 'It can't be…' she whispered. 'Father?'

'Hello Isime,' Kalu said. 'It's me.' Her knees went weak and she almost fell. 'And this is your little sister, Kissie, all grown up,' he said, smiling.

'Little Kissie?' Isime said. 'I missed you so much. You're so beautiful. Am I dreaming?'

Kalu held out his arms and she fell into them, sobbing like the child she was when they last held each other.

Chapter 36

Beb watched as Amira sprinted along the walkway towards the ramp. He hobbled after her as quickly as he could, leaving a trail of blood behind him. It was hopeless, the Mercedes was already out of sight. There was no way they could catch it on foot; running after it was desperation and he knew all about that. His breathing was fast and shallow as he tried to maintain his grip on reality. He had never envisaged a day when Amira would put Heba in harm's way. It was the unthinkable, unbelievable, impossible scenario. Fate had taken him from his family and now fate had taken his child from him. He was being punished again, for what he didn't know but he must have done something terrible to be cursed with such pain again.

When he reached the second stricken vehicle, they called for his help but he ignored them and hobbled past them. Amira was one hundred yards ahead of him. He looked at the empty space where the Mercedes had been parked and his heart stopped in his chest.

****

Isime was shaking, her eyes darting from Kissie to her father, trying to fathom if what she was seeing was real. It was too much for her brain to compute. They were much older than she remembered but it was unmistakably her father and sister standing in front of her.

'They told us you drowned. We thought you were dead,' Isime said. She choked back a sniffle. 'They told us no one survived when the ship went down. We thought we were the only survivors.' She looked over her shoulder, sensing Oke was standing in the hallway, watching them. 'Oke, look who is here. I can't believe this!'

Oke walked towards them, her hands pressed to her cheeks. Tears ran down her cheeks and her eyes were red and puffy. She was shaking her head in disbelief. 'Father?' she whispered. 'How can this be and why now?' she asked herself, looking up to the heavens. 'Father and little Kissie?' she said, eyes open in shock. 'I can't believe my eyes.'

'It is us,' Kalu said.

'What about mother?' Isime asked, her voice a whisper. Kalu shook his head and a tear rolled from his eye. She touched Kissie's face. 'But you made it, little one. You were so young.'

'Little Kissie,' Oke said. 'Can this really be you?'

'Yes, Oke,' Kissie said. 'It's me.' Kissie went to her and hugged her tightly. 'I missed you so much, sister. I thought about you every single day,' Kissie said in her ear, kissing her cheek. 'So much, you wouldn't believe. All the time when I was growing up, I wanted to tell you when good things had happened. I used to pray and tell you in my prayers.'

'I think I heard them sometimes, little one,' Oke whispered and held her tightly. 'I am sure I did.'

Kalu walked to Oke and embraced them both. Isime joined the huddle and none of them spoke for a while. They just held each other and absorbed the pain of loss they had shared and turned it into the joy of being reunited once more. The unconditional love that they felt engulfed them in the moment, like an invisible flame surrounding them.

'We have some more news,' Kalu said. Isime and Oke looked at him as if he was a talking bear, unable to comprehend that their father was there. 'We have found Beb too,' he said.

'But he died in the desert?' Oke said, shaking her head. 'Before we got on that boat.'

'He was taken by nomads and he lived with them for years but he survived,' Kalu said. The sisters were overcome with emotion. 'He's on his way here as we speak with his wife and daughter.'

Chapter 37

The woman who called herself Alice when she was working for Jet Unganu, was Belinda today and she was shopping in her hometown, Brighton. She hadn't spoken to another human for six days before exchanging pleasantries with the young man on the checkout till. He looked to be about sixteen, spotty and awkward but cute. She thought he was probably the ugly duckling type. He would grow into a handsome man and break hearts and make hearts. She enjoyed talking to other people when the opportunity arose, which wasn't often. Paranoia and nervous anxiety came with the job. Everyone was a threat and the shadow of the law enforcement agencies searching for her constantly hung over her twenty-four-seven. It was the price she paid to earn big money and not have to compete in the rat-race. Working 9-5 wasn't for her. It never would be. She would never be part of the herd, and the mundane lives they led. Her goal had always been to earn enough money to live in luxury and retire to travel. The thought of working until the government said she could retire was nauseating. Society could go and fuck itself. She had watched governments come and go and the fuckers were all bent, dishonest, lying bastards. The rest of the herd were nothing more than worker ants being taxed at every opportunity and treated like expendable assets, not individuals. Retirement ages were being increased and pensions squeezed. Life was too precious to waste because it wasn't guaranteed and she was testament to that, after all she had ended enough of them.

It was a cold day with the wind whipping in off the sea at a rate of knots, cutting through the thin material of her trousers and finding any exposed skin with ease, chilling her to the bone. Dark brooding clouds scurried across the sky, threatening to deposit their rain at any moment. It was a grey day to match her mood. Things had become complicated and uncertain recently, mostly down to Jet Unganu being at panic stations. Someone related to Harry Trainor had kidnapped and barbequed her uncle and now her auntie and a cousin were missing, although no contact had been made. Jet was convinced they had been kidnapped and that it was the same attacker. She was demanding Alice do something about it, blaming her for her misfortune when it was clearly her own fault. Jet had hired an assassin to do her dirty work in a brutal act of revenge. The mistake she made was letting it be known that she was responsible for Trainor's death as a warning to others. Sending messages to frighten people was fine as long as they weren't likely to reply with extreme violence. She couldn't have underestimated the response any more than she had. The Trainor family and their partners were bat-shit crazy and took no prisoners and Jet was reaping the rewards of killing one of their own. His position within the organisation and the manner of his death required a response of epic proportions. There would be no quarter given until anyone involved in his assassination was dead. Step into that world and you have to face the consequences. It's not a world where you can pick your football up and say you don't want to play anymore. Jet would have to pull on her big girl panties and face the music. She had a small army of soldiers, who would risk life and limb for her but they were not so keen to endanger their families, which meant they were no match for the depths of depravity some of the bigger cartels were willing to sink to. They were not in the big league. Their wives, husbands, children and extended families made them weak. Jet was well protected but her extended family and friends were vulnerable and no one was off limits. Men, women and children, pets and property were all targets and fair game.

Jet failed to grasp the nettle and admit that she should never have exacted revenge the way she had. Harry Trainor hadn't killed her niece. Suzette had sold him snide cocaine and he had demanded a refund and compensation, nothing more. Suzette was an arrogant bitch with no manners, no etiquette and no place in that world. She was always going to come unstuck and cause problems. Her death was almost inevitable. Now Jet was being hit where it hurt and she was frightened and looking to offload the blame. There was no one to blame but herself. Pointing the finger of blame at Alice wasn't cricket. Not one bit. She had indicated that she might be willing to leak the identity of the assassin to the Trainors in exchange for the release of her family members. It was only an indication said in anger but once said, it couldn't be unsaid. Jet was beginning to make threats and threatening an active, skilled assassin would get you killed. After all, that's what they do. Alice was beginning to think the only way to silence her and reset the game was to kill Jet herself. With Jet dead, the Trainors would probably let things lie. Probably but not definitely.

Alice was pushing her shopping trolley across the Tesco car park when her mobile rang. She looked at the screen and saw it was a withheld number, probably Jet again on a burner phone. A gust of wind made her eyes water and her hands ached with the cold. She stopped and pulled her hood over her head. It blocked the wind from her ears but the cold found its way to touch her neck and shoulders, making her shiver. Goosebumps covered her arms and her cheeks felt numb.

She had parked her car as far away from the entrance as she could to avoid other vehicles parking in the next bay. It was easier to spot anything suspicious parked near to her, such as big four by fours with blackened windows. They were the epitome of suspicious vehicles yet dealers across the planet opted for them. Ego trumps common sense every time. She looked at her vehicle and a transit van had parked nearby. It was next to a trolley shelter a few bays from her. Two men in overalls and high-viz were carrying a piece of timber from the van, obviously to replace a missing panel on the shelter. The rest of the area was clear of vehicles. She put her head down and pushed the trolley over the asphalt, struggling against the two front wheels which were determined to point in the opposite direction. They seemed to have a mind of their own.

She opened the boot of the Skoda and picked up the lighter bags first. The boot was immaculate and empty. She had it valeted monthly and only kept a vehicle for six months. Her properties were always rented and the six-month rule applied to them too. She always had short-term rental agreements and never had any contracts for telephone, broadband or social media. It was getting close to moving time again and if the Jet Unganu issue didn't resolve itself, she might have to resolve it and move sooner. It was a lonely life but very lucrative and she had made enough to drop off the grid and live well for the rest of her days. She had been thinking about walking away and going travelling for a year or two, maybe meet a wealthy partner and adopt a child. Men were vile and had no place in her future. If she was going to have a long-term relationship, it would be with a female who wanted to become a parent without the pain and inconvenience of childbirth. The more she thought about it, the more monotonous the Unganu issue became; it was so fucking tedious. Her voice was on replay in her mind.

'Someone is trying to kill me and my family, sort it out!'

'But you paid me to kill Trainor and I can't un-kill him...'

Alice was bored to fuck of her moaning. Her Teflon exterior was slipping and she was beginning to yearn for a touch of normality. Killing was no longer as exciting as it had been. She wanted to love and be loved and despite what she had done, she knew she was capable of putting her past in a box and closing it forever. She could love someone; she knew she could and she would.

She didn't hear the men approaching her from behind. A strong hand covered her mouth and she was lifted from her feet and bundled into the boot with her shopping. A heavy blow to the temple stunned her. She felt cold stinging liquid being poured over her and the choking fumes of petrol filled her airways.

'Say hello to Harry when you see him, bitch,' a male voice said. She heard a match being struck and there was a silent moment of complete nothingness before the whooshing sound of flames. The boot was slammed closed and she felt her flesh sizzling. She screamed but the fire cut it short as the delicate tissues in her nose and throat were incinerated. The pain was indescribable. It took longer to die than she imagined it would...

Chapter 38

Beb stopped in his tracks and he saw Amira drop to her knees, screaming at the sky. There were two suitcases and the Enfield rifle on the road but no sign of Heba. Beb felt winded as if a giant had punched him in the guts. There was nothing he could do. The Mercedes was gone now, speeding down the lower road towards Fotokol. He had a million scenarios in his head. Mo had used the pickup truck to ram the chain and then abandoned it across the road. They could use it to chase whoever had taken the Mercedes but it would never match it for speed. It was the only solution he could think of. He stumbled forward towards Amira. She was distraught, cursing every god that had ever existed, and screaming for Heba to be returned. His anger began to turn to guilt. If he had listened to Amira, he wouldn't have left them alone. He should never have walked across that bridge. It was stubborn and pointless. There was no way they could have driven across it but he was so determined to find a way to cross the river, he had put himself in danger. Amira had heard him fall and reacted. He should never have given her that choice to make.

'Hey, lady!' a voice called from behind a rusty Nissan.

Beb looked towards the voice.

'Hey, lady,' the voice called again. A woman came from behind the vehicle holding a child. The child was holding a toy giraffe. Heba's giraffe. Amira saw her and stood up, running towards her. The child reached out with both arms. 'The man left her on the road with your cases,' the woman explained. 'She was crying, so I picked her up.'

'Heba!' Amira sobbed.

Beb hobbled from the bridge and caught up. A group of people had gathered around Amira. One of the men went to help Beb.

'You need to wrap that foot,' he said. 'Bring me the first-aid box,' he called to his child. The boy looked to be in his teens.

'What happened?' Beb asked the woman who had held Heba.

'A man came from the lower road,' she said, pointing. 'He said the Mercedes was his vehicle and that Meta and his men had hurt his wife and stolen the vehicle.' She gestured to the cases. 'He had the keys to the vehicle and he opened it and unloaded the boot and your daughter. He said he had to take it back as he needs to take his wife to the hospital in Fotokol.' Beb was stunned and went to Amira and held her, kissing Heba on the head. 'Your daughter was crying, so I picked her up and gave her some water.'

'Thank you,' Beb said. 'Thank you for your kindness.'

'You're welcome.'

'Thank you,' Amira said, wiping tears from her cheeks. 'I thought we had lost her,' she said, holding Beb's hand. 'I'm so sorry that I left her.' Beb shook his head and kissed her cheek. 'I locked the doors. I did lock the doors. I wouldn't have left her in the car if it wasn't locked.'

'Don't blame yourself, dear. He had the keys,' the woman repeated. 'It was his vehicle.'

'I shouldn't have left you,' Beb said.

'You shouldn't have,' Amira said, kissing his cheek. 'But you needed to see if we can cross that fucking bridge. I understand you were just trying.'

'We still need to cross that bridge,' Beb said.

'We don't have a vehicle anymore,' Amira said, shrugging. 'What are you thinking?'

'We can walk across,' Beb said. She looked at his foot and arched her eyebrows. 'I can limp across. The walkway is intact all the way across to the other side.' Amira looked concerned. 'I know you're worried but what choice do we have now?' he asked.

'What will we do when we get to the other side?' Amira asked.

'Start again and find transport,' Beb said. 'We'll find a driver or buy a vehicle. One way or the other, we'll be fine and on the right side of the river in Nigeria.'

'Let me clean that foot,' a woman said, bringing a bowl and water. Beb sat down on the suitcase and slipped off his sandal. 'That's nasty,' she said, looking at the wound. 'You won't be walking far with that.'

The teenage boy came back with a first-aid kit. He gave it to his father. 'Keep it clean or it will get infected,' the man said.

'I will,' Beb said.

'I heard you say that we can walk across the bridge?' the man said. 'There's no way we can drive?'

'Didn't you see the Ford try?' Beb asked. 'There's no chance of driving across. That man and his family are dead in the water because he tried to drive across. The bridge is rotten but the walkway is built on top of the road structure, so it's stronger. If you spread out and don't carry much, you'll make it.'

'I'll bandage this and then you can get your sandal on it but it needs stitching.'

'My father is a doctor,' Beb said. 'We'll be seeing him soon, so I'll be okay. Thank you for your kindness.'

The man bandaged his foot and the group drifted back to their vehicles, each family unit discussing their options. If they wanted to go to Nigeria, they would have to walk into it. Beb slipped his foot into his sandal and fastened it as tightly as he could bear. The blood was already soaking through the dressing. He knew the risk of infection was high if he didn't get it stitched and antibiotics prescribed. They were stranded and against the clock in more ways than one. He knew they had to move before more people realised that the old bridge was the only way across the river from both directions.

'We need to move,' Beb said. Amira looked anxious and hugged Heba to her chest. 'Once we're across, we'll be fine. This river is the biggest hurdle we have to get over.'

'I know it is,' Amira said. 'I don't like water and I don't like heights.' She shook her head. 'And I don't like shitty old bridges.'

'That shitty old bridge is our only way across this river. Let's just walk along the footpath and don't look down,' Beb said. Amira nodded. 'Listen to me,' he whispered. 'Some of these families have a ton of stuff with them. We need to get across before they weaken the structure any more than it is already. The river is swollen and it's still rising. I don't think it's going to be there much longer.' Amira looked shocked. 'Don't worry. I don't think it will collapse right now but once people start crossing, it will become stressed. We need to go before that happens.'

'Are you sure we can cross safely?' Amira asked.

'Yes. If we go now before anyone else does,' he said, picking up the cases. He hung the rifle from his shoulder and walked towards the access ramp. 'You carry Heba and stay behind me.'

Beb set off as fast as his wound would allow him to. He crossed the metal ramp and stepped onto the pedestrian walkway. The stranded vehicle was still stuck and the family had given up trying to push it. He watched the father walking off the bridge towards the pickup truck. He climbed inside it and started the engine. Beb hobbled faster. The pickup roared as the man gunned the engine. Beb guessed what he was going to do but he hoped he was wrong.

'Come on, hurry!' Beb said to Amira.

'What is the matter?' she asked. 'You're frightening me.'

'That idiot is going to bring another vehicle onto the bridge. If it falls through the road, we don't want to be anywhere near it.' Amira jogged with Heba and they passed the vehicle and were a few hundred yards on before the father drove the pickup onto the access ramp. He had only driven a few yards when the sleepers beneath it snapped. The pickup seemed to nosedive through the road. The driver looked surprised as it dropped and then it vanished completely, plummeting into the river below. They looked over the edge and saw it floating downstream for fifty yards or so before sinking. Amira gasped as it vanished.

'Oh no,' she said. 'Why did he do that?'

'Because he's as desperate as we are to cross this river,' Beb said. 'And he clearly didn't understand how gravity works.'

'Don't be cruel,' Amira said.

'I'm not being cruel,' Beb said. 'His car had fallen through the bridge because it was too heavy for the old timbers and his solution was to drive a bigger vehicle onto the same bridge.' He was panting as they walked as fast as they could. 'Gravity. It's all about gravity. He didn't realise what was going to happen or he wouldn't have done it.'

They approached the hole made when the Ford had fallen. More of the structure had been washed away but Beb didn't point that out. He didn't see the need to frighten Amira more than she already was. 'Don't look down,' he said as they skirted the hole. The sound of the river had become deafening and they were soaked with spray from the weir. They carried on for another hundred yards. 'We're halfway,' he shouted. 'It gets a bit wet here for a while. Are you okay?'

'Just keep going,' Amira shouted. 'Get me off this fucking bridge!'

'I am going as fast as I can, we're doing well.'

They heard engines and turned around to see two of the vehicles from the convoy approaching the access ramp. It was the Nissan and a Toyota Camry. Beb was astounded they were even approaching the bridge.

'What are they doing?' Amira shouted.

'I don't know,' Beb shouted. 'Just concentrate on where you put your feet and keep moving. We're okay. Don't worry about them.'

He looked back and saw the Nissan mount the bridge, two wheels on the road and two wheels on the pedestrian walkway. The driver's side was two feet higher than the passenger side. Beb understood the theory of what they were trying to do but was absolutely sure it wasn't going to work in practice. Spreading the load between the walkway and the road was a clever idea but they had underestimated the decay. He wasn't a Master of Physics but he could safely say the bridge was fucked. The Nissan made it past the point where the pickup had crashed down and crawled past the stranded vehicle, which had now been abandoned by the distraught family. There were only a few inches between the vehicles as it slid by but it continued on. Behind it, the Toyota was wider and wasn't as fortunate. It couldn't squeeze past the stricken vehicle, although the driver was determined it would. There was the sound of screeching metal as he tried to force it.

'That car isn't going to fit,' Amira said. 'What a fool.'

'They're desperate, love,' Beb said. 'Keep going. This isn't going to end well.'

Beb watched in horror as it reversed ten yards and then accelerated to try and force itself through the gap. The impact was shattering and the sleepers that held the stricken vehicle cracked and the road disintegrated. Splinters of timber were launched high into the air. The rear of the Toyota dropped through the widening hole. It teetered on the edge, perched at an angle for a few seconds before the walkway began to collapse too. The handrail splintered and was catapulted skyward and the road sleepers began to fall like dominoes into the river. One by one they fell and the bridge began to crumble in both directions away from the crash site. The entrance to the bridge began to fold in on itself and sections were tossed into the air. The metal ramp fell away with a huge clang, sliding down the riverbank into the torrent. The Toyota disappeared from view, hit the water and drifted for a few yards before sinking beneath the surface. The bridge began to collapse and the hole grew towards the section where the Ford had fallen, one sleeper at a time.

The structure was reliant on the pieces of the architectural puzzle fitting together, each one vital to its strength, and they were falling away piece by piece. As each sleeper was washed away, the entire structure began to disintegrate. The weight of the water began to lift the remaining structure and it tilted to forty degrees.

'Run!' Beb shouted over the noise. They had less than a hundred yards to cover. He could feel the bridge being pushed over by the weight of the water crashing against the legs. The rigidity was gone and the entire structure twisted. They had to run at an angle to stay upright 'Keep going. We're nearly there.'

'I hate this fucking bridge!' Amira shouted, running past him. Heba was crying, cold and wet and sensing her mother's fear. Beb was hobbling but his strength was waning. He dropped the cases and pushed on as fast as he could. Without the cases, his speed increased and he caught up with Amira. They reached the far bank and collapsed in a heap, panting and sweating. The looked back to watch the bridge being torn apart.

The bridge timbers groaned like a dying monster as they were stressed and twisted to their limit. The centre stanchions gave up and there was a series of huge cracking sounds as they were snapped like twigs. A huge section of bridge was washed away and it floated like a jetty for a while until it was dashed against the rocks and turned into driftwood in minutes. The entire mid-section was washed away in seconds. All that remained was a twenty-yard section on the Nigerian side.

'You said you didn't think it was going to collapse right now,' Amira said, shaking her head. 'Don't let me ever listen to your advice on bridges again.'

'That was not my fault,' Beb complained. 'If they had walked across, like I told them, it would have been fine. I hadn't factored anyone trying to drive across a bridge with holes in it,' Beb said. 'What a waste of life,' he muttered shaking his head. 'Welcome to Nigeria,' he added.

Chapter 39

Kalu asked his daughters why they had been upset when they arrived, as both had looked as if they had been crying. They listened to Oke trying to explain what had happened earlier. It was distressing to hear her recounting what the soldiers had said at the fire. She was struggling to get the information out without choking up. Isime helped out when she could, filling in bits of the story, but they were both distraught.

'I'm so sorry to be telling you this, today of all days,' Oke said. 'This should be the happiest of days and we have this dreadful news for you.'

'You don't need to apologise,' Kalu said. 'I know what it feels like to lose children,' he added and Oke sobbed and held him so tightly, he could hardly breathe. 'Listen to me,' he said. 'None of this makes any sense.'

'What do you mean?' Oke sniffled.

'You think that your friend Nazia hid the children in the kitchen cellar because they heard the gunfire close by?' Kalu asked. Oke nodded. 'Then somehow, Nazia encountered a rebel who shot her, then the soldiers shot the rebel?'

'Yes, that's what the soldiers told us,' Oke nodded. 'And if the children were in the cellar when the house caught fire, they must be dead. It was burnt to the ground; we couldn't even get close to it.'

'Don't you think they would have called for help when they heard soldiers in the house?' Kalu asked.

'Maybe but if Nazia told them to be quiet no matter what they heard, they would have stayed quiet. They're good children and they do as they're told,' Oke explained. 'The eldest Najma would have been looking after the younger two. She always mothered them, even though she was a baby herself. The smoke would have killed them before they heard the fire, surely?'

'We don't know that, Oke,' Kalu said. 'And until we know for sure, we assume they're alive, okay?' Oke nodded. 'I thought all my children were dead except Kissie but you're all still alive and well. Sometimes miracles happen.'

'We need to go to the house and speak to the soldiers who were there at the time,' Kissie said. 'They may have heard the children and pulled them out of the cellar before the fire got a hold.'

'Kissie is right. We need the facts from the men who were there,' Kalu said. 'Let's go to your friend's house and see what we can find out.'

They drove the Pajero through the empty streets of Monguno, heading towards the furthest plume of smoke. The other fires had died down now. When they arrived, there was a single army jeep with two soldiers sitting in it. They were smoking and staring at their phones. The three properties were burned to the ground; smouldering embers and blackened brickwork was all that remained. Kalu pulled up outside Nazia's house and stopped the engine. He turned to his daughters.

'Let's go and see what we can find out,' Kalu said. 'These two men will be at the bottom of the pecking order, so don't expect miracles.'

'How do you know that?' Isime asked.

'Because they have been left in charge of a pile of cinders.' Kalu climbed out and walked towards the house. The soldiers looked irritated by their presence.

'Hey, you!' one of them shouted. 'Get away from there. There has been a fire. Can't you see the smoke?'

'I can see the smoke,' Kalu said, nodding. 'My grandchildren were staying in this house and we need to know where they are.' The soldiers looked at each other. 'They may have been taken by the soldiers who were involved in the shooting or they could be burned to death in the cellar beneath the kitchen. One way or the other, your commanding officer is responsible, so I'll be needing to speak to him immediately.'

'Who do you think you're talking to?' the youngest soldier asked, angrily. 'You do not tell us what you're needing!'

'I think I'm talking to a private, which is you and your corporal, which is you?' Kalu said. 'The people I need to speak to are way above your rank, so listen to me.' The soldiers postured angrily. 'Three children are missing. I am a British citizen born and raised in this town and I want to know where my grandchildren are.' Kalu shrugged. 'Someone is responsible for them. You're my first point of reference and you have the opportunity to help us to find our children or you can be mentioned in the report I make to the British embassy about how unhelpful you were. We could be looking at a murder investigation here.' The soldiers looked at each other again. 'I suggest you call your superior officer and tell him I'm here and need to speak to him immediately or my next call will be to London. I will have the police and press down here before you have eaten your breakfast in the morning. We want to know where our children are and we want to know today.'

Chapter 40

Beb and Amira walked the five kilometers to Gamboru with their daughter and the Enfield rifle. The roads were quiet with only a few vehicles passing by and as they reached the built up area, suspicious eyes were on them immediately. Beb's injured foot was becoming unbearable and he could hardly place any weight on it. They reached a crossroads at the edge of town and they were approached by an officer and two sergeants in a jeep.

'Where are you coming from?' the officer asked. He looked at the rifle. 'That's an old Enfield,' he said.

'It is,' Amira said. 'We tried crossing the river here but the bridge was blown up, so we drove north to Post Tango and crossed on foot.'

'That bridge is a death-trap,' the sergeant said.

'It's gone now,' Beb said. 'A few people tried to drive over it but it collapsed.'

'You left your vehicle on the other side?' The officer looked at his foot and frowned. 'You're injured.'

'I stood on a nail,' Beb said. 'It's a long story.'

'You're losing a lot of blood,' the officer said. 'Where are you heading for?'

'Monguno,' Beb said. 'I'm from there originally.'

The officer looked at him curiously. 'Do you have family there now?'

'Yes,' Beb said. 'At least, we think so. My sisters are in Monguno but they don't know we're going there. That's another long story.'

'Your sisters?' the officer said. 'Are they Isime and Oke?'

'How did you know that?' Beb stuttered. Amira was open mouthed.

'I have met them. You have a likeness to them. I can tell you're their brother,' the officer said.

'You know where they are?'

'Yes. They went back to the house where you grew up. I'm captain Mane,' he said, shaking hands.

'We have been hoping they would go home,' Beb said, hugging Amira.

'Let me have someone take a look at that foot and then we'll give you a ride home,' the captain said. 'We're done here. The local military are taking over, so we're heading back to camp. You're welcome to jump into one of the trucks.'

'I can't thank you enough,' Beb said. 'Can you get a phone signal here?' he asked.

'Let's get that foot sorted first,' the captain said. 'The other side of town on the Dikwa road has a signal. We'll be driving there on the way back to Monguno.'

'Thank you,' Beb said. He turned to Amira. 'Isime and Oke are there. Can you believe this?' Amira held him. 'We're going home.'

Chapter 41

Kalu waited patiently as the corporal made a call on his mobile and fifteen minutes later, a jeep came speeding into the street. The driver was wearing a pale blue helmet and next to him was an officer. He was dressed in pristine fatigues and a blue beret. His mirrored sunglasses looked expensive. He was gym built and tall with a jawline that looked to be chiselled from stone. The jeep stopped and he climbed out and walked over the Kalu.

'Doctor Sammi?' he asked, offering his hand. Kalu nodded and shook it. 'I'm Major Kazinski, on secondment to a peacekeeping unit here in Monguno.'

'You're American?' Kalu asked.

'Yes, sir,' the major said.

'It's a pleasure, major,' Kalu said.

'I've been looking into the events of last night as there was a shooting incident involving civilians.'

'My grandchildren were staying with a friend of the family who lived here and they're missing. They could be in the cellar.'

'They're not in that cellar, sir,' the major said. He removed his glasses. 'There were three US troops on patrol here last night and they reported that they witnessed a woman being accosted by a rebel. There was a scuffle at the front door and his gun went off. The lady was killed and the unit opened fire, killing the attacker.'

'Okay,' Kalu said. 'But what about our children?'

'The next sequence of events is unclear but the unit called in the contact and reported that a civilian was killed. Each civilian death has to be investigated, and while the unit were waiting for the investigating team to arrive, they heard children crying. Three youngsters were pulled from the cellar and in their wisdom, the unit put them into the back bedroom with a candle to light the room.' He shrugged. 'They say they went to the road to smoke and by the time they noticed the flames, the fire was established. One of the unit went around the back of the house and he reported that the bedroom was empty and the window was open but the children were gone.'

'Oh, my word!' Oke shouted. 'They're alive. They're alive. They're alive but where are they?' she looked at Kalu. 'Where can they be?'

'My guess is they would head for the lights and somewhere they were familiar with.' He gestured to the north. 'The hospital is two streets away,' he added.

Chapter 42

They arrived at the hospital and parked in an empty car park that was overgrown in places by tall weeds. The hospital looked neglected and uncared for. Some of the windows were missing and window frames were cracked and blistered. The Nigerian flag was hanging limply from a pole on the roof and it looked as weathered as the rest of the building, the colours faded by the relentless sun. A single ambulance was parked at the front, all four tyres flat and the windscreen shattered. A sapling was growing through the radiator grill.

They walked across the broken asphalt to the main entrance and waited outside until the major arrived in his jeep.

'It's good of you to come, Major,' Kalu said. 'Thank you for your help.'

'I know some of the nurses and doctors here,' he said. 'Did you work here too?'

'Yes, but it was a lifetime ago,' Kalu said. 'When I was training. I had a practice in the town centre when I was qualified.'

'Let's go in and see what we can find out,' the major said. They stepped into a sweltering entrance hall and the smell of disinfectant and floor polish was heavy on the air. A nurse was attending to her paperwork and she looked up.

'Excuse me, sister,' the major said, approaching the reception desk. 'How are you today?'

'Good afternoon, Major. I'm very well,' the sister said, eyeing the group of people. 'I hope you're not all in need of a doctor,' she joked. 'We only have two on duty and one of them is missing, probably drunk, and the other one is on his dinner break so today is not a good day to be sick.' Kalu and his children looked concerned. 'I was joking. How can I help?'

'We're looking for three children, two girls and a boy,' the major said. 'We think they may have got lost and headed here?'

'You're in luck. They were here early this morning,' she said, nodding. 'They weren't making much sense but when we were trying to establish who their parents were, they said their father was a Boko killed by General Bassi's chemicals and that their mother is called Oke.'

'I'm their mother,' Oke said. 'Where are they?'

'Was their father a Boko?' the sister asked, frowning. She looked at the group with disapproving eyes.

'No. He wasn't,' Kalu said. 'Their father was a doctor from Lagos. I'm a doctor too, Dr Kalu Sammi. I was a GP here in Monguno before the troubles.'

'Oh, I see.' The sister looked embarrassed and a little disappointed. 'I didn't realise.'

'It's not a problem,' Kalu said. 'They're my grandchildren. Where are they?'

'We sent them to the barracks,' the sister said, straightening her uniform. 'The major has a camp for Boko women and children at the barracks,' the sister said. 'Don't you, Major?'

'A camp?' Kalu asked. 'What type of camp?'

'The Nigerian authorities want anyone related to Boko isolated and questioned but no one from the government has questioned them and so, we have sectioned off several of the dormitories to keep them safe until they decide what is going to happen to them,' the major said. 'There have been several raids lately and they're targeting young women and searching for Boko widows and their children.'

'That's nothing new here,' Kalu said. 'So, the children were sent to the barracks?'

'Yes,' the sister said, nodding. 'We have a driver, Malik. He took them earlier today.'

'Okay, thank you, Sister,' the major said.

'Thank you, Sister,' Kalu said. His mobile buzzed and he turned away to answer it. 'Beb!' he said. 'At last. We were beginning to worry about you.' He listened and nodded. 'We have found your sisters,' he said, smiling. 'Okay. We'll see you there.' His daughters looked desperate for news. 'That was Beb. They're on the way to Monguno barracks.'

'Is it safe to drive here from all that way?' Isime asked.

'He's with captain Mane and his soldiers,' Kalu said, shrugging. 'He said you know him.' His daughters nodded, sheepishly. 'He couldn't be any safer.'

'Follow me to the barracks,' the major said. 'Let's go and get your children.'

Chapter 43

Beb and Amira slept most of the way to Monguno. They were emotionally and physically exhausted. Heba slept between them and they were woken by the sound of the trucks being unloaded and male voices barking orders. The soldiers were dismounting and being rowdy about it. Beb felt like his head was full of fog as he yawned awake. He felt butterflies in his guts. Amira looked a little groggy as she stretched and tended to Heba. Beb felt nervous anticipation about being back in Monguno. It was the only place he could truly call home and he had yearned for it every day since leaving.

'Did you get some rest?' Captain Mane appeared at the back of the truck.

'We slept most of the way,' Beb said.

'That's the safest I have felt since we set off,' Amira said. 'Surrounded by soldiers with machineguns, I slept like a baby.'

The captain helped them down from the tailgate. Beb's foot was swollen and painful to stand on. He grimaced as he took Heba and helped Amira down.

'Is that hurting you?' Amira asked.

'Just a bit,' Beb said, grimacing.

'You will need to keep your weight off it,' the captain said.

'Once we get home, I will.'

'Major Kazinski has called me,' Mane said, smiling. 'Your family are here already.'

'What are they doing here?' Beb asked, looking around.

'The major was a bit vague. They're waiting for you, I assume,' Mane said. 'Follow me and I'll take you to them.'

'Thank you for allowing us to travel with you,' Beb said, as they walked. 'I was very worried about driving, especially with this foot, and I know the Dikwa road is plagued with pirates. I've been putting my family in danger every step of the way. Is there still a lot of trouble in the area?'

'It's been sporadic. Not so much now we're here. They've moved further north but you're welcome, Beb,' Mane said. 'It's nice to be able to help the locals while we're here. I think your sisters will be pleased to see you. They're nice ladies.'

'You will know them better than I do. I haven't seen them since we were children,' Beb said. 'I remember them as little girls. It will be emotional to say the least.'

'I'm sure it will be,' Mane said.

They walked towards the main building and turned a corner and Beb could see his father and Kissie, standing next to a Mitsibushi with two women. They saw him coming and pointed. There were soldiers crisscrossing the yard between them. Oke put her hands to her face and Isime covered her mouth. They held hands and walked towards him, all tears and smiles.

'Brother. You are all grown up,' Oke said, holding him and looking at his face. 'I can see the boy I knew in the man before me.' She kissed his cheeks. 'We thought you were dead in the desert. Mother was broken when we lost you. We all were.'

'Look at how big and strong you are,' Isime said. 'My little brother, you're so handsome. I can't believe this day has come and you're here with us. It's a miracle.'

'It's more than I could ever have dreamed off,' Beb said, holding them both. They stayed like that for a time. 'I missed you all so much. You have no idea.' He paused and turned to Amira. 'This is my wife, Amira,' he said, smiling. 'And this little beauty is our daughter, Heba.'

'You are so beautiful,' Oke said, kissing Amira. 'Your eyes are so pretty,' she added. 'And your daughter has your eyes. It's wonderful to meet you.'

'Thank you,' Amira said. 'It's so good to finally meet you. I've heard so much about you both.'

Beb went to his father and Kissie and greeted them. 'What took you so long?' Kalu asked. He hugged him and shook his hand.

'It's a very long story,' Beb said. 'We were lucky to meet the soldiers from here or we would still be in Gambornu, looking for transport. What are you doing here?'

'My children are here,' Oke said. 'We have come to collect them and you can meet them and we can all go home.'

'I see,' Beb said, confused. 'How many children do you have?'

'Three. The eldest is Najma, the middle one is Rida and my boy is Kareem. He's the youngest.' Oke said, smiling. She looked excited. Beb nodded but she could see he was confused. 'They were involved in a fire and became lost. They made their way to the hospital and they brought them here.'

The major appeared with a stern expression on his face. Kalu knew bad news was coming. 'What is it?' he asked.

'We have checked every possibility but your children never arrived here,' the major said. 'They're definitely not here.'

'What does that mean?' Oke asked, beginning to panic. 'The hospital said they sent them here. Where can they possibly be?'

'I think we should stay calm,' Kalu said. 'We know they were alive and well at the hospital. The sister said they sent the children here with a driver called Malik.'

'So, what does that mean?' Oke asked.

'It means we need to speak to Malik.'

'We need to go back to the hospital?' Kissie asked. 'To find this Malik character and ask him where the children are.'

'Yes,' Kalu said. 'Let's go to the Pajero and we can go to the hospital and find out where Malik has taken the children.'

'But where would he take them?' Oke asked, her hands shaking. 'Wait a minute! They told the people at the hospital their father was a Boko.'

'What are you thinking?' Isime asked.

'What if this man Malik is a Boko sympathiser?' Oke said. 'What if he's taking them to Boko?'

'We don't know any of this,' Kalu said, shaking his head although his eyes belied the truth. 'Let's remain calm and go back to the hospital.'

'Where else would a stranger take my children?' Oke asked. 'Oh no. My girls. They're just babies. What if he's a paedophile?'

'Calm down, sister. Let's get to the hospital and track Malik down,' Beb said.

'I'll follow you with some of my men,' captain Mane said. 'If that's okay with the Major?'

'Yes, of course.' The major said, frowning. 'Go and find your children.'

Chapter 44

Kalu and Captain Mane walked into the reception. The sister he had spoken to earlier was gone. Kalu explained the situation but the nurse on station had no idea what he was talking about.

'I don't know anything about any children,' she said, scribbling on her paperwork. She seemed disinterested in his problem. 'The sister is back on duty tomorrow at nine o'clock. Maybe you could come back then.'

'We need to find our children, now, today.' Kalu tried to remain calm. 'I'm Dr Kalu Sammi and my grandchildren are missing.'

'Oh, I beg your pardon, Doctor,' the nurse said, paying attention. 'What did the sister tell you?'

'The sister said the children were sent to the barracks with a driver called Malik.' Kalu said. 'Do you know him?'

'I know him, yes,' she said, looking concerned. 'Are the children female?' she asked.

'Two of them are,' Kalu said. 'Why do you ask?'

'Because he's a letch,' the nurse said. 'I wouldn't trust him with any female, especially young ones.' She looked around. 'I shouldn't tell you where he lives without permission but under the circumstances, he has a smallholding on the F258, at the junction for Wulari Nomadic and Adamari.'

'I know it,' Kalu said. 'Thank you, nurse. I'm very grateful for your help.' He turned to the captain. 'It's a few miles east of the town on the nomad road.'

'The last few raids have come from the east,' the captain said. 'If you know where it is, we'll follow you.'

Chapter 45

Kalu drove the Pajero as quickly as he dared with his precious passengers aboard. Conversation was down to a minimum apart from Heba chunnering to herself and the strangers around her. The captain and his two sergeants were close behind them. Their presence was reassuring to say the least. They left the built-up areas of Monguno behind and travelled through miles of scrubland and swamp. Buildings were replaced by tall reeds and thick bushes with dark green waxy leaves. A heat haze hovered above the compacted clay road, shimmering and mysterious. When they approached the junction, he could see a low building patched together with corrugated metal sheets for the roof and breeze block walls. It wasn't built by professionals, that was clear and it looked like it had been extended a few times when new materials were sourced.

He indicated that he was turning off the road and drove towards the building. There were goats foraging in the green patches around the plot. The ground at the front of the building was compacted red clay, baked by the sun and a pack of skinny mongrels were basking in the shade of the trees to the right. The arrival of two strange vehicles spurred them into action and they mounted an attack, barking and snarling aggressively, circling the Pajero as Kalu pulled it to a halt. Several more dogs appeared from the rear of the building and attacked the jeep. There were a dozen or more growling canines, drooling like rabid animals.

'Don't open the door,' Kalu said. He studied the building and surrounding areas through the window while the dogs slavered and snarled at the vehicle. They looked hungry and aggressive. Opening the door wasn't an option.

Kalu beeped his horn long and loud. A scruffy man appeared at the door. He was dressed in denim three-quarter shorts, sandals and a basketball vest. A cigarette hung from his lips. His eyes focused on the soldiers and he appeared to be weighing up the situation. He clearly wasn't impressed by the visitors. Captain Mane shouted something to him that Kalu couldn't hear and his sergeants stood up in the jeep, rifles raised. The man stepped out of the house and walked towards the jeep, keeping a distance from the soldiers.

'What do you want?' he asked. He looked inside the Mitsubishi and focused on Amira immediately. His attention was broken by the captain.

'Are you Malik?' Captain Mane asked.

'Who is asking?'

'I am,' Mane said, drawing his sidearm. He pointed the Glock at Malik's face. He stepped back and held up his hands. 'I won't ask you again. Are you Malik?'

'Yes,' Malik said, nodding. 'What do you want, coming here to my home with your guns?'

'Call your dogs off or we'll shoot them,' Mane ordered.

'They're not my dogs and they don't listen to me,' Malik said, stepping back again. 'They're wild and they don't like strangers. Especially strangers with guns. They're not trained, they're wild.'

The captain fired three shots into the air and the dogs scattered and ran to take shelter in the trees. With the safety of the trees, they skulked and faced the vehicles, teeth bared and haunches raised. The soldiers climbed out of the jeep.

'Stay in here,' Kalu said, opening the door. Beb followed suit and they walked to where Malik was standing. He looked nervous and uncomfortable and couldn't make eye contact with anyone.

'You were sent to the barracks with three children earlier today but they never arrived,' Mane said, standing directly in front of Malik. 'Where are the children?' Malik took half a step backwards. 'If you're thinking of making a run for it, sergeant Ahmed is the fastest man on the barracks and he's a nasty fucker if he has to chase anyone, so think again, think quickly and tell me where the children are.'

'They ran away,' Malik said, pawing at the dirt with his foot. The captain slapped his face hard, snapping his neck violently to one side. He fell to one knee and covered his head with his arms. 'Okay, okay!' Mane held up his hand again. 'Don't hit me, please!'

'Where are they?'

'Attack!' Malik screamed. The dogs leapt forward as if they were one, snarling, frothing mass of claws and teeth. The attack took everyone by surprise. They covered the ground with frightening speed. Malik took a hunting knife from the back of his belt and drove it beneath the third rib of the captain. He sprang up, turned and ran as the howling pack launched their attack.

Kalu only had seconds to react before the first dog was on him. It sprang for his face, teeth gnashing and eyes wild and focused on him. He managed to raise his arm between him and the animal and he felt its teeth sinking into his forearm, piercing the flesh and puncturing the muscle. The force of the dog knocked him backwards and he lost his balance and fell onto the clay. Two more dogs were on him in a flash, slashing his skin with razor claws and tearing his flesh from his hands and arms as he desperately tried to fend them off. He heard teeth snapping near his face and heaved with all his might to keep the dogs from his throat. One of the dogs changed the angle of attack and savaged his left ankle, teeth ripping the thin layer of skin and scratching his bones. He kicked out to shake it off but the dog clung on and bit down harder. Kalu heard himself screaming for help.

Captain Mane fell onto his back and pressed his hand to the terrible knife wound. He knew that the stab had been aimed with precision by a man who knew where to strike to kill. He would bleed to death in minutes unless the bleeding was controlled quickly. The dogs were on him and the scent of blood drove them into a frenzy. He couldn't fight them off with just one arm and he couldn't release the pressure from the stab wound. One of the dogs latched onto his face and he felt his nose being torn. One nostril and part of his cheek were ripped from his face. He felt around for his Glock as another dog bit into his neck, below his ear. The screams of the other men around him were deafening.

Beb tried to reach the captain but two dogs were on his back, ripping and tearing the flesh from his shoulders and neck. The weight of the attacking dogs knocked him down. He tried to cover up with his hands and felt the little finger of his right hand being attacked. The bone cracked and it was torn away below the knuckle. He felt another dog attach itself to his injured foot, the blood like a magnet to the berserk animals. Beb knew if he stayed facedown in the dirt, he would be torn apart. He glanced towards the sergeants and they were nothing but flailing arms and legs beneath a seething mass of blood and fur. Blood loss was weakening him. he heard his father screaming and then the light began to fade.

Chapter 46

Sean Trainor looked at the message on his mobile phone and nodded. There was a certain amount of satisfaction in the knowledge that the assassin who killed Harry was frying in the boot of her car. The bitch deserved to burn and more. He hoped she would be burning in hell forever and a day. She had ended more lives than most in her profession, probably because she was a normal looking female and no one saw her coming. Her gender had been an advantage until the end when she was picked up like a parcel and dumped into her boot without a struggle. The physical strength of the men who had taken her out was overwhelming and she hadn't had the time to defend herself. Live by the sword and all that nonsense. She was an evil bastard and died a horrible death. Happy days.

He climbed out of the van he was driving and opened a metal shutter at the front of a lockup. The row of garages belonged to a tower block which had been empty and derelict for years. He drove the van inside and then closed the shutters behind him. The strip lights buzzed and clicked into life, making him blink. He could see that Jet's auntie and her son were awake. They were fastened to chairs, back to back, naked, frightened and freezing. He felt no sympathy for them. They were nothing but pawns in a huge game of chess, pieces that could be sacrificed for the sake of the greater good. He would film what was going to happen to them and send it to Jet, making sure that she was well aware that she was responsible for their horrific deaths. It would be the last communication he would send to her because the next time they spoke would be face to face. It was all arranged for today. She would be snatched and brought to him by her own people. Trainor had got to the families of her personal security guards and they were terrified, terrified enough to give her up. Everyone has a price. He checked the three barrels of acid were at the correct level, two for her relatives and the other for Jet herself.

Chapter 47

Beb heard a gunshot and the weight on his back was immediately lifted. Another two shots rang out and he heard a howl and a high-pitched whine. He heard the dogs snarling and barking. One of them bit his leg and he staggered to his knees and clubbed it with his fist. A piece of calf muscle was ripped away as he broke its jaw. It squealed and tried to bite his face but he held it off.

Captain Mane felt his fingers touch his Glock. He heard gunshots ring out and the dog at his throat howled and released its bite. It collapsed on his chest. He raised the pistol and shot the dogs on his legs. Another shot rang out and another animal cried out. Someone else was shooting but he didn't know who. A dog snapped at his face, barely missing. The captain put three rounds into its head.

Kalu heard the gunshots and the dogs on him were sent into a frenzy. They were desperate to attack his face. Another shot and one of them fell away. A second shot and the other dogs ran away howling.

'Get them into the truck,' Amira said. Beb could hear her voice giving orders. 'We need to keep pressure on this wound,' she said, kneeling over the captain. 'The stab wound is deep. He will bleed out if we don't control the bleeding.'

Beb turned around and saw Amira holding the Enfield. His sisters were tending to Kalu and Captain Mane. She ran to Beb and checked his wounds.

'We need to get you to the hospital,' Amira said. 'Captain Mane has been stabbed and his men are badly mauled.'

'We need to find Malik,' Beb said, trying to walk, but his foot couldn't hold his weight and he collapsed.

'He won't get far,' Amira said. 'I put one in his leg as soon as he ran.'

'That's my wife. Find him, Amira,' Beb said, losing consciousness. His eyes rolled backwards.

'I have the captain's weapon,' Kissie said. 'Let's go and find him.'

One of the sergeants staggered to the jeep and radioed for help, before helping the captain and his fellow sergeant. 'He went around the back of the house,' the sergeant called after them. 'Take my weapon from the jeep,' he added.

'Shall we split up?' Kissie asked.

'No. We should stay together,' Amira said. 'Follow me.'

They crept around the ramshackle building, Amira following the blood trail. It led her to the rear of the house and then towards an outhouse a hundred yards further on. There were goats milling about and a couple of the dogs were weaving between the trees at the edge of the clearing. She shouldered the weapon and followed the blood. The outhouse had a padlock, which had been opened and dropped on the floor. Blood pooled around it.

'He's in here,' she whispered. Kissie nodded.

Amira opened the door and aimed the weapon inside. Malik was sitting on the floor, holding his knife to Najma's throat. She stepped inside and Kissie followed. Rida and Kareem were in a makeshift cage fashioned from wire mesh and wood. They were teary and frightened.

'Women with guns?' Malik chuckled. 'Did the dogs take care of all the men, eh?'

'Hello Najma,' Kissie said. 'I'm your auntie.' Najma started to cry. 'Don't cry, little one. And you must be Rida and Kareem. We'll have you out of there in a minute.'

'I wouldn't be so sure about that,' Malik scoffed. 'I will use this knife to skin these little urchins and then skin you both.'

'Let her go,' Amira said. Malik grinned, exposing yellowed teeth.

'I don't think so, woman,' he said, shaking his head. 'They're Boko brats and this one will be a Boko bride. She'll be popping out her own little brats in no time.' He laughed. 'Boko will be back soon and this time, they'll be back for good and you and all the other bitches who have forgotten your place in this world, will be put right back where you belong. Kitchens and bedrooms are all you're good for.' He grinned but looked nervous. 'I might keep her for myself. She's a petty little thing. I will teach her how to show a man some respect.'

Malik didn't hear the bullet that killed him. A dark circular hole appeared in his forehead and the back of his skull exploded, spraying his brains up the wall.

Epilogue

Six Months Later

Beb limped to the storage shed and opened the door. Three women walked in and loaded up their baskets with tins of food. They carried them to a handcart and unloaded them.

'How are you settling in?' Beb asked one of the women.

'It's amazing,' she said. 'What about you and your family?'

'We're all here on this street,' Beb said. 'The children are being spoiled rotten by their aunties and uncles. It's taken a bit of work the get the houses in a decent state but we're getting there.'

'We've found some paint in an empty building near the Mosque and there was enough to paint all the houses in our street,' the woman said. 'A man from the next street is handy and he's fixed up all the doors and roofs.'

'It's like one big family,' the other lady said. 'Thanks to your father and Major Kazinski for getting us out of that camp. We have started a school for the children too. They're loving it although we need more books.'

'My father is arranging a collection of books from charity shops in London and they will be sent here soon,' Beb said. 'They always have too many, apparently.' Amira came out of the house. 'Have you met my wife, Amira?'

'Yes,' the women said, nodding. 'How is the morning sickness?' one of them asked. Amira put her hand on the growing bump and smiled.

'He's kicking already,' she said.

'You know he's a boy?' the woman asked.

'He feels different to Heba,' Amira said. 'I'm convinced he's a boy. It would be nice to have one of each but it doesn't matter if he's a girl.'

'Of course, it doesn't,' the woman said. 'We'll share out this load of food to the newcomers. They've taken homes near the old market square but they haven't brought much with them.'

'There's enough here to feed everyone until things return to normality,' Beb said. 'We'll see you soon.' They waved as the women pushed the cart up the road. 'Shall we go and see how Oke is?' he asked, frowning. 'She's taken a turn for the worse.'

'Oh no,' Amira nodded. They walked to the house next door and knocked on the backdoor, opening it before being summoned.

Oke was lying on the settee, looking poorly. Kalu was standing over her, patting her head with a damp towel. Kissie was watching from the armchair. She looked at Beb and shook her head. Beb and Amira exchanged glances.

'How is she?' Beb asked in a hushed tone.

'Not good,' Kalu said, shaking his head. 'I think she's terminal this time.' He frowned. 'She's not going to make it.'

'I'm here you know and I can hear you. You might think it's funny but I'm sick as a dog,' Oke said, sitting up. 'I am never drinking red wine again. My head feels like it's going to explode and all you can do is make silly jokes.'

'It's self-inflicted,' Kalu said, laughing.

'Self-inflicted?' Oke said. 'You brought the wine here!'

'I didn't say drink it all,' Kalu said. 'It was good to see Captain Mane again and catch up. He's a nice man. Anyway, me and Kissie need to be at the hospital in twenty-minutes. So, keep hydrated and abstain from wine for the rest of the day.'

'Thank you, doctor,' Oke said, standing up and walking to the sink for a glass of water.

'Are you on the mid-shift again?' Beb asked.

'Yes.'

'How's it going?' Beb asked.

'Better now people are returning,' Kalu said. 'We've got two more doctors at the hospital and a dentist in town. Supplies are not a problem anymore. The soldiers at the barracks have driven the raiders across the borders for now.'

'Father is thinking of opening his practice again,' Kissie said, smiling. 'Aren't you?'

'Good,' Beb said. 'We're going to need a doctor if we're staying here.'

The door opened from the hallway and Isime walked in carrying Heba.

'Here's your uncle Beb,' Isime said. Najma, Rida and Kareem ran to him and hugged his waist. 'Ask him to read you a story. He loves reading you stories!' Isime said, winking.

'Will you read us a story, uncle Beb?' Kareem asked, skipping around him. 'Please, please, please, please!'

'Which one is your favourite?' Beb pretended to look thoughtful. 'Is it the one about the three little pigs?'

'No, no, no,' the children shouted.

‘Chicken little?’

‘No!’

‘Pinocchio?’

‘No, no, no, uncle Beb. The dragons!’

‘I don’t know that one,’ Beb joked. ‘How about Billy Goat Gruff?’

‘No, no, no, no!’ Kareem shouted. ‘The magic dragons!’

‘Ah, the magic dragons of Anglesey?’

‘Yes, yes, yes, yes!’

‘Okay, then,’ Beb said, sitting on the mat. ‘Come and sit down.’ He picked up their favourite book and opened it. ‘Once upon a time on the beautiful island of Anglesey, far, far away, lived an old dragon. She lived beneath a mountain and her name was Hen Goch, which means Old Red.’

THE END

Printed in Great Britain
by Amazon

44064316R00169